T0115447

# THE COLLECTED NOVELS OF CHARLES WRIGHT

# THE COLLECTED NOVELS OF CHARLES WRIGHT

THE MESSENGER, THE WIG, AND

ABSOLUTELY NOTHING TO GET ALARMED ABOUT

## CHARLES WRIGHT

INTRODUCTION BY ISHMAEL REED

HARPER PERENNIAL

NEW YORK • LONDON • TORONTO • SYDNEY • NEW DELHI • AUCKLAND

*To My Lady of the Hats, Midge McKenzie*

# CONTENTS

# INTRODUCTION

Whereupon, I went to the washbasin, picked up the Giant Economy jar of long-lasting Silky Smooth Hair Relaxer, with the Built-in Sweat-proof Base (trademark registered). Carefully, I read the directions. The red, white, and gold label guarantees that the user can go deep-sea diving, emerge from the water, and shake his head triumphantly like any white boy. This miracle with the scent of wild roses looks like vanilla ice cream and is capable of softening in sufficiently Negroid hands.[1]

SINCE AT LEAST THE 1920S, in order for a Black writer to achieve literary success they would need to find a White individual or organization to sponsor them, whether it be a wealthy Park Avenue patron, the Communist party, or, currently, bourgeois academic feminism. The uncontrollable and brilliant bell hooks said that she was told by White feminists that in order to succeed, she had to write for them. There were Black writers who were contemporaries of James Baldwin, who wrote as well as he, but those who dictated trends in Black culture did not find their works comforting. John A. Williams and John O. Killens

---

1   Charles Wright, *Absolutely Nothing to Get Alarmed About: The Complete Novels of Charles Wright* (New York: Harper Perennial, 1993).

who was introduced to us by James Baldwin. Here was a writer who spun a tale based upon a character's attribute, as he did with Lester Jefferson's hair. The two wrote in different styles. What they have in common is that, as bisexuals, they might view reality from a different perspective than those who are of one or another persuasion, sexually. Their basic difference is that Baldwin, in the words of Chester Himes, was "ambitious," while every time Success knocked on Wright's door, he wasn't home.

Hair is such an issue in Black culture that in 1992, the late sociologist Kennell Jackson, a professor at Stanford, taught a seminar called Black Hair as Culture and History. The *Wall Street Journal* published a column about the course that was written by David Sacks, then editor of the conservative student-run newspaper, *Stanford Review*. Kennell replied in a column so brilliant that he sat his conservative critics down.

While Whites can wear any style of hair they desire, Black hairstyles like the Afro have been controversial. A Black newscaster was fired for wearing cornrows. Charles Wright exploits the politics of hair in *The Wig*, which allows him to create a fantasy about a magical wig.

Charles Wright's memoir, *The Messenger*, had gotten an endorsement from James Baldwin. Both were bisexual, but except for Rufus in Baldwin's *Another Country* and Giovanni in *Giovanni's Room*, Baldwin's readers were not ready for the taboo-breaking cast of characters found in Wright's *The Messenger* and *The Wig*. Baldwin's readers would have found them repellant. They're either drinking liquor, smoking pot, or occasionally shooting up.

> All day I had been drinking: wine, beer, gin, scotch, champagne. I ticked them off in my mind, maybe to prove to myself I was still sober. I had taken six bennies to ward off a high and smoked a little pot.[2]

Turning tricks has a literal meaning in *The Messenger* and *The Wig* but also reflected the miserable characters who, in

2 Ibid.

words, resided …n …se" of the 196… … 
hustlers, prost… a… …d those wh… …s…
… were ambigu…s. 

… defined th… … …aracters. The… …p…
…e tricking th… …se …ng that they … …e…
…ovie stars. Mi… …S… …r of *The Wig…*
…lner, Bette Da…s, …wanson, and … …a…
…mile. Lester Je… …rs …gart smile."
… some played …ne …e of luring a… …u…
…l a promise … s… …ake off with …
…hese charact… …on themsel… …U…
…ve the real …i… …z… …cariously in … …
…es.

…ke Baldwin, …w… …l… … down the co… …et…
… Himes, Ric… …r… …ngston Hug… …s,…
… Wright h…d …n… …o with the … …u…
…an token …va… … sons slay t… …
…laughters s… al …th… …Richard Wri… …s…
…on, was subje… …e… …d rubbing in … …A…
…s the literary …o… …t the time. It … …g…
…ething to do …it… …ns the publish…
…s, had with W…h… …oirs, Phillips… …n…
…Wright's anti-… …n… …countering l… …i…
…s wrote, "U…l… …e… …ght was swe… …nd…
…ived in his b… …n… …vas in his ar… …A…
…therefore no… …rt… …ican continge… …n…
…French."[4] This… …s…a… …le.
… only did Ri… …ar… …ve in a circle …
… expats like t… … …llie Harringt…
…s and others, …n… …h friends wer… …i…
…ir and Jea… …au… …rtrude Stein … …e…
…." Near de…t… … …essed to Ric… …l…
…r Julia that h… …na… …cholars write… …p…
…n's attack o… …ic… …without und… …u…
…s behind it. R… …h… …asn't the onl…
… by Baldwin.

… Baldwin, "Ever…b…y'… … …tisan Review, Jun… …9…
…l am Phillips, *A P…rt…* …n … …in & Day, 1983).

Langston Hughes was hit by Baldwin in the *New York Times*, March 29, 1959. He wrote, "I am amazed all over again by his genuine gifts and depressed that he has done so little with them." Both Richard Wright and Hughes were his patrons, and in Richard Wright's case his benefactor. About Chester Himes's *The Lonely Crusade*, he wrote "[He uses] what is probably the most uninteresting and awkward prose I have read in recent years," adding that Himes "seems capable of some of the worst writing this side of the Atlantic."[5]

Charles Wright refused to audition as a hatchet man contestant in the Manhattan token wars in which only one Black writer is left standing during a given era. When I asked George Schuyler, author of the classic novel *Black No More*, why he, at the time, hadn't received more recognition, he said he wasn't a member of The Clique. Tokenism deprives readers of access to a variety of Black writers and smothers the efforts of individual geniuses like Elizabeth Nunez, J. J. Phillips, Charles Wright, and William Demby, whose final novel, *King Comus*, I published. In the 1960s, when literary-minded editors influenced publishing, such a rejection by a master would have been thought unthinkable. A woman acquaintance advised Charles Wright to be more sociable. You know, network. Every attempt to take him "uptown," the image of cultural success, was rebuffed by the author. His bad manners sent an interviewer from a prominent women's magazine scurrying after he decided to urinate in public. He despised the elite and their mannerisms. He called members of the Black middle class "cocksuckers." He found both the Black and White "silent majorities" contemptible. Ridiculed their pretensions. He judged Black political leaders to be charlatans.

His community was that of the outcasts, the rejected, the freaks, who would eventually make it into the mainstream. Some of his characters would now be referred to as sex workers. Restrooms, in some places, are now all-gender, and those outlandish characters in Wright's novels and nonfiction, though not given credit, led to these reforms. They fought the vice squads at Stonewall and in San Francisco.[6]

---

5   Hilton Als, "In Black and White," *New Yorker*, May 27, 2001.
6   Ishmael Reed, *Why No Confederate Statues in Mexico* (Montréal: Baraka Books, 2019).

woman with a child. Sometimes, he appears to be a Midwestern kid lost in the big city. Like other minority writers he writes about the indignities experienced by those whose color makes them a target of racism, but he does it with an originality. With humor. Dealing with racial profiling, he includes an anecdote about the police making him run for their amusement after he boasts he's a good runner.[10]

Wright chooses a comic surrealism (among the painters he cites is Salvador Dali) to point out the experience of a shit-colored Black man in the United States. While writers like Baldwin and the underrated Louise Meriwether might condemn the absentee landlords who abandon their tenants to the lack of heat, bad plumbing, cockroaches, and rats, Himes and Wright use these conditions to spin some tall tales. Himes's rat has created an apartment within a box that includes the rat's provisions, such as condoms. The rat reads comics. Wright's lead rat is named Rasputin.

After Baldwin's classic *Go Tell It on the Mountain* was published, the marketers must have told him that in order to cross over, he would have to give some White characters a major role in his novels. And so while heterosexual relationships are the pits in *Another Country*, it ends with the White bisexual, a person of means, Eric, awaiting his lover's arrival from Paris. In *Giovanni's Room*, another well-off White American male, David, journeys through the novel trying to choose between heterosexual and gay relationships; he decides that he is gay after having cast aside lovers both heterosexual and gay. Vivaldo Moore of *Another Country* exercises his White man's burden by trying to rescue Lena from Rufus and Rufus from himself.

The White, Black, and Asian men in Wright's books are too busy trying to get high to engage in such square tasks. Their expressions of their sexual inclinations are out front. They are not sexual Hamlets. Their communities are fleeting. There are no long-lasting commitments. Wright shares a woman named Shirley with a doctor. He has a platonic long-distance relationship with a woman named Maggie. If he loved anybody, it was his grandmother.

---

10 Charles Wright, *Absolutely Nothing to Get Alarmed About: The Complete Novels of Charles Wright* (New York: Harper Perennial, 1993).

... are not even ... each other ... for sex and ... the novelists ... Testosterone ... women as ... luck, for ... Wright and ... works of a ... and Baldwin ... the style of wo... are made up.

... and Mrs. Lee ... uffing, ... cleverly ... black suit. ... down with ga... pearls, a ... brooch, and ... bangle ... scarf dropp... carelessly ... a garnet ve... perched ... old hair, fluff... was not ... and Pi... ...re French ... the face of a ... b.[11]

... boy, sho... ... cover of ... Charles had plenty of ... with both ... His cousin Ru... ...uction to the ... Charles include a ...

... ouse. I know ... told you ... she could, belie... good- ... Women are going to ... White, ... They're going to ... get into ... if you take ... old fool, ... When you ... of your ... played-out to... ... thirty-five ... how rotten ... te it on ... the bitter, Son... ...who can't ... themselves ... was born ... voice to tea... ... Well, kid, ... damn well ... ...ng being ... could have ... ...ing born

11 ...
12 ...

Critics use the term "jazz" loosely when referring to poetry and fiction. A case can be made for its existence in *The Wig*. The tempo and wealth of allusions fly by so fast that one has to reread some of the sections as one would go over the notation of, say, Bud Powell's piano solo for "Tempus Fugit."

> Everyone seemed to jet toward the goal of The Great Society, while I remained in the outhouse, penniless, without "connections." Pretty girls, credit cards, charge accounts, Hart Schaffner & Marx suits, fine shoes, Dobbs hats, XK-E Jaguars, and more pretty girls cluttered my butterscotch-colored dreams. Lord—I'd work like a slave, but how to acquire an acquisitional gimmick? Mercy—something had to fall from the tree of fortune! Tom-toms were signaling to my frustrated brain; the message: I had to make it.[13]

Baldwin sought solace in the blues and spirituals in his work. Wright liked jazz. Wright was Charlie Mingus. Wild. Expressionistic. And though the form of a dialogue between him and his straight man reminds me of Langston Hughes's "Simple" series and desires to be the literary son of Ernest Hemingway, author of the poem, "Nigger Rich," his syntax leans more toward that of the Beat master, Lawrence Ferlinghetti. Besides, surrealism is a hard sell to publishers who believe that Black art should be pedestrian. Imitative of The Masters. But Wright's surreality is closer to the reality that most Blacks have experienced since their arrival here. Every day you might encounter a surreal situation. Like my being racially profiled while relaxing in a famous landmark cemetery. In a nod toward the Neo-Slave Narrative novels of today, a term I created in 1984 to describe my novel *Flight to Canada*, a slave shows up in *The Wig*.

> "What are you doing over here?" I said severely. "Don't you know beggars aren't allowed over here?"
>     "I ain't no beggar," the man said. "I'm a runaway slave."

---

13  Ibid.

the circle that Himes moved in was Pablo Picasso. I asked him if Picasso had offered him a painting. He had. Himes rejected it because he thought it was absurd.

Charles Wright remained in the United States and took his licks, psychologically, spiritually, and physically. The character Fishback, the necrophiliac, says of the United States that it is filled with "nasty images." They're rounded up in Wright's work. The memorable phrase from both my and Wright's mentor, Langston Hughes, can apply to Wright's work. "Laughing to keep from crying."

When I read passages from *The Wig* cited in the Knickerbocker review, I figured that a writer had arrived who would break Black writers out of the aesthetic prison that critics had placed around them. A Faulknerian quagmire of cluttered baroque prose. Copycat Black Modernism. If young novelists have extended his experiments, Whitehead, Beatty and LaValle, it was Wright who began the jailbreak. After reading the review, I called my friend poet Steve Cannon, now a gallery owner and magazine publisher, who was subjected to a lengthy profile in the *New York Times* magazine,[16] and told him that this might be the guy.

We sought him out. He was living at the Albert Hotel. As we approached his room, we found him engaged in a tussle with another guest. His life was a tussle. From the time of his childhood when he was taunted by his schoolmates for being yellow, he was an outsider who found companionship with other outsiders.

The final stages of Charles Wright's career weren't as dire as the *New York Times* described in their obituary. Ironically, it was a grant to Mercury House from the National Endowment for the Arts that was responsible for his comeback, the same National Endowment that denied him an individual artist grant when he really needed the money. I have photos of Charles Wright taken at a dinner in his honor at a downtown restaurant. He didn't seem to me that he had "vanished" in "despair." Others were taken at a book party held at Steve Cannon's Tribes Gallery.

---

16  M. h. Miller, "A Blind Publisher, Poet—and Link to the Lower East Side's Cultural History," *New York Times Style* magazine, February 9, 2018, https://www.nytimes.com/2018/02/09/t-magazine/art/steve-cannon-david-hammons.html.

...ay, Richard Pryor ca... ...me in the Be...
...a package of wr... ...nted me to p...
...up routine in ...d... ...gues and o...
...t had includ... ...Pryor wanted...
...al of my frien... ...warned hi...
...ring his com... as... ...ne to Ber...
...rselves as m... ...edge. Our...
...ta, ironic, s...r...l... ...American...
...s delivered i... r... ...onic style...
...black lette... ...nts who...
...ment of slave... ...hen as n...
...ply, Pryor... h... ...m down. N...
...at the chan... ...He was the o...
...his work. Li...le... ...that Charles...
...dly written th...ir cr... ...d wanted to...

Ishmae... R...

# THE MESSENGER

........................................

*In memory of Billie Holiday and Richard Wright*

I AM ON THE STOOP these spring nights. The whoring, thieving gypsies, my next door neighbors, are out also. Their clientele is exclu-
sively male. Mama, with her ochre-lined face, gold earrings, hip-
swinging beaded money pouch, flowing silk skirts, is sitting on her
throne, the top step. She went to jail the other day, made the *Daily
News*. She had clipped a detective and tried to bribe him with ten
bucks. The gypsy kids are out also. The girl is five, the boy six.
They sell paper flowers. Some moron walking with his girl gives the
boy a dime and tells him to keep the flower. He takes his girl's arm
and they go off laughing, doing the slumming act. The sweet-faced
little gypsy boy looks up at me and mutters, "Cheap c———." The
gypsy girl, when her face is clean, looks as if she had been born to
wear a confirmation dress. She works men with her sad angel's
face; tears fall like soft rain from her eyes. Most men are not
deceived and then she jumps up and slaps them on the buttocks,
always the wallet pocket.

This street is a pretty spring night's dream, Forty-ninth Street
between Sixth and Seventh Avenues, with its frantic mixed bag of
colors. Chinese and French restaurants, the Gray Line sightseeing
buses, jukebox bars catering to soldiers and sailors and lesbian
prostitutes, parking lots and garages filled with people returning
from the theatre. And tourist hotels.

Later in my apartment, five stories up, nothing obscures the

Nothing lasts forever, I remember telling Shirley. She had called to wish me a belated happy birthday. It had simply slipped her mind. Oh, she was fine. When she felt the need to come over, she'd let me know. "Well, you just do that, cupcake," I had said. "I'll keep you waiting on the stoop five hours like Easter." She hung up without a good-bye. We have been fighting and making up for more than two years now. This always happens when people are unwilling to give up even the carcass of an affair.

I must remember not to flush the cigarette butts down the can in the hall. I'll need them to make this place look unlived in. I'll sweep up and move back in when the Housing man has come and gone.

boxes of dresses to the garment district. How I hate that place. Laura Vee models in that gilded Buchenwald.

Later Pepe, Tommy and I—fellow messengers—are in the subway john drinking Gypsy Rose wine, the champagne of winos. We are killing time. It has begun to rain.

"Shit," Pepe says. "I've gotta move. We just moved into the projects and we still ain't got enough room. My folks are fighting worse than usual. You can't shit straight in the projects."

"I'm saving my money to buy a pick-up truck," Tommy says. He is eighteen, a Tenth Avenue Irish lad. "I wanna go into business for myself. I've saved up almost two hundred dollars. Everytime the boss tells me to ride I walk and pocket the thirty cents."

"Shit," Pepe says. He's Puerto Rican and speaks with a Southern Negro accent. He lives in Harlem. "That's no bread. I'm gonna get me a whore or something. Right, Charlie?"

"Oh, yeah," I assured him. "You've gotta have something working for you."

"My old man hasn't worked in over a year," Tommy tells us. "I've gotta help Mama. I really want that truck. Hell, I don't know if I'm coming or going."

"Shit," Pepe says. "I give my old lady fifteen bucks a week and send my baby sister five a week. She has TB and lives in Puerto Rico with my aunt. The climate is good for her. I'm buying a guitar on time. I don't have five bucks left when it's all over. Shit!"

"Let's drink up, boys," I say. "Let's get this show on the road."

That afternoon, as I walked through the concourse of the RCA building, sneezing and reading Lawrence Durrell, dead drunk from the explosion of his words, I suddenly looked up and encountered the long face of Steven Rockefeller. He seemed startled. Doesn't he think poor people read?

NING I was w... Fifties, going ...

... a bench ... Hemingway's ...

... ddle-aged ... British ...

... e, jostled ag... "Excuse me, ...

... is guarde... y. "All youn...

... Hemingway." ... when I firs...

... ally like Hem... a front?

... large collect... ly rare. Most ...

... d you care ...

... wardly and s... ell.

... is Mr. Benn... ront of his tea...

... drawings in ... *Street Journal* ...

... e. A Marc ... English down ...

... the firepla... Japanese prints ...

... rink a doubl... Swedish crystal ...

... a dozen gla... sign to a wom...

... d to Sutton ... cked as if she ...

... pier in the ... s, she lived in a ...

... e South.

... was offe... Dutch cock...

... ng I must t... ty-year-old ...

... nd all. I nev... pass out. A...

merely a brace for my spine, the fine oil for my reflex gears.

If I could only be alone with that wall of books! But Mr. Bennett said, "I think I'll return to North Africa. So simple. The Arab boys will do anything—for a price, of course."

He sat down on the sofa beside me like a careful old maid. His voice was fatherly. Sweat trickled down my armpits. My heart rose or fell a little, as it does at times like this. I bet I can't get an erection, I told myself. That seemed funny. I laughed secretly, and then I felt his hand on my buttocks. This queer would get nothing but his feelings hurt.

So I rose, smiling, and made my exit. I didn't even take a last, hungry look at that wall of books.

WE... O... ...UMPETS though... ...the music i... com...g... horn. Some o... ...y... ...am ocky, ar... n... ...ways been alo... ...a... ...oped wha... the...ee... ...r my protecti... ...st... ...came over. O... ...quitting the... me...ng... ...a better job, s... ...down pay... me...on... ...arry Shirley.

...e... ...rely in my sa... ...r her dark... eye...ta... ...g. There was...on... ...and lovely ab... h... ...rose in a vas... ...shed back ca...lly... ...a tailored w... ...skirt, and Fre...h-... ...mps.

...e s... ...other like prou... ...engulfed in the...ig... ...y Saturday n... ...thoughts The...w... ...the room, save...or... ...e of moon cut...g... ...indow. The roo... ...ght, had ove...ri...

...th... ...s going to be a...pe... ...Shirley com pla...d... ...I thought we'... ...a little fun I di...t... ...y over here jus... ...tment."

...ll... ...rising. "Wait... ...We'l go do...to... ...But I thought e'... ...et evening tog...er... ...of champagne o... o...

"You and your quiet evenings," Shirley cried. "I don't like quiet evenings. Not anymore. I'm twenty-two years old. I want a little fun out of life."

I started to say, "Get the hell out of here then. Go on the town with your rich doctor." Instead, I finished my cheap port silently.

"You're nothing but a wino," she said, and she wasn't joking.

"So what?"

"I bet you don't even write anymore."

"Is that any sweat off your Goddamn back?"

"I told you about cursing at me."

"I'm sorry. But what the hell are you trying to do to me?"

"And what are you trying to do with me?" Shirley shot back, her voice fighting one of her terrible whimpers.

I poured another glass of port, thinking, I'm through with the Village, the intellectuals. I know the Village and now it is merely a place *not* to go. I want quiet evenings alone with you. My face is bright, I have a youthful stride, but I am getting old. I ought to stop wearing sneakers. My hair is getting gray at twenty-nine and there is nothing distinguished about that. The lines on my forehead are more or less permanent. My energy has been sucked up; I have given, traded my youth for both good and bad values and what mind I had has been ground fine as chopped meat.

I said none of these things. The moon has disappeared. The room was dark. I got up and put my arms around Shirley. She pulled away quickly, as though I were a leper.

Roughly, and with one quick movement, I grabbed her face in my hands and kissed her hard on the mouth.

Shirley broke away. "For God's sake, stop it! You don't own me."

She left angrily; off to her rich doctor. Well, I could sit on the fence and watch love freeze too. Actually I felt like a sea lion landlocked. I sat alone listening to the noises drifting up from the street.

SDAY EVENING Tr y ... and said he wo ...
with his wife, S ... year-old so S ...
quite a shock. I ... rs ago at the V ...
rr. These were ... s, and if Tr y ...
ainly had half f ... hared the sam ...
ed a hard, butter ... tainer of black ...
of us had a steak ... y received a sp ...
from home H ... at N.Y.U., whil ...
ropology. Ah, ... mes we rode ...
the world-bound ... p would read ...
se newspapers ... *the Daily Fo wa* ...
the passengers ... ought they were ...
g nightmares. O ... ook me to the ...
austairs Gallery ... enth Street wh ...
tch kids. They ... swinging, and ...
place the follow ... ero sandw he ...
d Dubonnet, and a ... e supply of ga ...
ped in. I introduced ... Mantle, a fr ck ...
In the green spring ... oy and Susan sa ...
to get married.

Troy received a ... ly anthropo g ...
married and ... Paris and ...
use of Troy's stu ... born there. No ...

back in New York and were coming over to see me right away.

I went out and bought two fifths of scotch for us, milk and oranges for the baby.

The bell rang. I heard Troy's gravelly voice coming up the stairs.

Susan, brown as a berry, all smiles, was wearing what appeared to be a camel-colored Berber's robe. She ran to embrace me. "Oh, Charles. It's so good to see you!"

"I've missed you kids," I said, releasing Susan.

Troy came up to me. He had on blue jeans, sweatshirt, and a floppy safari hat. Three-year-old Skipper was glued on his back, Indian fashion. Troy dropped Skipper to the floor, and gave me a man-killing slap on the back.

"Charlie, old man," he said. There was warmth in his voice and smile.

"Jesus Christ," I exclaimed, stunned.

"We got in this morning," Susan said. "You're the first person we've seen."

"Yeah," Troy added. "Had to see you. Had to find out what's been happening."

"Oh," Susan moaned, looking at her son. "We almost forgot the baby!"

"Skipper," Troy commanded, like a stern, proud father, "Say hello to Uncle Charles."

Three-year-old, tow-headed, Troy Mantle Lamb pouted and played with his fingers. He wore a little striped suit with matching cap, mischief-like lights sparkled in his blue eyes.

I am very fond of children. The neighborhood kids get all my spare change. "Hello, fellow," I said, picking Skipper up. "Did you kill any tigers in Africa?"

Skipper gave me a long serious look, which in an adult might have meant, "I know you, I know your kind."

"Nigger," Skipper said in a clear, small voice.

For a brief second, human breath was suspended.

Then Troy said angrily: "Shut your trap, you little bastard."

"Oh, Charles," Susan said, shaking her head sadly. "I'm sorry. Honestly, I don't *know* where Skipper heard that."

MY FRIEND ... ... ...ver my bod... ... ...e-
thing to w... ... ...less hymns ...b... ... t is
well-cor... ...it. I must e...te... ...of
queerdo...

So to... ...e-and-only ... ...'s
a scent of ... ...using my b...yi... ...ve
had three ... ...l the lights ...re ... ile
quietly, a... ...and peril...s ... le
eunuch g...id... ...ere is the p...op...
ent...l hous... ...elling of ho...d... ...st
tanned w...t... ...e an oarsm...n. ...d.
set like st... ... ...ossible for h...
of it, but h... ...a flicker of ...nt...
I take ... ...covered i... ...
Empire pai... ...the fruit-w...d...
ple lines; ... ...nged white ... s

There a... ...n in the room, ...
drinks, the... ...around the ...od... ...le
of the au...... ...piss-elegant ...ag... ...e
well-to-do, ... ...eep thinking if...
real life, ...ow ... ...eir sex lives ...o...
And the a...sw... ...esn't.

"Wri...er... ..." They kne...

might be fruitful if I came to cocktails next week. I need to get away to the Cape, or Fire Island. A writer needs solitude. I don't look like a messenger. (What does a messenger look like?) They're all round me, talking in their prissy, cultured voices and I'm thinking, Jesus, Jesus, the latest hunk of meat to be tossed into the arena.

Dinner in a shimmering black and white dining room. Real linen napkins, candlelight, three wines. Polite small talk. And now, shall we retire to the den?

We're all good and drunk now. To hell with good breeding, we're for real. Several of the men have suddenly become their favorite actresses. Gradually, the lights are lowered, one by one. Men are lounging in chairs, on sofas, the floor, in various poses. Shirts open or at least unbuttoned. Trousers: open or down. Most of them went about their business silently, except for a few who whispered in tense voices, cooing of love. It was a grotesque scene with wild, quick body movements, groans, great murmuring sounds.

No one had touched me. I have a feeling that they are waiting for the main show, *me*. When it came, it was the little man who had sat next to me at dinner, a jolly man who told amusing stories. But now he was like a man stumbling through the dark and afraid.

Nick and I left at three a.m. I wanted a drink. We stopped in a neighborhood bar.

"Oh, you were sensational!" Nick beamed. He seemed very pleased, like a mother when baby takes his first steps alone. "You're going places, Charles. Didn't I tell you, didn't I?"

I didn't answer him. I drank my drink, his drink, and four more.

It was an experience, nothing more. And if I felt like it, I'd do it again. It was as simple as that.

But Nick talked on. My anger rose. With a rock-and-roll singer on the jukebox yelling, "What is the price of happiness, what is the price of love?" I leaned over and tried to crack Nick's head with my glass.

EL as if I'm being s... y the sophisticate s...
by those ... making it tow...
what it take ... New York...
s this sophisticated ... from me? The ...
he priest in blue ...
breathless, girlish ... coming up sta...
... now Tik ... me, one at a time
clicked on the ti... she stage-c...
ng. You have v...
he door and M... me puffing
body cleverly ... black suit. She
with garl... els, a large g...
and exactly ... bracelets. A s...
seven skins ... houlders; a ga...
was perched ... -gold hair, flu...
was not ... le and Pike, her
...ch poodle. S... of a warmhea...

Mrs Lee sighed ... Charles, you ...

the door and w... You're looking won...

...by," she ... ught you ... 
...pa ne."

I put the champagne in the ice box and waited for the soliloquy. Mrs. Lee was posed grandly on the sofa bed.

"I was thinking of you, Charles darling, of something you once said, 'You are not defeated until you are defeated.' Remember Adolf? . . . Where he got that German name I'll never know. Oh dear, I was wild with grief, stayed in bed two days. I couldn't eat a thing, darling. But on the third day I was starved. I went to Schrafft's and had a feast. Over dessert I said to myself, 'Lee, dear, let's face it. Adolf was a first-class son-of-a-bitch!' Well he was, darling. And these two little sweethearts knew it all along." She paused to look lovingly at Tike and Pike. "Adolf would sit on the sofa beside me, and Tike and Pike would jump on the sofa *facing* us. Never once did they sit on *our* sofa. That's how I smell out rats. With Tike and Pike, the dears."

On cue, like guards of honor, Tike and Pike pranced over and sat elegantly at their mistress's feet.

"I had a little party last night, Charles, and I called you. Where were you, darling? It was only half-past-eight, and Chico had left. . . ." At this Mrs. Lee paused and tears began to play hell with the three layers of makeup. "*Left,* darling. Saying the most impossible things. Oh, dear."

Mrs. Lee has had a succession of lovers and suffers no illusions. Her heartbreak is only on the surface—the same act played with a different male lead. Mrs. Lee, an aging, ageless coquette, dressed in gold and lavender tea gowns, matching ribbon in her hair, dancing through an army of Puerto Rican gigolos, small pretty young men, manicured like dolls. Or Mrs. Lee, her face powdered chalk white, a headache band around her hair, yards and yards of black chiffon, screaming, "Go! This very moment! Back to your Goddamn island!" Or Mrs. Lee, motherly, chiding, "Your English hasn't improved. What are you going to night school for? No more pointed Florsheim shoes. No suede jackets and those tight pants. *Understand?*"

"Oh dear," Mrs. Lee was saying, "I need someone like you, Charles."

"Chico will come back," I tried to reassure her.

"Of course," she said coldly. "They all come back, the rats. But Charles, *do* you think I'll have another lovely, lovely affair? Like last summer?"

Remembering the champagne, knowing what she had come to hear, I nodded and said in a soothing voice, "As sure as the sun rises."

... over this afternoon ... ...terious bottle. ...le
...e, his tiny, glass bead... ...leaving my face. I
...p of the bottle and to... ...The smell was too
...g.
...an. It's cough syrup ...g," Mitch invited.
"...it at any drugstore. ...cough like ma... I
...ne... ...trouble. I'm so ...cir... ...I have TB."
...pot was your speed."
...me a long hard star... ...you got anything... It
...ns this boy is buste... ...to get my nerves
...make a score. Real bad
...at was coming. ...nee... ...ney myself," I said.
"I...id till Tuesday."
...right," Mitch ...d th... ..."You ought to give
...nger job. You' ...lost... ...with that body of

...your stall, daddy," I... ...head, remembering
...d once told me. "I... a million dollars'
...r I discovered I could s... ...will sell when not-

...it's morals," Mitch... ...eyeing the brown
...e you gonna drink that ...
...short nip and it tasted... ...d glue. Mitch took

the bottle. "Man, I got so high that I walked all the way down. From West Seventy-second Street."

I took another drink of the cough syrup and after a few seconds, my head was slightly light. I wanted a drink but I wouldn't stand Mitch a drink. A shot wouldn't do him any good. On moneyless days, we used to boil water and make a cup of tea, throw in a generous amount of cinnamon, inhale the fumes and drink the scalding tea down in a gulp. Today, I can't stand the smell of cinnamon.

"Mitch, have you ever drunk lemon extract?" I asked.

"What? Come again."

"Lemon extract. It's got eighty percent alcohol in it."

"Take me to thy vat," Mitch hammed.

We went into the closet kitchenette. I opened up a bottle of Seven-up, got a tray of ice and a ten-ounce reserve bottle of lemon extract, and poured them into a water pitcher. I stirred until the tangy mixture was chilled.

"This is something a cook in the army taught me," I said, giving Mitch a sample glass.

Mitch took a careful sip, his beady eyes pointed dead on me. He licked out his fox tongue and took a long drink.

"Ba-bee," he exclaimed, "this is a fucking groove. Man, we can bottle this shit and sell it!"

"Oh, sure," I agreed, pouring a glass. "We'll call it lemon juice."

"Yeah," Mitch hee-hawed. "Lemon juice."

We downed our lemon juice, poured another round, went into the living room, and exhausted the possibilities of lemon extract, joking about the crazy Bronx-Brooklyn kids who get high on marijuana mixed with store-bought oregano and catnip. Mitch used to push that stuff. The kick came from following the leader and because it was the fashionable thing to do.

"Awright," Mitch said. "Awright. With this codeine and lemon juice I can't help but score tonight."

"Do you mind if I have some more of this shit?" Mitch asked.

"Knock yourself out, baby."

Mitch returned from the kitchenette, a deep, one-track expression on his face. He fished in his pocket for a cigarette and out fell his red plastic toothbrush.

...hbrush fell to ... ...idn't say any...
...inkled up the ... ...p and I saw ... ...eth...
...t a smile. ... ...adly. "I'm ... ...
...d. "Those wh... es... ... The Tombs. I ... ...go...
...can't bail'm o... ... ...oked out of ... ...
...one-and-only ... rd...
...ough," I said... ... ...h as I sounde... ...Why
...rk the eastsid...
...ig those piss... ...ag... ...n frowned. "... ...you
...orals. I got to ...g...
...oofless, baby... ...to...
...gonna be one ... ...ght. You ju... ...ch
...te. Awright!"
...e all right," I ... ...m He was ne... ...re

...ing my nerves ... ...e said. "I got ... ...ing
...eal nice."
...said slowly, "... ... ...a place to flo... ...me
...re."
...s smiling th... ...re ...l...ng like hell ... ...he
...ve me a warm ... ... ...n... "Charlie, ... ...re

TODAY I WALKED and walked through the rainy New York streets. I had deliveries downtown, uptown, westside, eastside. I walked until my feet were soaking wet and I could feel water coming through my raincoat, sweater, and shirt. I made my way through hordes of New Yorkers, and commuters, all walking, running, shoving, cursing. Finally the last delivery was over, and at 7 P.M. I climbed up my five flights and locked the door. I didn't even bother to take off my wet clothes, just lay down on the bed and asked myself what I was doing in this city. I knew some answers. After my grandmother's death there was nothing to keep me in Missouri. I had always been a travelling lad, and so I came to New York.

But I cannot connect the fragments of my life. These dirty, white-walled rooms, the mixed cheap furniture, the decayed scent of this old midtown brownstone, the constant hum of voices, music, and impatient traffic which comes up from the street— what do they have to do with me? The Chinese say that the first step is the beginning of a ten-thousand-mile journey. But what is the first step?

With my head burrowed in the pillow, I try to think of beginnings; my past.

"*One of these days, you gonna die, pretty baby,*" a voice sings mockingly from the jukebox of the bar on the ground floor.

...mous effort, I... ...he bowels of...
...Missouri. It... ...es me bac...
...m that four-y... 
...only been sick tw... 
...a crowded co... ...ling from the...

...ng. Ain't he swe...
...give cousin M...
...know what it i...
...ng. Ain't he swe...
...my father, sta... ...king lost, altho...
...with us anymo... ...big tall man...
...stache, in a blac...
...re, Sonny," he s... ...playfully rub...
...hands through... ...me a bowl of...
...After the ice... ...ick my finger...
...went roun... ...les.
...there was m... ...ding in front...
...looking down... ...our daughters...
...ght and she c... ...chief in her ha...
...cry. I did not... ...they had alre...
...was a long, lon... ...did not wake...
...Afterward... ...the sky and in...
...did not believe... 
...was the fun of... ...la and Grandm...
...licking th... ...ons. Fishing w...
...through the... ...with him, list...
...ones and their t... ...Missouri River.
...and I am ve... ...ow the child...
...kes me. My m... ...e are fights wi...

..."
..."you is cute."
...ger like all the... ...of...
...ain't nothing bu... ...igger."
...bastard."
...pretty, dark... ...eyes. She...
...braids. She sm... ...cess. I gave...

Years go quickly. I become the best-liked boy in the community. "I think it's simply wonderful the way you are raising that boy." This is said to Grandpa and Grandma.

I'm thirteen now and teaching Sunday school. I become a man in the sexual sense.

Mary Ann's grandmother was a sewing-circle crony of my grandmother. One hot, summer afternoon they went out, leaving Mary Ann and me alone. We drank lemonade and had a couple of half-hearted games of blackjack. Finally the card game petered out. Sixteen-year-old Mary Ann began telling ghost stories. The setting was perfect. An old Victorian house filled with dark, heavy furniture, stiff, dusty drapes at the windows and between the doorways, the odor of hothouse flowers. Very little sunlight entered. I was always fascinated by Mary Ann's house; it was like suffocating in a delicious dream.

Suddenly, Mary Ann became sleepy. I began to leave, believing she was trying to get rid of me. On the contrary, she wanted me to stay. If I wasn't sleepy, at least I could stay until she fell asleep. I could usually be talked into things which did not interest me. Not really talked into, but still I'd go along like a good sport. Already I had discovered that it caused me less worry, less arguing and explaining.

So I went into the bedroom and carefully turned my head while Mary Ann undressed. I caught a view of her buttocks and legs as she deliberately pranced in front of me, talking a mile a minute. Her naked body aroused my thirteen-year-old mind. I would have liked to ask Mary Ann to stand still so I could take a good full view. But I was too well brought up.

Mary Ann got into bed; I sat in a slipper chair, very uncomfortable, digging my nails into the palm of my hand.

"Come and get into the bed with me," Mary Ann giggled.

"I don't want to get into bed," I argued. "I don't take naps anymore."

"You know this old house is full of ghosts," Mary Ann said, sitting up in bed. "Remember my Aunt Sarah died in this very room. If you don't get in bed with me why she just might come wandering in here. Honest, Sonny."

I did not really believe in ghosts. But I wasn't going to take a chance. I jumped into Mary Ann's bed and pulled the covers tight over my head.

...gled her nervou... ...bing my body ... ...s ...nd then it d...w... ...we were playing ... ...summer afte...n... ...undress... ...moved my body as ...though ... did ... ...humping up an... ...g. I was t...se ...ing what would ha... ...Ann's grand- ...The climax ca...e ... ...my body and ...nd Mary Ann. ... ...press far her, ...was too great. An... ...still a little s...ep- ...it, I was certa...ly g... ...again. ...ere was a who... ...girls and... of ...Ann. She kept me s... ...contracep...ves ...winter boots. ...ternoon that su...m... ...aged min...ter ...ited me int... h... ...in back of the ...

"...ld are you?"

"...Sir."

...g to be a little ...a... ...i...er said. "I've ...nday school. So... e... ...ke a fine d...ci- ...You have got ...e... ...you act ...ry ...hat it takes. No... l... ...you to think I'm ...nto becoming a ...a... ...I: I want yo...too ...'d make a f...ne ...n... ...ld do a lot...or ...

...ng to be a little ...n... ...ister grin...ed. ...an, and I be...al... th... ...are crazy about ...

...tood by my ...ha... ...head, look...ng ...ng expression in hi... ...you hav...all ...ving you aro...nd... ...whopper." ...evenings gr...w... ...aid, Gran...pa ...epe...t, "This w...ld... ...me." He...ad ...local paper the N... ...phic, and the ...prised and slightly... ...But I did...ot ...ndma. We...ere... ...pt our sec...ts ...s. At the tim..., th... ...verything...ad ...adolescent m...nd... ...a was not the ...

man of fishing, ice cream days. I was getting older, almost fourteen.

Grandpa's mind drifted as he felt that this world was not his
home. People began to talk. They were very decent about it; everyone knew my grandparents. We were a quiet, respectable, church-
going family.

We used to sit on the big front porch during the Missouri summer evenings. One night Grandpa tried to fight with Grandma. In
the past she had always been able to outwit him or at least calm
him down. But that night she was powerless. Two neighbor men
came over and put him to bed. The doctor arrived and was going
to give him an injection. But sleep had overtaken him, sleep that
turned into death by eight the following morning.

Then Grandma and I were alone in the paint-peeling, white
frame house during the long days and short nights of that fourteen-year-old summer. We became very close.

I began to be aware of something at this time, something perhaps I had been born with, and which was never to leave me.
Loneliness.

And this consciousness is here with me now, in this small, dark
room in New York. I get up and look out the window. It is still
raining.

I WALK THROUGH the early morning streets still ... numb, self-centered ... The bars are closing and a ... indefinable magic ... the cool air. Early Sunday morning ... that subtle, quiet quality in New York. Lonely people ... know that time of morning. Slow, uncertain footsteps ... own distorted reflection in darkened store windows, ... furtive, envious, eye-lowering glances at passing couples ... recognize other solitary fellow travelers. Both of you ... separate ways, moving with the cold edge of Sunday ... cigarettes, tap water ... the nearly empty half-pint, and the feeling of having missed out on Saturday night's jackpot prize. You give up at Waterloo, mount the stairs, unlock the door, turn off the light ... across. You pace the floor and finally try to sleep, comforted by nothing but the prospect of another sunrise.

You say ... everything; you get in the world ... and polish, sophistication, and ejaculations delivered ... the country. Everything.

You are ... now buried in your own misery ... I've got to leave New York. I am leaving my nickels, dimes, ... and this winter will go away.

Now the Sunday sky is serene and pale blue ... in the east a ballet of soft, white clouds. The rising sun hurled ... through shafts of gold ... as if God had suddenly opened His ... ful hand on the world. My heart bows its head in the presence of this force. I am suddenly at peace in this early morning. The sun comforts me; I am swaddled in the folds of those wonderful clouds. Let the rays of the sun touch your body and you will be made holy. Shirley used to say I was saintly, I had missed my calling, I should become a preacher. *You've got the makings, boy. Why did you stray so far from home?*

FRIDAY. Faded blue ⸺ . Ninety-three-degree ⸺ at. Jammed traffic ⸺ grind of the cro⸺ ⸺

Maxine the pi⸺ ⸺colored seven-y⸺ old ⸺ in. She lives on the ⸺ and has the mind of ⸺ a old.

"Did I scar⸺ ⸺" Maxine throws her ⸺ and me. "I've got ⸺ ⸺ One of my ⸺ ⸺es. Look!"

I look up slowly ⸺ Maxine loves the ⸺ ⸺" Now she is ⸺ ⸺ taking in the ⸺ ⸺ and the fat bags ⸺ ⸺ two-day beard⸺

Maxine has gi⸺ ⸺national children⸺ ⸺ ⸺s on an abstract ⸺ ⸺ firm; the color⸺ ⸺ her once to the Museum of ⸺ Art, but she ⸺ ⸺ the gods of Mo⸺ ⸺ fers her own a⸺ ⸺

Maxine's pictu⸺ ⸺es, circles, crisscro⸺s ⸺ green, yellow, b⸺ ⸺

I try to sho⸺ ⸺ despondent. "⸺at is ⸺i? I give up."

"Oh, good ⸺ know anythin⸺ It's ⸺ ⸺ parking lot with the ⸺ ⸺g down on it."

"And it's b⸺ ⸺aking another ⸺ ⸺ picture. "I'll p⸺ ⸺n."

"No, Charles ⸺ ⸺'t have any ligh⸺ ⸺ ⸺"

Evening arrives with the sudden press of a familiar inky stamp. I look out the window at the soot-caked, blank, brick wall of Tip Top parking and the grim, red-brick façade of the Elmwood Hotel. TV and mistily yellow lights glow in Elmwood windows. An unreal face appears at a gold-curtained window and withdraws, a shy ghost.

I grow old in the terrible heart of America. I am dying the American-money death. "There's plenty of money out there, Charlie," Al, my messenger boss says, waving his expensive cigar. "You only have to figure out a way to get it."

Why doesn't America let me die quietly? No. This country smiles on; the smile is a stationary sun. The sin is believing, hoping. But I am too tired, too afraid now to commit this sin.

...G S DROP since the ...ive ...kari, the stoc...
...ing Tuesday, May ...ly a quarter o...

...g and one gruff ...nl... ...k...s are quite pub...
...noses. Nervous ...s... ...tension? Onl...
...s...he sanitary turn-... ...handkerchie...
...k Avenue branch o...ce... ...Street firm. I am...
...te stocks and b...r...s... But the ticker...
...ret. Everyone is ...ra... ...ll I want to do...
...up and go home. T...e... ...ge of fortune ha...

...an elevator opera...e... ...says, "The big...
...ing up but good. So...e... ...i...the gravy, you...
...ottom dollar on the... ...levator opera...
...u...ed dollars in th...d... ...ix children an...
...ar... fifty dollars in...l... ...He lives in...
...o...o Avenue walk-u... ...ng on with his...
...n...l daughter is eigh... ...serious opera...
...n...sn't helping thing... ...ant to visit his...
...to...orrow and he...e... ...e should go to...
...t is, if he doesn't get... ...ing drunk Sat...
...e s...a moderate drin...er... ...ears old, slen-...
...jer...y movements of a p...e...i...d. He has the...

pallid looks of a man who spends eight hours a day in an automatic tomb with his thoughts, his eyes straight ahead.

But here, fourteen stories above Park Avenue, the air is jubilant. If the voices, the laughter, are slightly on edge, the feeling nevertheless is that we've made the day. One of the brokers cracked: "Well I won't have to go to the blood bank after all." This is followed by lusty, breathtaking ha-ha's.

Now picture, if you will, a room about sixteen by twenty feet: ivory walls, deep gray wall-to-wall carpeting, reproductions of English antiques, steel filing cabinets painted pale green, Chinese-style lamp bases, and silk shades covered with clear plastic. The east wall has a large, plate-glass picture window. This is the operating room where the wheeling and dealing is done. There is God, or his earthly counterpart, the ticker tape. Phones ring. Brokers pick their noses and watch the vice-president as the ticker tape glides through his smooth, firm fingers. The brokers doodle with pencils, make notes. Now and then there's slight disagreement. The voices become angry. Warriors after an uncertain truce.

"I feel sorry for the girls downtown," the vice-president says, "printing the stuff. They must be really boiled. Every now and then they print the wrong number."

The lights in the glass-enclosed room are fluorescent and under that naked glare, I discover that all of the younger brokers need a shave. The older brokers are clean shaven.

The vice-president is the star, with ruddy good looks, a full flowing crop of white hair. He is wearing a black suit with matching vest and gold watch chain. He resembles a magnificent Irish actor. His black eyes are polished like marble and they are quick, too quick. His manner is friendly, even with me, the messenger. Perhaps that is why he is a vice-president. But there are moments when his nerves give and he overplays his role.

"Jesus!" he says, "six o'clock, and it's still coming in. Can you beat that! My wife and I, Jesus. Whiskey and soda all night long."

One young broker wants to cut out. I don't like his looks. I doubt if I would have him working for me. He looks like an overgrown prep school boy who will soon have a prominent stomach. He has been fucking around, walking in and out of the glass astronomer's cage. He wants to leave. Who will phone him on the outcome of the market? No one says anything. So he

Already he has the slow relaxed stride of an old man. I am certain he is around my age, twenty-nine.

Then the vice-president steps smartly from the cage. He smiles, rubbing his hands together which I know are never cold.

"Sorry to keep you waiting, sonny. Do you know how to get down there? Fine. Take it to the seventh floor. They're waiting on you. Thanks again, sonny."

I take the stocks and make it. And so that is how it was on May 30, 1962, at the Park Avenue branch office of one Wall Street firm. Earlier I had heard the vice-president exclaim, "We're making history." So in a very, very, vague way, I too helped bring this historic day to a close. And me, I don't have a Goddamn dollar.

ONE AFTER... ...me to Esso Res...ch ... Park, New Jers... ...th...e-mile hike afte... ...in.

I star... b... ...ation about five...irt... ...eave for New ...k...ou...

The s...y...w...h the promise ... ...a...l...ged man and ...n...dusty, beat-up sta...w...and asked if I ...u...a...t. I said yes and s...ed...the backseat. ...to sit up front wi...ni...sus. So I did. T...ned and smiled at...l...ay.

"Than...fo...s," ...said, trying to m...

"Thin...i," the man sai...e...ning wheel wit...an...bit into a plu...f...co. "Glad to...g...

"Pa an...a...s...up hitchhikers," ...We got a boy...d...I...wrote and told...to get a ride, ...n.

"You i...?"...man asked.

"Out."...

We roc...le...e until I said, "...ght have a stor..."

"Yeah,...d, ...king another ch...at are you, Pu...o...F...pino?"

"Neith...n...lored."

"I see," said the man thoughtfully. "Would you like a woman?"

The woman started crying before I could answer.

"Alfonzo," she moaned.

"Boy, I asked you if you wanted a woman."

"I don't know," I replied weakly.

The man turned off the highway and went down a road lined with tall green trees. It was a dead end. There were the ruins of a decayed farm. The man left the motor running. It made a whining noise.

The man put his arms around his wife. "Hold still, Elvira," he said.

"Oh! The things you do to me," the woman cried, trying to escape from her husband's grip. "The things I have to go through."

Then the woman turned toward me. I sat rigid, listening to the raspy sound of the motor and feeling as if a ball of fire had dropped between the woman and myself.

"What you do to me," the woman wheezed mournfully, pressing her body against mine.

She made a drooling noise like a baby who hasn't learned to talk. I felt her soft, fleshy leg.

"Let go of me, Alfonzo," the woman said. "He's got me. Take your hands off of me. Take'm off, Alfonzo."

The man released his wife and did not say anything. He did not look at his wife when she embraced me. He rested his head against the steering wheel. Toward the end, when his wife screamed joyfully, the man put his hands over his ears.

I straightened up in the seat. "I have to go," I said. "I have to catch a train."

"All right," the man said.

"No," the woman said forcefully, grabbing the steering wheel.

"Elvira, the boy has to go," the man tried to explain.

"You ruin everything for me," the woman said.

They let me off at the highway and I thanked them. I watched the car disappear into the darkness. It was drizzling now. I thought of the expression on the man's face. It was like something terrible had happened to him once long ago that had destroyed his sense of being a man, but it didn't matter much anymore. Whatever it was, resignation had settled in the creases of the pale, puffy face and under the tear-filled, forlorn eyes.

I walked to the station under the black sky, smelling the fresh earth.

I WAS IN Claudi... ...laudia, the Grand... ...lous Negro ... ...es down the st... my friend and ... ...to speak of as a ... a swinging br... ...getting dolled... Claudia cru... ...the subways... picked up by ... ...o, after the sh... accompany ... ...rever asking po... tions. By the ... ...made up his fac... he has gone ... ...transformatio... woman.

Today, wh... ...was on the ph... That is to say ... ...is great doe ey... ford had noth... ...ad on a simpl... gown, a stri... ...e wasn't weari... expensive wig ... ...belonged to a... Without the w... ...very feminine...

Claudia w... ...ng high, laughi... jeweled, whit... ...a glass of grap... Italian sailor), ... ...might talk for a...

Claudia p... ...curls lovingly a... white teeth. ... ...tell you. I br... home, and ... ...ad to put him... through in t... ...please, Miss T...

Greek muscles. Muscles, just gushing. Oh honey, quite facial. We had one old ball. I was so unlovely when I woke up. Not a curl in my head. Miss Bobby tried to get him and couldn't. Greedy bitch. Miss Thing, I gotta hang up. Charlie. Yeah. Miss Thing, I've gotta hang up, child. Press, honey. Get something to grace my bed. Okay, child. Good-bye."

"Oh, honey," Claudia sighed, banging down the receiver. He trotted over and sat down at his concert-size electric organ. There was also a large gold harp in front of the bay window.

"Let's sing 'Nearer My God to Thee'," Claudia said with great dignity.

"Baby, what turned you on?" I asked.

Claudia threw back his head and displayed the evil giveaway, his prominent Adam's apple. "Child, your mother is stoned. The Queen's head is tore up. But I must pray for those poor bastards."

"What the hell are you talking about?"

"Didn't you read the paper? Didn't you read about those children at the UN?"

Claudia gave me a stick of pot. I lit up, taking a deep drag, and held it in my head. "Oh, yeah. You mean those Africans at the UN. I did glance at the headlines."

"Child. Those were no Africans. Those were BM's from uptown. Harlem, child."

"You kidding?"

The Grand Duchess struck a heavy trembling chord, blinking his great eyes. The bold, red mouth bordered on a big laugh. The jeweled hands waltzed over the keys. "Nearer my God to Thee. . . . Amen."

"Carry on, girl," I said.

"Jesus!" Claudia shouted. "I caught the BM's on the eleven o'clock news. They were fighting like crazy. It took two guards to handle one child."

Claudia paused and shook his head, banging down on the organ. "I hope they show those damn fools on the Late Late Show. Jesus. Give me a drag. I've got more in the vault."

"What did the NAACP have to say?"

"Child, those were Muslims or something. They're not connected with the NAACP."

"That's right," I said, reaching for the pot. "Those NAACP

bastards are the busy writing ass in Washington. I wonder who's blowing who in the Oval ...

"Oh, honey," Claud said with great drama. "I ... through the Pentagon in a wet drag and get my dick a big general!"

"That would be a real democracy."

Claudia and I ... again and I left.

Back to my own place ... my white-walled, dark room

To score on the smart eastside without good connections, you have to know the right bartenders in the right bars who will set Johns up for a cut. But male and female hustlers are always telling me in sad voices, "Gee, kid, you should have been around during World War II. Or even the early fifties. Things jumped then. All you had to do was just walk down Third Avenue. You could even afford to be grand. Turn down tricks."

Now the scene has changed. Big new office and apartment buildings, bright new street lights, the cops clamping down like the great purge. Johns are also not as easy to come by. This is an age of elegance, stupidity, and fakery. Fags giving off an aura of wealth are often nothing more than glorified office boys, struggling like hell for the privilege of living in a walk-up on the East side. And those Harvard tones give under three martinis.

Still, Third Avenue has a little seedy, fashionable charm and sometimes I wander over, step through all that rich dog shit which peppers the sidewalk like a mosaic and peer into antique shops, knowing that some freaklina will accost me. I'll be picked up for ten-plus-drinks, or by a Vassar-type of girl who will want to discuss jazz.

But that evening I had been walking around about an hour, and nothing was happening. I was getting fed up with freaklinas baiting me like a bitch in heat. I was certain two bulls had spotted

They were ... table at First Av... ...th Street. I saw ... ...ird and Fifty-f... ...t young men ... the cool pose ...spaper repor... ...unkie. They co... ...t minds which ... ...cessful pose.

I made it into ... ...venue bar, an ... ...ion of a Iri... ...with the smel... ...ds, poodles, ... ...women. The r... ...special mal... ...developed cage... ...kers.

...went to the ... ...next to a ha... ...silver-blue ... ...able scotch ... ...ld nurse his ... ...thing turned up...

The woman ... ...people alon... I... ...w this too, for ... ...ed her elegant f... ...had eyes like ... ...e. The simple ... ...e strand of p... ...l, bored express... ...ested me. She ... ...and damn sure ... ...ortant, she see...

Presently ... ...en with a line... ...ed up and b... ...was the cutest ... ...ld he buy me ... ...ry head, thou... I... ...ful to be charm...

After the pluc... ...e woman turn... ...with the ... ...al smile. The... ...her daiquiri, ... ...This was my ... "Thank you," ... I had lit her ... ...ned to her pr... ...led rum and li... Later the wom... ...to go for a spi... The bar closed ... ...ther. The wom... ...hrysler like a ... ...he stoplights, g... ...nsboro bridge ... ...we were on L... There was a ... ...ld smell the sea... Niki—that was ... ...on the fifth dr... she had said: ... ...Wythe—Niki ... ...house as eleg... ...herself. As we ... ...yer, I thought ... ...appeared in th... ...r above a Chi... ...ed a haircut an... ...ed, button-do... ...ed khaki trous...

We made small talk for an hour amid the cool tones of a harpsichord playing on an old Atwater Kent phonograph. Niki had expertly sidestepped my flirtations. The only thing she had done was caress my face in the foyer. Her soft hands sought out my face like a blind man groping for his favorite chair.

"How smooth your skin is. Like baked bread. You remind me of my son, Robin. He was killed at prep school."

That had been all and finally I came on with, "It's getting late. Let's turn in."

Niki sat primly in her black Empire chair with both hands fingering a scotch. She closed her eyes like a woman who has never seen the dawn or the early morning light of peace. Perhaps she didn't want to see.

I couldn't stand the silence. I took off my shirt, walked drunkenly bare chested and stood in front of Niki. I tilted her head back with my hand. She turned angrily. She cringed. I felt her body stiffen.

"Don't be so ladylike," I taunted.

I leaned over and put my hand on her shoulder. She held her breath, let it out in deep, spasmodic gasps.

"Say the word, baby. It's getting late."

Then I jerked her up from her chair and held her in my arms. With the hate people vomit up in moments of weakness I said, "Look at me, white woman. Look at what you want and what you don't want. I know you'd pass me like the plague on the street. I know my looks got me through that front door. Otherwise back door, Boy! So, just say the word."

"Please," Niki moaned, "please try to understand. . . ." She broke off. Her lips grazed my neck. Her tears ran down my bare chest.

We went into her bedroom. A beautiful, cold, gray and white room. She was crying softly as we got into bed. I tried to comfort her grief and tears. I held her gently in my arms and stroked her silver hair until she went to sleep. If I knew or understood nothing else, I knew and understood loss and loneliness. It's like having all your breath sucked up in a balloon or like when you are in a dark room alone and you are certain your heart is beating for the last time and it doesn't matter. Anything is better than being aware of your own breathing.

IT IS F... o... ol... out my wind... a ... above the to... rin... s, solid, and u... a... ...epolo's mauve... ea... ...d oft blue clou... d... here in New Y... ...a pleasant breez... ...as suddenly a... f... ...he...d on the wro... ...en the policen...'s... ...ed horse's tail is...

An... ...here they go, th... ...laughing goo... ...rers. They hav... ...e in this world... ...g to make dam... ...know it and tha... ...tempt anything... ...ens to destroy... ...rgeois right dow... ...ear and there go... ...le dark dots i... ...ck and white, ... ...ces like mad... ...ogged traffic... ...city's nausea. I... ...belong down th...

One... ...from Tip Top... ...ver at me. The... ...ng green uniforr... ...sist in staring?... ...pty?

The... ...*a de Paris* have... ...ette: a gypsy ba... ...he elegant rear o... ...aked, eating a... ...oy's mother does... ...pping dance,... ...ge, cat-shaped... ...on an approach... ...sailor in stiff w... ...his right han...

There is no air. I watch the paralysis of mummified Americans waiting for their cars to take them back to suburbia.

Now the sky is an evaporating pearl gray with watery mauve patterns. Evening is here like a heavy, hot, dusty, velvet curtain. The Grand Duchess, Claudia, is leaving with Lady P, his tiny Egyptian dog.

Later, Shirley called and we quarreled as usual. "Sometimes I feel so close to you," she once said. "And then at other times, I don't feel anything. You're here. I can see you. Oh, I just don't know."

And then I heard the super call me. I did not answer. An oppressive stillness which I cannot break.

...messenger work for the ... world. It is ... near the famous, husky ... Tallulah Bankhead ... Irene Manning lo... with pincurls ... does over footlights, and ... brews a ... Julie Harris is a ... the long ... a b... snowy night. ... his wife, Ann... always excited upon receiving ... But not all ... to the famous. Some ... delivery will be ... actress on the way ...

...ivery was my job. ... to a you... lower east side, on a side ... the bargain capital ... Orchard.

...enement. Plaster peeps ... the dirty cra... colored hallways. It was ... but it was ... I had to strike a mat... the names on the ... actor's name was ... the name of the ... have to ask the tenants. ... on several doors and, ... answer, walked ... aky stairs. A door wa... and I heard ... noise.

... on the tin-covered ... my head in. ... said. A PR woman ... arge of a p... looked up at the ... her head as ... ful noise was coming from ...

There were two other PR women in the room in black dresses and black cotton stockings. They had fine mustaches and carefully braided white hair. They eyed me curiously.

"Yes?" the woman on the bed asked. She folded her hands and bit her lips. "Police?"

I couldn't make head or tail of what had happened. The room smelled as if a thousand people had lived and died in it, although the window was open and the room was cheerful with starched, white curtains and green plants growing on the window ledge.

"*Media, media*," one of the old women said.

I turned and saw that she was pointing at a small bundle lying in a corner of the room near an unpainted chest of drawers. The bundle lay on the glossy blue linoleum floor as if waiting to be picked up and taken away.

I went over and examined the bundle. Inside lay a dead P.R. baby about a month old. He was naked and his head was turned on his left side. A circle of blood had dried and was caked around his mouth, and his little chubby hands were high above his head. There was a blue-black mark on his right cheek, as if he had fallen against something or had been hit or kicked.

I re-covered the bundle and looked over at the woman sitting on the bed. Her whole body shook but she had stopped making that strange noise. She rubbed her hands together and looked at the two old women but she did not look at me.

I held out a pack of cigarettes to her. She took one but her hand was shaking badly and I had to put the cigarette in her mouth. It fell from her lips. She put her hands over her mouth, trying to hold in that strange noise. I put my arms around her. She fell against my chest like a dead weight.

One of the old women went into the kitchen and the other came over and stood and looked at me. Then the old woman returned from the kitchen with a cup of milk-coffee. I forced myself to drink it because it seemed the thing to do.

Gradually the noise ceased and the woman asked for a cigarette. This time she could hold it. She took long, deep drags and said that her husband had come in drunk, demanding money. She would not give him money and so he beat her. In a final show of revenge, he had picked up the sleeping baby and had thrown him clear across the room.

That had been last night. After he had left, the woman had

called her two ... ved down the street. ... sitting silent ... unable to move. ... woman
said, sniffing ... the smoke billowing ... low
ceiling ... come to see her. ... always
dropping ... but not today.

I said ... all the police, ... me.
The two ... followed me to the ... ter,
learned that ... actor had left the ... before
for Bratt ...

IT IS ONLY June and I am drunk with dreams of leaving New York, of going to Europe, going any place. I have always been a traveler. I remember the first time I left home. I was eight years old and Grandma had just bought me a pair of brown and white shoes. That summer afternoon I squeezed a couple of peanut butter-and-jelly sandwiches into the shoe box and started out walking to my great-grandmother's house. She lived in another town, thirty miles away. I had gotten three miles when a family friend spotted me on the highway.

At fourteen I hitchhiked to Kansas City and St. Louis every weekend. It alarmed Grandma, but I had to move. What would a fourteen-year-old boy do alone in a city? Well, I walked and walked, met all types of people. I went to movies, museums, the library. I remember a little old lady in a Queen Mary hat who went around the library in Kansas City giving notes to young boys.

"Are you lonely? Very well then. Come with me. I will feed you and cheer you up," was scrawled on pink, scented stationery.

I followed her one hot Saturday afternoon to a cluttered walk-up above a secondhand book store at Twelfth and Vine. Miss Sally lived with two dozen white pigeons which flew around the taupe-colored room. The roller piano tinkled merrily with barrel house music and Miss Sally danced around the room, a hop and skip,

48

ooping like a d... ...refused to ta...
refused the ou... ...ate, and later a...
Sally cut me d... ...my table hum...
Sambo."

I remember... ...s City at four...
went to the b... ...acked out on...
tended to g... ...ame up and s...
tion. "Would I... ...olice and sleep a...
...ase?" I followe... ...as I emerged fro...
out his arms an... ...id, "Son, your ey...
into bed." I wa... ...hat had happe...
breakfast. I fel... ...in the half-world...
...ciousness, I h... ...thing was happen...
part of my bod... ...ad to scream, I...
turned on that... ...ollywood bed w...
...ory-and-leathe... ...ith brass nail...
were dying di... ...God to let what...
...g end. And th... ...he man said, "H...
...o dollars and... ...of here. My w...
...on."

By the tim... ...ned him, I wa...
...as a rainy Sa... ...was sitting in...
...partment. So... ...d up like an el...
...striped suit... ...gleamed in...
...oked down at... ...tion from his...
...feet, and sto... ...rench at me. I...
...d we walke... ...this mad ma...
...ked. I wanted... ...was more than...
...as a beanpole... ...We went to his...
...à terre, as h... ...ere many pain...
...X talked and... ...nce did he tou...
...that he sai... ...pause" of his...
...ondered if Mr.

And then th... ...es singer. I ne...
...knew my... ...ght have. I use...
...at four o'cl... ...ternoons. She w...
...then and wo... ...oss. "Hey, you...
...Get me a b... ...ou? Go down a...
...And if you... ...ip—I'll tan yo...

hear me? Where in the hell do you come from? If the cops ever come here looking for you, and sweetcakes, I know plenty of cops, they'll put your little ass under the jail. Do you hear me?" She had many boyfriends and gave them all hell, throwing cups of coffee or empty gin bottles at them—"Yes, Goddamn it, I made a mess, but I pay the freight here, and that's why I have a cleaning woman,"—But once we were in her pink convertible and started for the club, the bitchy woman vanished. "Sweetcakes, you're gonna sit ringside tonight. At the best table in the joint. And if you want a whore, just say the word. Don't blush. You're a sassy little tomcat. . . ."

In my sophomore year at school in Missouri I began to read everything that I could lay my hands on. I was the best customer at the Sedalia Missouri Public Library. I shall never forget those wonderful women at the library. They even allowed me to read the so-called adult books.

But, after a while, Sedalia, St. Louis, and Kansas City weekends were not enough. The undiscovered world beckoned and one Sunday night, three months before graduation, I climbed out my bedroom window and with a carefully saved seventy-five dollars, I headed for California.

I caught a ride with a pleasant truck driver who was going as far as Albuquerque, New Mexico. I remember passing through countless grim, quiet, small towns, and I remember when we swung into the wide open, sunny, dusty face of Texas. There wasn't that "grand sweep" that I had read about. The landscape was a land of plains and rivers frozen over. Too many trees had been cut down and the towns all looked as if the hands of time had stopped. I remember driving down the short main street of one Texas town and reading a sign: "Nigger Don't Let The Sun Set On You In This Town." I closed my eyes, fell asleep, and when I awoke, it was the end of the line, Albuquerque.

I got out of the truck and discovered that it was morning again. There was a brilliant, turquoise-blue sky, serene Rocky Mountains; a red-pink sun was coming up behind the mountains. A heavy wind rose and then a sandstorm. I thumbed vigorously at the speeding cars and trucks. No one stopped, not even Negroes. I stood there all day and toward evening two young guys in a beat-

I remember finally a bearded man with a tarnished silver crown who said he was the son of Jesus and a woman in a man-tailored suit, built like a boxer, saying: "Come unto me, son. This is the day of your salvation." And in a sense she was right. I discovered Maria was pregnant, and my cousin, Ruby, came for me from Missouri. We rode back to Missouri on the Greyhound bus and didn't say one hundred words to each other. I never knew whether or not Maria had the baby.

Back home, I worked on and off, hitchhiking back to Kansas City on weekends. I read a great deal and tried to avoid the kids I had grown up with. At eighteen, I had had my first slice of life and I wanted more.

I was searching for something, I would tell Ruby. What? She would ask. I don't know, I would say. But I'll know when I find it. Shit, Ruby would say.

...n cousin, use... ...cking and f... ...s n't nothing... ...e to get out of...

...f st time I saw... ...o visit me and... y grandfather... ...ate August to visit... ...w sitting in the... ...room, rocking... ...b cked, oak r... ...was a cigarette... ...ht she was the m... ...nan I had ever... ...w skin was sm... ...the nose was... ...egro face. Her v... ...ways seemed... ...of a smile tha... ...She wore her... ...ge boy, and it... ...houlders. She... ...g npowder e... ...ed to give off... ...ga e people a... ...ruel glance... ...men say, "Tha... ...woman. She... ...nothing from... ...h eyes of hers... ...irough you."

..., Grandma," R... ...in a voice... ...but cold and i... ...were reciting... ...aper. "My bab... ...fu and died... ...and left me, an... ...with a white...

"Sonny, you'd better go outside," Grandma interrupted.

"Let him stay," Ruby said, blowing smoke rings. "It's no good hiding things from kids. They'll only get the dope from the streets."

Ruby had been a singer up in Kansas City and now her voice was shot. She couldn't make twenty-five a week in a ginmill unless she hustled on the side, and she wasn't ready for that. Grandma suggested she sing at the Hughes Chapel Methodist Church until she got her voice back in shape. No. Ruby would get a domestic's job and if her voice came back, fine and dandy. She had had a good voice; she no longer had a voice. Everything with Ruby was black and white, no buts and ifs.

The next day, Ruby and I both looked for jobs. Ruby found a job in a hotel as a chambermaid. I would need money as school was nearing. I saw an ad in the paper: busboy. I went to the back door wearing my white-folks smile and was told the job had been taken.

The ad continued for another week. I returned to the café, thinking the new busboy had quit. The man met me at the back door again and bellowed, "Boy, can't you get it through your thick skull, we don't hire niggers." It was like being slapped hard across the face or dashed with a bucket of ice water. I was standing on the back stoop of the café and the man was looking down at me. He slammed the door in my face because I couldn't move. It was a heavy, old-fashioned screen door and slammed shut like a giant mousetrap.

Next stop was a large store, the nearest thing to a department store in that Missouri town. I got the runaround there too.

So I made it to the hotel where Ruby was working. She was in the linen room, sitting on a pile of dirty sheets. She counted sheets and she listened to my tale of woe.

Finally I became furious and jumped up from the box where I had been sitting.

"The sons-of-bitches. I'd like to kill'm all!"

"Kill'm?" Ruby asked. "There ain't enough time."

"Yes, kill'm," I sneered. "Kill'm, line'm up. All the white bastards. I'd go BANG BANG BANG until I couldn't see another living white face."

"Oh. Talk that talk," Ruby mocked.

of an old fool, you'll play it cool. When you get into the prime of life, you'll be a played-out tomcat. I've spent thirty-five years discovering how rotten life is if you waste it on nothing. Never be bitter, Sonny. Only people who can't face life and hate themselves are bitter. Maybe I was born black and lost my voice to teach me a lesson. Well, kid, I learned. I know damn well I learned something being born black that I could never have learned being born white."

I looked at her in wonder, listening to the clear flow of words, turning them over in my mind, which was not a boy's mind, nor a man's mind, but something in between.

Ruby lit another cigarette with the butt of one that was only half gone. I saw the wrinkles on her forehead and her eyes which now gave off a light, warm and small as a candle.

"Being black taught me humility," Ruby said, beginning to sound tired. The fire had gone out of her voice. "Another thing I learned was the meaning of compassion. I sang at the Blue Room in KC. We had so many white country-club folk coming in that we had to turn them away. Can you imagine? Rich white folk, wanting to hear colored blues. They weren't slumming. I know that kind. I asked Finkelstein who owned the joint. He said, 'Ruby, you know true blues is about suffering. Troubles. They know about these things too. That's what true blues have, compassion. Ruby gal, you reach the people.' And Sonny, I started watching those white faces out front. They were like the faces of you and me. Anybody."

I am brought back to the present by a neon light shining in on the seven-by-nine photograph tacked above my fireplace. It shows a boy, aged one-and-a-half, in a white knitted suit with matching knitted beret and white shoes and socks. He is standing in a peeling wicker chair. He's a cute, fat, healthy-looking kid. A golden teddy bear. But the eyes, large, too beautiful, are strangely adult. They seem to be staring beyond the photographer. Great, sad eyes. I would like them to tell me what they see, but they are silent.

THE DIVINITY STU...

...tones and qu...

...ing, dead drunk...

...is healthy, ha...

...and the living...

...my ears to h...

...of his twenty-thr...

...ly was still or...

...half was ris...

...bly in my arm...

...sobs shook...

...slithered down...

...the young Epis...

...God he...

...es which keye...

...the cries of men...

...ying. I sat the...

...ette, and tried...

...to doze then...

...uddenly as Br...

...my arms. He...

...lapsed back in...

...to be a troubl...

...ette had gone...

...relit it, wa...

...turn to elect...

...The air w...

...would be a s...

...sound from...

...was nothing t...

...to think an...

...awn.

...ing fitfully, c...

...owing afternoon

...the sofa...

..."Boy," he s...

sad announcement, running his pale hand through his mushroom-colored hair.

I had the bromo, orange juice, and black coffee ready. He wanted none of it. He wanted a drink.

So I gave the former teetotaler a water glass of gin straight and he put it down nicely, wincing slightly.

"The bastards," Bruce said with finality.

"Who?" I asked.

"My family," Bruce said, eyeing me steadily. "Give me another drink." He nursed his second straight gin bent over, resting his arms on his legs. He had the somnolence of a frog basking in the sun.

The afternoon was cloudless and humid, with the promise of rain; the room had a murky gloom.

"The bastards," Bruce said again, rising, and saying no more except, "Thanks, and I'll see you later."

THE GREAT D...her has arrived. Dusty ... like snow over ...is ...y; ...i...e are a washed-out ... ...le...suspended days ...ak...d ...t. A...insane jungle ...ve...y ...u...night. It is neve...qui...e ...ot ...ven in the soft...our...s...s...a...n. I d...not go o...t un...s I...ve...o. We tenan...s...av...co...open, ears pric...d, a...:...ootsteps on the stai...s...a...t...i...g to the store. Wal...q...do...? How soon w...t...h...e...returi...?"

I...ave...i...t...o s...ay in this whit...wall...s...ti...il the sum-mer...end...g...he...march out, le...t...he...l...nlike Lot's wife...eve...ol...ck. The messenger...en...s...ig...e day and at...t...s...g...ac...here, sweat...y, t...h...chilles feet thro...ng i...e...fla...ed heart. I ask...ha...i...t...ith me. I'm one...th...o...n...s American as...p...l...t...I cannot, simp...car...t...a...ask and suc...e...a...eet, secure bitch...aid...American life.

S...m...m...n...my fifth-floor w...do...t...the young Ame...are...t...e town, he...l...t...nte...d as moth...he...fac...s indistingui...ha...le...ass. Look how...app...t...hey are united and o...c...ld become one...th...m...sp...te the fact that...rl...ember the black...ots...re...white fields...ou...ing about writi...a...t...orruption of this c...y...d the fate of m...ki...d...et a soft, safe...v...i...save the coins, marry, and all in the name of middle-class sanctity.

I remember one Monday I played hookey from the messenger service. I shaved very close that morning, glued on my average, boyish, American smile. This smile is no different from the average, boyish, white-American smile. After all, the Negro has been fucked through the years and in many different positions in this country. He has been the faithful, unpampered watchdog of the whites. Above all, he knows that white is right. Witness skin lighteners and all those magical oils, lotions, creams. They will not only take away blackheads and pimples, but your dark skin as well. Hence, the average, boyish, American smile. I donned my only good suit, white shirt, dark silk tie, picked up the Sunday *New York Times* classified section, and made it.

There were twenty or more men around, waiting for the fifty-seven-dollar-a-week midtown mailroom flunky job. All types, races, ages, backgrounds. It was a cross section of America. Several looked extremely intelligent and several were very well-dressed.

I filled out the application and middle-aged Mr. Personnel called me first. Twenty-three envious faces were on me. How did I rate? Nowhere, baby. I knew nothing about mail rates and they wanted someone experienced. Personnel was sorry. He would have liked to take me on; I seemed bright, on the ball. Personnel and I exchanged shitty grins. I exited and went down to Wall Street and applied for a brokerage house trainee. Seventy dollars every Thursday. The company paid the agency fee. Before reporting to Personnel, I dug the sorry-looking jokers in the "cage," sorting stocks and bonds like so many automatic monkeys with their white shirts, sleeves rolled up, and wearing impossible ties. They were the kind of young men who went bowling and, after four beers, became "cards," the kind of young men who took their girlfriends to Chinese restaurants on Saturday nights, the kind of young men who would say, "Let's get a couple of beers and pick up some dames." The only thing they could pick was their noses. I have double-dated with them and their vague pigs, and I know.

If I worked with these slobs, I would be stoned from nine to five, I thought. The average jerk, going along like a cog, questioning nothing, seeking nothing. I've heard tell that these young men are the beefsteak on tomorrow's menu.

But the n w  b  be wrong abou  he  ay
to find out w  ul   with these yo  n

Personne  wa   this time. A s  er
self. She p  me    nced at my a  li  n  en
looked up,  s   sked me if I    k
Puerto Rican

"Neither,   i  and making xi  o.
You'll hear fr m   dor."

That afte no    ed to the me gs  a
prodigal son eg   ess.

AT EIGHT O'CLOCK Monday morning, Shirley walked in as casually as if she lived here. She put her beach bag on the bookcase and smiled roguishly. Her eyes were bright.

"Don't look at me like that," she said. "Surprised?"

"Are you working today?"

"No. I had my schedule changed. I worked yesterday. Channing said you didn't go to the beach because it was too crowded."

"Who said I was going to the beach today? I've got to work."

"Charles," Shirley warned, "don't be difficult. We won't have to borrow Tony's radio. My *friend,* the doctor, bought me a transistor radio."

"That's nice."

"Isn't it? Oh, Charles, he's such a wonderful person. He is all I ever wanted in a man. We're getting married in the fall."

"Congratulations."

"At least you don't have to be so dry about it."

"All right, I'll try to show a little emotion in my voice: Congratulations!"

"Goddamn it. Get dressed."

And now we lay under the boardwalk at Coney Island on an old army blanket, sheltered from the hot sun, staring out at the sea. Low clouds with the brilliance of a cold snow seem to bank at the

...ge of the sea. ...ze and then ... back like a... ...iendship a wa... ...chnician have ...es out to ch ...be... ...eath.

The dazzlin... ...ld. Giant wh... ...arby, a grou... of... ...w chilly. S... en...

"Want to go... I a...

"Do you wa... o...

"Not yet."

"All right the..." ...queezing my ha... ...ently until a... ...ny... ...er ten p.m.

...adio plays mu... ...ong hands cla... ...o! Would thi... ...head of love?... ...heart in chec... ...y-colored girl...

Dusk arrived ...the sparsely... ...boys played... ...in my arms.

...per attacked th...

WHAT IS WRONG WITH ME? Yesterday, I got drunk. Al said I'd better take a week off. Now I am jobless and broke because I blew the works last night. I have a talent for getting too involved with people. One crisis follows another like the second hand of a smooth-running watch and this great republic might blaze with prosperity under fair skies, but each time I make a lunge for the dollar, the eagle flies in the opposite direction. The Negro Bernard Baruchs have a fence around their park benches.

I tell you, I've got to get out of this city, this city which will accept victory or defeat with the same marvelous indifference.

And my friends: a twenty-one gun salute to madness. Laura Vee, spitting icicles. Claudia, chained to the organ, composing his first drunken opera in English, singing at the top of his voice, "Oh, my most noble love, return. . . ." Bruce is having a financial tumor. Channing is not very warm these days because I said he was not a square but an octagonal fool. Last night, I swallowed my pride and phoned Shirley, begging forgiveness. But she was mesmerized by melancholia.

This pad looks as if the devil just stormed through and I've got exactly sixty-five cents. That ain't nowhere.

I left my place at eleven-thirty this morning and looked around for a fast hustle. Tee-shirted with faded, tight Levis, which is the

"How old are you?"

"Old enough."

A wise smile lit his face. "You're cute . . . Don't blush."

"What time is it?" I asked.

"One o'clock. Are you in a hurry?"

"No. Why?"

"You know why. Have you got a girl?"

"Yeah."

"Are you good to her?"

"I hope so."

"I know you are."

The punch line made me feel as if I were about to be raped in Rockefeller Center.

"Would you excuse me for a minute?" he asked, looking up. "I have to make a call."

The cops? He's going after his gumshoe partner. You had a crazy feeling all morning. Should have worked the Village.

Cool it, baby. The voice. No cop could bring off that voice. Cool it, now. Don't queer the deal.

Here he comes. All smiles, strutting jauntily, swinging his attaché case. Portrait of a successful, young businessman.

"Want to take a ride down to the next station? The first car. It will put us off at Exchange Place."

The train pulls in. I linger back. The stupid joker is motioning toward me. As if I wasn't going to make it.

I stand against the door nonchalantly. He is sitting on the opposite side of the car, watching me.

Exchange Place filled with people on lunch. There is tension in the air and on the brooding faces. People are walking fast like ants scurrying from rain. I remember this is where the money is.

We go up a side street to a small sandstone building. "Give me ten minutes," my boy said, patting my shoulder. "Get off at the ninth floor. The elevators are automatic."

"Okay. If somebody stops me, I'll say I'm a messenger."

"Fine," he nodded.

The ninth floor has been freshly painted. Not a stick of furniture. "Our main office is in midtown. We're getting our furniture wholesale. All good things take time." The last sentence with a leer.

Now he was facing me and I could see his Adam's apple working like mad.

"Sorry I _____ _____ rink."

"That's _____ _____ould have used _____
_____ch, depr____ _____ _____Wonder what h__ _____

Then __ __ __ _____ front of me. __ _____ __
_____isty. He st__ __ __ _____ I was reminded _____ __ __
with tall, bl__ __ _____

He push__ __ __ _____vall roughly. I st__ d __ __
_____ling and s__ __ _____over.

"My nam__ __ _____d. "What's your _____ __

"Char____ __ _____

"Do you __ __ _____

"Yes," I __ _____ y wallet and gav__ _____ __

"Could I __ __ _____ s?"

"Oh, sur__ _____

"Your pa__ __ _____ __d?"

"Just _____ __ _____ Diamonds. That_____ a __ __ __ __ __
play with _____ __

"I see, __ __ _____ "I'll give you a _____ __ __ __
__d."

"My folk__ __ _____ug__," I came o__ __ __ __ __
_____ their m__n __ _____ u__ kids out of th__ __ty__

"You w__u __ _____ __?"

"Woul__ y__ __ _____

Keith _____ __ _____ _____oothly grea____ _____
_____nty. "N__w __ _____ __nd watch that __ __ __
"Sure __h__ __ __ _____ __d left.

Keith w__ as __ _____ __ive me any pho__ __ __
a damn wh__t _____ _____re real, and m__e__ _____
And m__? __ __ _____ __ther and fath__r. __ _____
have to tel__. __ _____ __op__e are peopl__ __ __
you. If you d__ __ _____ __t go to bed wi__h _____
Milksh__ke __ _____ __t. Take "A" tr__ __ _____
_____eet. Clam__ __ _____ A quick bour__ __ _____
_____thing ha__p__ __ _____

The Bil__ie __ _____ __m. Lovely, s__ __ _____
_____ongbird. S__ng __ _____g. __ had to have _____
Milk, __a__ __ _____ __ench bread. Ch____ __
_____wberri__s. __ _____ __tt__s, six beers, a__ __h__
_____ne and, __dl__ __

TONIGHT I FINISHED taking my shower at eight o'clock, stepped from the bathroom nude, singing happily, and encountered a freckled, baby-faced sailor who was lumbering up the stairs. He had the dumb expression of a forlorn pup.

He walked up, took in my nudity, and grinned. "Hiya, sport."

I smiled faintly and nodded.

"Is number fourteen on this floor?" he asked.

"This is the top floor," I said. "The highest number is eleven. And that's my pad."

"Well, where are the whores?" the sailor asked. A look of alarm covered his face.

"Well, dad," I said, putting my towel over my shoulder, "there are no whores in this house."

And if it is possible for such a dumb face to sink deeper into the pit of confusion, the sailor's did. He fumbled in his white middy shirt and pulled out a piece of cardboard about the size of a book of matches. The sailor studied the cardboard intensely.

I took a deep breath and thought: How do you tell a man he is a sucker when he is not a friend?

Finally I blurted out, "Baby, you have been taken."

The sailor looked up quickly. His shoulders seem to rise as if they were suspended from balloons. His hazel eyes were moist, on the edge of heartbreak.

"You'd better ask to see the broad before you put out your

cons... ... ..." ...d then you ca... be... ... ... sure. Any
way... ow... ... ... ... e score. How ...ch ... ...u?"
"... ...was... ..., he said, kick... ...his ... ... the steps
"Twe...ty f... ... ... rs. Jesus! I sho... ...ha... ... ...tter."
"...Ye...h ... ... ...kes," I said ...n ...gen ... ... ...one.
"...ah" ...th... ...greed.
I ...ur... for... ...d.
T... ...a... ...e...d back dow... t... sta... ... ... perfec... vic-
ti... ...f th... ... ... ...ne.

The ...ur... ... ...played every ...t ... ...g ...orhood. A
year... ...p ... ...ed overtime ...g ... ... ...d summer.
A... e... er... ...e ...l Murphy Ga... ...p... ... ...oth talker
and g...neral ... ... v... dressed.
I... ...ds ... ...c... the incident ...th ... ...l...at Shuffle
Al...g was ... t... neighborhood ...is s...
Sh...ffl... ...l... ... ...aster of the M...ph... ...e ... is a Negro
of in... ...ctu... ...e ...omewhere on ... ...ot ... ...d ...rty—with
the h...ght ...l... r... f a twenty-year ...ld. ... ... olly confi-
denti... man... S... a Claus and ...esse... ...ood sports
clo...he... ...ts ... ...rty-five-doll...r ...lig... ... ... e shuffles
along k... h... ...ts ...m of mules in ...rt... ... ...though a
ball and ...ha... ...o... been attache... ...o h... ... ...ps th...t is
wh... ...M... p... ...n is his professi...
T... M... ... ...n is nothing bu... an ... ... ...eet co...ner
or ...ng ...a... ...c...erving a man ...th... ...ok, a man
who, ...ou ... ...l... intelligent th... yo... ...l... ...rike ...p a
co...ve...ation... ...nd in a few ...a... ...ull... ... ...ds, which
mu...t ...ut... ...a... y... inform the ...a...tl... ... ...get hi... a
good ...ot... ... ...n fee. First he ...st ... ... money—
"you ...o... ...b... ... ...hores are." Y... tel... ... ...wait until
you r...art... ...n't return. O... ...ou ...a... ... into ...hat
hot...l ...d ...l... r ...ou'd like a ...o... ... ...or with a
we...s... ...n... t... ...e man will thi... you'... ...p with a
priva... ...od...
V... frie... ...n ...n't play the ...ph... ... ...ess he has
smok... ...a... ...s... ...ks of pot. He'... ...ll ... ...king, ...ut
has n... ...uts ... ...A...ng is someth... else ... ... as nerves
of s...e... B... ...e ...r... t door was lo... ...d... ... ... over the

landing and saw Shuffle Along talking with a man. Shuffle Along held out his hand. The man opened his wallet and gave Shuffle Along three ten-dollar bills. Shuffle Along said, "Daddy, I'm the house man. What are you gonna give me?" So the man forks over five and one single. Shuffle Along departed slowly. Once he reached the street, he would take wings of the morning. The man started knocking on doors, seeking his nonexistent woman. In most cases, these men are not drunk. They simply have sex on the brain.

The young boys pose a problem. If you are a professional Murphy player like Shuffle Along, you know that some of the college boys think they can get a woman for two dollars. Shuffle Along has solved this problem magnificently. He will say in his confiding Uncle Tom's voice, "Now, boss. Ya know we been having trouble with the cops. And you look so young. Do you have any ID?"

The young man hands Shuffle Along his wallet.

Shuffle Along will give the ID card a quick glance, checking the money.

If the money is substantial, Shuffle Along will say, "Boss, I is sorry. You is straight. But like I say: we can't take no chance. Now what kind of woman do you want. I can get you a young one, old one, fat, skinny, black, or white."

The young man gives Shuffle Along fifteen or twenty dollars. Shuffle Along takes a piece of cardboard from his jacket. There are two identical numbers written on the cardboard with red pencil and Shuffle Along tears the cardboard in half and gives one half to the young man. The other half goes in his pocket and he says, "This goes to the big boss. He don't take no fuckin' around. Now you jest take this number next door and ring bell four."

The young man departs eagerly with his number and Shuffle Along scampers up the stairs and out through the trapdoor leading to the roof.

My messenger job allows me encounters with all kinds of people and I admire Shuffle Along and the men and women of the Murphy Society. All they do is tell you a story and hold out their hand. The Murphy Game is flourishing in June of this year. The hayseed tourist has arrived; the ships are in. And, of course, there are always the sports from Jersey and the Bronx.

CHT, I AM CO LID II. ... n he East Sixties. ... h
, brown, and gre n li ... n f a town house ... ly
Korean pal, b oug at ... a e three other m ... u
Everyone is nde f ... e ights are low.
arry, the ho t, l o i ... i y-two and his al
with the Da s sl ch ... s ort shirt, and tl b
e shoes. He i in e ... s ess which he in i i
cle, and pla s th s ... s
was helping ys f t ... s tch when he ca e ... t
en sticks of pot E e ... estrained, but e
ever left the pot n ... o e table.
Daddy rea he o e ... k up two sticks o oc ... [
show on t e r ...
Cool it," a etty in ... ughs and takes st i
Daddy.
he guy sittin ne t t ... the pot. He ha ... k
, desperat ju k ... around Sixth e
ht.
You know w at e a ... etty blonde gig d
Keep it up," he a ... "Keep it up.
ur head."
Oh, shut up ' t e b ... You're a l k
too damn are ... mes have I to

leaving the Goddamn needle under the soapdish in the bath-room?"

I looked at Barry. He was blushing.

"This is good shit," I said.

"Panamanian pot, baby," Big Daddy added.

"I don't want any of that shit," the pale junkie said scornfully. He got up and Barry ushered him upstairs.

Another guy, who hadn't said a word since I had arrived about an hour ago, followed them quickly.

A girl, a typical Village type with long stringy hair, man's shirt, and paint-splattered blue jeans, bolted up and yelled, "Wait for me, you greedy bastards. You think you're going to get all the goodies."

Then Jelly Roll struts in like a proud rooster. He was a Korean War buddy of mine and Big Daddy's. Round chocolate bear, nuts for ballet. He makes his living now playing drums in a rock-and-roll band.

Jelly stands in the middle of the living room grinning, jerking his shoulders, rubbing his fat hands together as if for warmth.

"Charlie, my man, Big D," he said, "what's the haps?"

"Everything, baby," Big Daddy mumbled. "I've got to ration myself on this stuff."

"Ah, come on," Jelly laughed. "Man, I want some H. Some horse."

"Talk that trash," a girl named Louise said. She put her bourbon down and gave Jelly the eye.

"Yeah," Jelly amended. "Take me to thy keeper."

"Come on, Charlie," Big Daddy says, getting up. "Let's get this show on the road."

Jelly turned to me. "Baby, I knew you'd finally get hooked."

"Hell," I grinned, "I just wanna see the orgy."

"Tell me more," Louise said. She came over and took my hand and we followed Jelly and Big Daddy up the carpeted stairs. A group of landscape prints decorated the stair wall and there was a chandelier of frosted glass. And because of the quiet, it reminded me of a funeral home.

Barry and the pale junkie were in the bedroom sitting on the floor. They reminded me of guys down at Wall Street with Big Deals brewing. Stoned junkies have that same cocky air.

They are the to    d          hey feel that th     a
        There was   gi          the bed who
stairs.  She  sta  d            or  perhaps  sh   w
thoughts lik   pl  to           e jungly wallpa    r.
glazed like a  ca  s.           radio was  pla   g
jazz and she  ke   ti          music, snapping    r
        Louise  we     w      l Barry and the
his eyes closed,    o          l.
        "Who's  go   a          Big Daddy  asl
ish expression    h
        "Yeah,"  Jel   e          sperate voice.
        Barry  looke   u        n the boys on."
        Ellie was  t  e          n the bed.  "     a          d,
rowning.
        "Turn the   ys
        "Oh su  ,"  lli          eaving her drea   w
        Ellie got  u   r          a very busines  k          nt
over to the  m    r            r.
        Jelly gave l   r          stare, but Big        d
rolling up  h     ev
        "Easy  d l,  as          ig Daddy grin               c
my veins. I go   b            e arm and they   d          i
the feet."
        Ellie di  n  lo          k a smile. She  p  ce          i
spoon, and  s    k            d prepared the   j          a
the same b re   na            doctors giving    o
        Ellie  p ng  d          n Big Daddy's    r          l,
expertly, sw t  d            cotton.
        Big Da dy  xl          e had suddenly    ee          a.
great weigh .
        Ellie g are  xl          lly.
        He ease l   t          rozen grin. His  p          a
if he were on  t  v          am.
        Ellie sh t  n.          "Oh, bitch, su   r
        I left the  w te          ouse at about f   r          v
ing afternoon  nd          n the quiet,  e   n          i l
street. I de ide   d          an. My energy       l          ui.
But I didn't  ca   a          rosstown bus  h   e.

MRS. LEE CALLS: "Charles, pet. Are you alive? Fine, fine. Listen, Charles, I have a most delightful idea. We'll round up a party and go to Jones Beach in a rented limousine. What mad fun we'll have. I bought a portable beach tent—yellow, green, and red. Oh, it's *too* much, pet. Cleo going down the Nile. Now, there will be Diego—you haven't met him, have you? What charm! Like taffy melting in the sun. He wants to be a cabinetmaker. Laura thinks he's adorable. She's coming. She has the most marvelous French bathing suit. A bikini. All red knit. A scream, Charles! I thought we'd ask Sade, too. Oh, sorry, pet. I forgot you were not on friendly terms. But I could ask that sweet little Jewish boy . . . what's his name. Oh, you know who I mean. And Lena. She's such fun. I hear she's out again—have you seen her? And what do you think of this pet? I've got champagne for you. Just for you, darling."

"Oh, Jesus," I moaned, on the verge of tears, and hung up.

Then Claudia, the Grand Duchess, dashes in like a mad potentate. His eyebrows are plucked. The makeup is wearing off and he resembles a spotted wild animal. He's giddy from the aftereffects of an all-night sexual drinking bout.

"Gimme a cigarette," Claudia said, swooping down in the chair like an exhausted bird. "Oh, child, I really had a ball last night. I really enjoyed myself. Those children carried on. Let me tell you: they carried on like there was no tomorrow."

comes in, waggin  tail like a sh

Claudia croons. "          walky-walky. And              se a lovely  na          ho  ped steak fo                aby will have.

                the petite, silent           y   it, grand-
ope

WORKED LATE AGAIN TODAY: seven p.m. There was nothing waiting for me at home and I walked over to Amsterdam Avenue for a drink. This was poor Alice's turf, and I thought of her and felt like saying a prayer. She got such a bang out of just living; the prostitution and drugs had nothing to do with it.

I remember Alice once leaning out the window and tossing a handful of coins down to the kids who lived in my block. "That's right, ya little bastards! Get'm! That's what you'll be after the rest of your life. Bastards!" This was followed by a great peal of laughter which could scald a sensitive heart. Bruce tried to convert Alice. "If St. Peter opens them pearly gates for you," Alice would tell him, "I think he'll open them for me. Yeah. That's right, baby."

About a year ago she got syphilis. A month later Alice was nearly nuts. Then, one windless, pale, March afternoon, she made crazy designs on a man's face with a beer bottle in her West Eighty-fifth Street room. She called me, her voice giddy. I thought she was back on heroin. "Charlie, come up quick. I think I killed somebody," Alice giggled.

"Who?" I asked. "Alice, are you high or something?"

"Yes, baby," Alice said. "I got a jolt this time. Some bastard is conked out on the bed, bleeding. Come on up, baby."

I arrived an hour later, and there were only blood stains on

. There was on... ...the room, the
... blue. The wind... ...the pink, pla-
...led. I looked ou... ...there was...
...he garbage-litter... ...ba...
...t now it," the s... ...fully, displaying
...teeth.
...you say that?" ...ke...
...frowned. "You... ...pi...?"
...slowly, trying to... ...ager. "I'm her...

...P... ...the super's line... ...s paid til Satu...

...ago, and in this... ...emembrance, I
...Down bar on A... ...te... There were
...woman in the... ...ntimate, neigh-
...rs. The bar was... ...et. The telev-
...on its throne ab... ...wall and th...
...ot'n 'em up, but... ...l.
...urbon with bee... ...ny usual spo...
...the street scene... ...ould watch th...
...ed that they wer... ...about me.
...e end of the bar... ...crew cut. H...
...ealthy appearan... ...blue eyes. H...
...ce with his mac... ...khaki trousers
...n shirt, and slim... ...ust have com...
...Park West.
...time he would... ...bottle beer a...
...direct and cold... ...wife inspect...
...t the butcher's... ...im shake...
...why he wasn't... ...cowboy movie
...artoon of monk... ...chorus girls.
...a, a redhead, wa... ...Collins. She
...ed Rubens nude... ...ess, cut low
...reamy tits alm... ...the bar. Th...
...busy with hi... ...ing the red
...eyes stayed dow... ...flushed. Th...
...a few healthy... ...
...e, this joker wit... ...beginning to
...was putting awa... ...bon, feeling

cool, grateful that tomorrow was a holiday, and trying to collect my thoughts. My hair is cut just as short as his, though the quality is different. I am clean shaven. I don't look in the least unusual. At least that's what the reflected, mirrored image says.

I go to the jukebox and play a couple of Lady Day sides. "*Yesterdays*" and "*Ain't Nobody's Business If I Do.*"

Crew cut is drinking his bottle beer like there was no tomorrow. Well, I decide, I'm going to stare the bastard down. These eyes are going to the market; appraise and set a judgment, look right through him.

Okay. Now set your drink down with lowered eyes and then look up. "Aw right," as Mitch would say, "you've shook him." Now he's got a mean frown on the ruddy face, and he's knocking ashes from his cigarette. He won't look at you.

Now he's smiling with his eyes as well as his mouth. I half expected to see caps on his fine white teeth. What the hell is so Goddamn funny? He must be nuts, lonely, has a problem, or is queer. It might be interesting to find out his story.

Have another bourbon. He'd got his Goddamn blue eyes on you. I'd like to put a good solid one on that firm, proud mouth. He's looking up again. A bold smirk on that Ivy League mug. There is nothing to do but stare him down.

The bartender ambles down to me and sets up a bottle of beer. He has a bright, wise look on his owlish face.

"It's for you," he says knowingly.

Crew cut raises his bottle beer in mock salute, buddy-buddy fashion.

I nod and give my boy a shit-eating grin.

Then he got up and walked toward me, and I discovered that his left foot was a club foot. He had on a pair of highly polished, cordovan brogues; the bottle of beer in his large hand like a flag. Now his smile was warm, boyish. But I had my doubts.

"Hi," he said, brightly, by way of introduction. "You have crazy eyes. Did you know that?"

I downed the last of the bourbon and started on Crew cut's beer. I certainly wasn't going to make conversation after that opening.

"What was the Mets' score?" he asked.

"I don't know," I replied, without looking up.

ook a beating ... he Mets were ... easily and said ... he Yankee-

Tig... ny? Man. Twen two ... must have
dru... ith that one.'

he Yankees to ... tha...
... e a Yankee fan.
...y-five, the Tig... and ... tics played
alm... I id, springing ... oas... ... ge.
... w cut said in a... ... e, and then
look... d, horn-honk... raffi... you li...e to
go t... ... round the co... I've ... hard stuff
there

... owly, without ... nkin... ... ...ain Grew
cur... ... g.

... club-footed y... g m... lived high
ab... est, in a mello... wood ... ...en... with a
hig... n old hunting ... ... bo... conceal...d
a b... i... ent. Peter was ... ou... la...ghingly
said ... have to get a ... ...g... two-fi...ty a
m... ...s rarely met ... ne... ... l...ue eyes
expr... ... pain of a shy, ...ng a ... a...n't making ... ...im—I had m... ... ...escen...ing,
ric... ... -thinking jerk... ...a...on that
m... l; but all of thi... ...d ... ...e good. ...
re... ... had gone to ... var... ... to Cam-
bri... ... had an opi... of ... ...he Cl...n-
ning... ne... floating in ... f... ...round he
has... ope. Poor l...t... ...l... ...has l...ved
ab... ...n years, mostl... Pa... ...nows less
ab...

... ored person I've ... ... aid, gr...p-
ing ... t is, except m... ...id."
... I said sweetly.

... ...t...?"
... agreed slowl...
... and tonic; Pe... ... ... ...er out of a
silver...

"Do you like tennis?"

"No."

"Opera?"

"No."

"Interested in politics?"

"No."

Peter set down his silver mug carefully and smiled. "I bet you like to screw."

Oh Jesus, I thought, depression settling in. I wish for once that I'd meet someone who would surprise me. I've been studying people closely for twenty-nine years and it is agonizing to be able to put them in slots like coins in a cigarette machine. Was Crew cut queer? You see the queer kids in the eastside bars lapping up beer, only beer. It is only the less affluent homosexuals who buy mixed drinks. I'm rather free sexually, but I'm a little sick of the queer scene. The queers are not really honest and their fear has nothing to do with it. With the straight squares and the police, the whole business is made up of fear, hate, money-making. The greatest problem of the American male is proving his masculinity. I myself find that I do not have to lift weights, wear heels with clicks, to assert my maleness. Claudia, the Grand Duchess, once said, "Oh child, one of these days we'll have a faggot for President. In high drag. Won't that be a bitch?"

Crew cut's voice cut in on my thoughts. "You know, I don't like niggers." He was sitting on the sofa, his feet propped up on the slate-topped coffee table.

I sipped my gin and tonic, looked over at Peter, and smiled.

His blue eyes flamed with hatred and his face was very red. "Well, what are you going to do about it, nigger?" he asked, his voice quivering.

I burst out laughing and shook my head sadly. "'Drown in my own tears,' Ray Charles sings. What do you want me to do? Beat the living shit out of you?"

"I like to be hurt a little," Peter said. "I like to have my hands tied behind my head. Then I'll do anything you want."

N...-T... A lustreless pearl sk... ...mer rain. The cl...cl... ...up... and shuffle of fee... ...ward. The truck dr...r's ... morning song, "...et ... i... ass in ge-aar." Th... so... ...urban drivers cre...pi... ...Top Parking. I lo...ou... w at the bumper... ...fic blocked to Fi... A... ...ars are like a ...ea... in... cap... of Rockefel... C... ...ender trees lini...g ...e... ...ike cheap corsa... ... veil of rain, the ...m... ...uilding looks ye...lo... ...rning. No sign o... li... ...nwood Hotel ex...pt ...or ash blonde m...kin... ...ce with a hand m...or.

...ft... ...staccato tone of ...au... ...street voices. Th...co... ...ouch of autumn... A... ...mes in to tell m...er... ...lice raid. It doesn... i... ...At five o'clock, th...ar... ...s like the early ...sh... ...The blaze of ne...cu... ...aching darkness. ...o... ...enc... of summer, an...oi...

...la... ...y pops in from ...r... ...ked out with sli...ye... ...t and matching ha... ...the doorway, he...her... ...p observers of th...s... ...oor. Then she ru...ov... ...own beside me... ...d. "Charles, the po...e v... ...hispering her b...g... ...we...re here this a...noo...

"Yes, cookie," I said. "I heard them. Must've been a false alarm."

"False alarm," Maxine reflected. "Then it was a mistake, wasn't it?"

"That's right, cookie. How was the art class?"

"All right, I guess. Clay."

I have an idea of Maxine's prima-donna, natural-born-leader attitude at the Museum of Modern Art's children's classes.

"They're such babies over there," Maxine sighs. "We worked in clay this afternoon."

"I loved working in clay," I said. "You can make a lot of fantastic things with clay. I had a lot of fun when I was a kid."

Maxine looks up solemnly. "Did you, Charles?"

"Yes. It's a lot of fun. But you have to be very careful. It takes time and it's something new for you."

Maxine removes her coat and hat and folds them neatly over a chair. "I like clay. But I don't like to make boys and girls and dogs and houses. I like to make fantastic things. But the teacher says no, make boys and girls and dogs and houses."

"Well, if you're a good girl. . . ."

"Good?" Maxine laughs. "You know I'm always good, Charles."

Then Mitch calls me to the phone and when I return, Maxine asks, "Who was it?"

"Shirley."

"Oh, her. Is she coming over?"

"No."

"You like her, don't you?"

"Oh, I don't know, Miss Fancy Pants."

"Charles! There you go again. You'd better stop that. I mean it."

"Shall we have tea, Miss Fancy Pants?"

"Have you got any cookies? I don't like tea without cookies. But I like iced tea."

"You know I've got loads and loads of cookies. Mucho cookies."

"Mucho cookies." Maxine laughed and then added, looking me straight in the eyes, "It's been a long time since we've had tea and cookies. You don't even buy Ritz crackers anymore."

"They don't go good with vermouth," I joked.

The deep sigh and the I-know-that-Charles expression Max-

...adds another ro... scoreboard...
n, Miss Fancy Pan... ing up and ki...
d. "Let's have tea."

the tea," Maxine... grown very ta...
n light the back bu... e."
ght, cookie," I said. ...ng to be a big...
axine exclaimed, a... pt from the c...
...uoting a litany, "I... fresh milk an...
eth and bones."
gives a dazzling sm... he stove. I...
outh.

ly drink a lot," M... "Mama said
take down is all bee... y bottles."
me, Miss Fancy Pan...
and stop calling m... s."
ll call you?"
cy Pants, you jerk.

ake a walk. Going... Maxine retu...
athroom.
where are you going...
said sharply.
y," Maxine slamme... ur cool."
ht, cookie," I gri... ed the stairs...

TODAY I HAD a delivery in the serene, green world of Manhasset, Long Island. A group of nursery school children were playing in front of a large Tudor-style house. One little boy, with space helmet and Davy Crockett tee-shirt, aimed his yellow plastic water pistol at me and shouted, "Hey you! Chinese boy!"

I ducked the spray of water and reflected that this was the first time I had ever been mistaken for a Chinese. I had a sudden impulse to set the record straight. But then I thought that the kid *had* the right tone of voice, if the wrong nationality.

I have always known what I was—if I might have had a brief lapse of consciousness, there was always a sign, gesture, or word from the outside world to help me bear in mind my race. Even with my closest friends among the whites, there are these little reminders. Even Troy Lamb, of Scotch-German parentage with a trickle of Jewish blood, reveals now and then that his feelings are mixed on color. Yet I must be at the hospital at the birth of his second child and meet his in-laws. Laura Vee, the model, with new coiffure, Paris dress, takes my arm proudly and defiantly as we emerge from my building to encounter a sightseeing bus of southerners. But too, Laura Vee can angrily shout, "By God, you treat me like I'm white." I bow, because Laura has bowed often before my black throne.

I have moved like an uncertain ghost through the white world.

of my Missouri childhood was no worse than a sand-
in. As a six-year-old    of the twins whose
ver) my grandfather     I used to go to
es, though they never    me. White Penel pe
played as brother and s   til we arrived at the
welve. Afterwards, very po    formal.
r one white boy name    e was a cripple  d
His house was the first whi   se across the tracks.
ld be at his white picke    e always greeted me
ar." I always laughed  n  d his crude shu  le.
ould do a quick some    he sidewalk in fr  n
Then I'd jump up and say   tight, crip. You  ry
nced the score.
l movie, I had to sit in  e  ny on hard woo  en
tairs, the seats were  p  red with maro  n
t it was very dark up t  e   balcony, and us t-
ys would sneak smo   s a   with the little  l-
t was something the w  ce   downstairs could  't
were too bright.
me I spent a weekend   d   with white peop  e,
, very shy, and late for    ey were waiting  or
yed coming dov n. I g  e    es an extra shi  e,
air again. Despite the   a    had just bathe  I
rmpits. At the t me   n   that Negroes sm  ll
I didn't really believe i   e people said it v  s
vere always righ . And a     down the carpe  d
rd my fifteen-year-old     le, a Missouri st  e
Maybe he won't come   w   se we ain't got   o

r laughed hearti y at h  t, but there was   o

ord in Negro argu   y childhood w  s
" or "shit-colo ed b   metimes us yello  ,
ds stuck together as    f protection  T  e
rown colors of  ur s    o to our heads;  e
Though a few o  my   childhood cla  -
in this respect w en    ler.
s sixteen, I got  job    at Harry O M  -
bowling alley.

"Hey, Harry. See you have a coon back there."

Harry O'Malley made no reply. He merely looked away.

"Take a shot at the nigger, baby."

"Oh, honey." (This with giggles.)

"Look at that nigger go. Fast as lightning."

I was nicknamed 'Lightning' because I was fast. I worked there a week, frightened, and overly conscious that I must do a good job. This had been pounded into me in my colored neighborhood.

"Sonny, now you act right. Be the best."

"Yes. That's what white folks expect of you."

"Say 'yes ma'm' and 'no ma'm' and 'sir'."

"Get the lead out of your ass, boy."

"You should be proud. The first colored pinboy up there."

I did work hard and fast, and the second night I was handling two alleys. The next League night, Harry gave me the slow teams (which a pinboy accepts as a honor and a burden). This became a custom. A fast pinboy speeds up slow bowlers. The compliments of Harry, the envious glances of the white pinboys, and the egging on of other Negroes did very little for my ego. I knew I had done a good job. I was tired. That was that.

I often took the long way home from the alley, passing the courthouse square and going up a neat, white, residential street that gave onto a bridge, the railroad tracks, and home. I liked the old, crumbling, Victorian houses up that way.

One night the police stopped me.

"Nigger, where you going?"

"What?"

"I said, where are you going?"

"Home."

"Do you live up this way?"

"No. . . . I. . . ."

"Get in."

The police station. I remember standing in the center of an empty-looking room thinking, What will I tell Grandma? Above me was a harsh, unshaded light, just like the movies I thought. But I was frightened, surrounded by four policemen. My heart thumped like crazy and my eyes darted from man to man and then at the wall behind the rolltop desk. A portrait of Lincoln, the American flag, and a nude, calendar girl decorated the cream-colored wall.

ally the policeman at the desk looked up. "Wha...
...p there?"

...work at O'Malley's... ...and I like to ta...
...me. It's very quiet and... ...track."

..."...that so?"

...s, sir. I'm pretty fast... ...the track team a...
...policeman at the desk... ...and smiled faintly...
...ke your hands out of... pockets," he...
...'em, boys."

...searching police... ...quality handkerch...
...ippo lighter, and a... ...counting four one-d... ...at...
...ent piece, three quarters,... ...one penny.

...policeman at the desk... ...up his lips and...
...ed hand through his... ...ped, gray hair. "...
...er been arrested. L... ...des . . . and you...
...m. Is that right?

..., sir," I said brightly... ...of truth and...

...L, GODDAMMIT. START... ...ROUND THIS ROO..."

...an running. He... ...s arched at... ...
...slow and easy like a... ...horse.

...et," a policeman yelle...
...sure can go," and here...
...God, jest like a rabbi..."
...er, boy!"

...ed up speed. The room... ...like an overbal...
...pped out on my face... ...little streams down...
...tee shirt was wet and... ...body like a...
...ach time I swallowed... ...seemed to contra...
...eyes once. The room... ...in like a top.

...er?"

...ld hardly get my... ...continued tak...
...bout half an hour... ...egan to give...
...in my leg muscle... ...ot seem like a...
...d, dazed eyes in the... ...faded cloth...
...sed in a washing... ...e, too; my fee...
...ttom.

..., boy," the policeman at the desk said rising...

...ped against the desk... ...and wiped my fa...
...f my hand.

"That was damn good," the close-cropped, gray-haired police-man said. He reached in his pocket and threw a nickel on the floor. "That was a miteee fine show."

The nickel hit the floor dully, rolled, and fell on its tail as if on cue. I kept my eyes focused on that nickel. (I still remember that nickel. An old Indian-head nickel.)

Then I knelt down and picked up the nickel because that was the only thing to do.

"You sure can run fast," another policeman said, handing me my wallet.

"Never saw a nigger who couldn't," another policeman reflected.

"Yeah," the gray-haired policeman agreed. "But stay across the tracks. Do you hear me?"

"Yes, sir," I replied firmly, quickly, and walked out of the Sedalia, Missouri, police station, trying not to think of anything.

It was a quiet summer night. The small town street was deserted and the crumbling, Victorian houses faded like the night from my dreams.

As I grew older, the white world beckoned. They wanted me. Now I began to wonder what they wanted from me. I certainly didn't have money. Were they trying to prove something to themselves, using me as a reassuring springboard? Only a few of the young white women I became friendly with wanted to sleep with me.

Young Negroes were another matter; the type of young men I met at liberal white parties and chic black parties. Quiet, turned out in Ivy League garb, usually with a pipe and mustache. Perfect gentlemen: sophisticated Uncle Toms. I certainly don't go for most Negro girls who have gone to a good college. They are usually phony intellectuals. The swinging Negro girls were more likely to be those who had gone to secretarial school—waitresses, maids, promising singers. They knew the racial score; they had paid their dues.

If you disagree on race relations with another Negro, well, you're asking for a fight. I remember the fights at school about Lincoln. What did he *really* do for the Negro? The fights would take place around election time, the man's birthday, or when we were studying a particular period in American history.

Born black, not actually without color, brightness, or evil.

Bl... ...s. Rather, the fash... ...lat. Half and
ha... Bla... ...amily is almost ...d ...etween the
...es... ...dark. I am tan, ... ...wn exposed to
th... ...t I emerged from ...m ...womb. Beige. I
ar... ...ma... (f... ...o. La Ronde bega... a... ...esters sailed in
fro... Af... ...e the day of their ...u... ...her... many sea-
so... in a... ...hell.

...men ... why ... ...ed in their
na... Th... ...e an outsider. A... ...a minority.
Th... ...go as a child, be... ...rred to kinks.
Th... su... ...at these kinks fo... ...crown. Negro,
Ne... oid, ...lack, brown, an...b... ...nit-colored.
Bu..., be... ...e result of genera... ...d Anglo Saxon,
Af... an, ...k, and Choctaw Indi...
...e Negro, southw... ...ri Stevensons.

LENA IS BACK on the scene. I am at Bobby's apartment in a small West Side hotel.

"Ah! There's my daddy," Lena says, grinning from ear to ear. "There's my sweet little motherfucker."

‹ Lena then bounced over in a yellow, baggy, Italian sweater and form-fitting blue slacks, her buttocks quivering evilly. She planted a mouth-smacking kiss square on the top of my head.

"Hiya, doll," I said, bringing on a happy smile. "When did you get out?"

"Tuesday morning," Lena said, patting her tight spit curls which were geometrically arranged on her head like a careful bird's nest. "Yes. I'm operating again. Clipped a joker for two hundred bucks last night."

Lena threw back her head and cackled; her teeth were a miniature Fort Knox. Then she started jazzing me—huddling close, her long thief's hand lunging for my head as if trying to pull out a hunk of hair. Then she bends down, licks my arm with her sharp witch's tongue, and sinks in her gold teeth savagely.

I squirm and give her another painful grin. "Take it easy, baby."

"Miss Lena," Bobby says, pursing up his lips like a dried peach. "Child. You're trying to eat that boy alive."

Lena bolts up. "You're just a jealous bitch. Faggot."

trick in the subway. Don't try to be piss-elegant because Charlie is here. I know you from way back when. Now get out in the kitchen and fix me some food. And a plate for Charles, too."

"Lena, I don't want anything," I said.

"Oh, make that faggot work. You need to put some meat on those bones anyway."

Bobby blinked his eyes and stepped gingerly into the kitchen. Lena flopped back down into my lap and sighed heavily. I massaged her shoulders, and soon the heavy breathing stopped.

"That feels good," Lena groaned, closing her eyes outlined with navy blue mascara. The beat lines showed through her pancake makeup.

"Are you going to move into a pad or hotel?" I asked.

"Pad? Hotel? I wish I knew, Charles," Lena said without opening her eyes. "I'm so tired. Think I'll save my loot and move to California. I wanna make a new start with my old man. He gets out of Sing Sing next year."

"That's a good idea," I said. "But then, you'd better be careful."

"Don't I know it," Lena said. "I can't afford to get busted again. Hustling up by the Park Sheraton is out. But if I'm a good girl, will you help me?"

"Oh sure, doll," I said.

Last summer, Lena and I lived in a place off Third Avenue in the Fifties. I didn't work because Lena liked to have me around the house. She was out a great deal and there were many phone calls. Lena is a prostitute and a professional thief. Like the Murphy Game players, she works best in the summer. She'll meet a John in a bar, talk some trash. Once the John leaves the air-conditioned bar and hits the humid streets, he's Lena gravy.

The first score only whets her appetite. She used to come home, say at two a.m., hand over the first take, change clothes, have a drink, and hit the streets again. She would still be hustling after the sun had come up. Lena had discovered that there were good scores to be made in broad daylight between six and nine a.m. But this was usually on Saturdays. But it was on an early Sunday morning that Lena got busted in the doorway of a Fifth Avenue dress shop. The John said that Lena had cleaned him for a hundred and seventy dollars. Yet when the cops took her down,

ninety in h        ever said what    p
other eighty  v      aising drive a    n
ew a lawy          . A week later,     n
. Even Bruce k       hn was from c
five-hundred-        dropped.
war  a scandal       trial and Lena
got busted ag        was against h e   e
aying I was aga      le-class, res  c   h
ck to Philly         clerks, and rai   a
al workers, ea       wo years.
ena had studie       tnapping.
ay in my arms,       ied chicken, g
he n with a w        at," he said.
olls. "Wake up       at this dumb b    h
he d and smile
for some God
Bobby exclaim        to all this tro   e

p and rubbed         you got anythi    o
house?" she d        tta go out a   e
og for the lia
a," Bobby said
d at Bobby a         d sadly. "Liste   o
?" she said, h       errily as her v   k
d in her mind        my eyes, fre      n
o. There's this      dying to work     's
ub. Soft lights,     floor. I'm goir    n
y dear. Like th      ami. I'll spen
s across the b       ut with a hun     d
Now what             h? Miss Sub      y

Claudia swep         the ever-pres
The queen's h        Claudia cackled
ed the door ar       Miss Claudia,

and bitch," I         you been in

" Claudia sig        haughtily as if
ible royal cou        , Miss one—"

But Bobby interrupted: "Really? I don't see how you go in drag. You're not femme. You have buck teeth."

Claudia threw back his head and snapped his fingers. "Ain't no man asked me for teeth yet."

"The kind of men you have," Bobby huffed. "Butch sissies."

"And when have *you* had a man?" Claudia asked. His large, doe eyes seemed to be larger.

"Why my boyfriend, Hank—" Bobby began.

"You stupid faggots make me sick," Claudia said. "You wouldn't know a man if you saw one. You don't think a real man would sleep with a hard-ass faggot like you?"

"I don't have to take that," Bobby cried.

"Oh, please, Miss Thing," Claudia laughed. "There's only one real man in this room. It's Lady P."

or the stoop w h           r holds the air.
: the neon signs c           lticolored can-
front of the ho s           nts like wilted
ple who live on           oo hot to sleep.
ll buildings glea           sts and create a
he smell of fre           wars with the
m the litter bas           t, burned sofa
nanas (the gyps           rushed Iceburg;
-moon of ham:           l bun. Broken
gin bottle, a pi           smeared with
nocks over the li           usually sits in
like a piece of ch           den sculpture.
n and pick it up.           he bars do no
e haughty, hom           g by, cursing,
udenly is drown           de, imploring
b singer from           "*I wanna be*
le proclamation.

ips up like a shy           essed in white
, her dyed str           air has been
ers me a swig           a silver purse
bird is in the re           e has to walk
-five-dollar I.           her hell. Miss
ly prospect and           c

Two more prostitutes. This begins to seem like a union meeting. They're Negro and do a land office business downtown. Sally and Sue. Sally is very dark, with short slick hair and a great body. She looks like some rich jungle fruit that has been carefully preserved in waxed paper. Sue is delicate, light-skinned, very ladylike. Sometimes Sally and Sue use me as a front and turn an occasional trick at my place.

Sue and Sally came rushing up, breathing hard, and shaking like jelly on those spike heels. The cops have run them off Broadway. They have to rest and get their bearings.

"I don't feel like working tonight, anyway," Sally says hoarsely, chewing gum avidly. "And, baby, I can't afford to get busted. Went to the can last Wednesday night and was picked up again Saturday night. I'm trying to talk those cops into letting me go. Maybe give'm a little free pussy." She laughs. "Anyway, baby, so they take the doll to the West Fifty-fourth Street station. Way up on the top floor. And then, in the squad room, all hell breaks loose. The cops run out. Baby, they shouldn't have done that. Leaving me there all by my lonesome. I took off my heels and crawled down those four flights and pressed."

We laughed. A young rookie cop is suddenly on the scene, swinging his nightstick, walking stiffly like he had a board up his ass. He comes up to the stoop and demands, "What're you girls doing here?"

Sally, cracking her gum, looks over the cop's shoulder at a crowded station wagon pulling out of Tip Top Parking. She swings her fine brown legs and begins humming "John Brown's Body."

"You girls ain't talking, huh? I bet if I took you in, you'd talk plenty. Didn't I see you about an hour ago on Broadway?"

"Officer, we ain't doing nothin'," Sally drawled. "We just trying to cool off."

"Cool off at home."

I decided to speak. "These girls are friends of mine," I said firmly, looking the cop straight in the eye. "And we're sitting here cooling off. We are planning to sit here as long as we feel like it."

The cop was stunned. "Oh. Is that so? Who the hell are you, their pimp? I can take you in too, you know."

"I've lived on this block for five years," I said, rising. "I know

have enough ... ke... ...without bother... ...
trying to cool ..."
...have very litt... ...cemen, because ...
...ets enough to ... ...cops really wo...
...would overflo...
After my ...ma... ...quickly and ...
...nue. He st...l m...e... ...board up his ...
"A tough cop-...
Finally Sa...y a... ...ready to sign i...
...ning shift.
...I go up to my ...a... ...ine pops in, wa...
...I haven't gon... ...
"I'm goin' to t...cc... ...ine said. "Not ...
...kids. I'm goin...o ... ...th my *grandm*...
...going to Ca...da ... ...er been to Ca...,
...les?"
"No, Coo...ie," ... ...places, but ne...
...re a lucky girl...

SAW MY OLD ARMY BUDDY, JELLY, on Sixth Avenue this morning, standing at the subway entrance, wolfing down a bag of French pastry. His brown face seemed paralyzed with terror.

"Charlie, my man," he whined. The day was pleasant, about sixty-five degrees, but sweat poured down Jelly's face. Jelly gave me a panicky grin and said, "Where you going? Let's get a beer."

"Sure," I said.

We started off and were almost at the corner when Jelly stopped. "Wow," Jelly exclaimed, the panicky grin still glued on his sweaty face. "Look, Dad. I don't want any beer. I've gotta have a fix and I know where I can get a twenty-dollar fix for fifteen dollars and it's real good shit and Charlie, my man, I don't wanna hit you like this but I swear I'm dying, my guts feel like they're coming loose. Oh baby, I gotta have that fix or I'll go nuts and it only costs fifteen dollars fifteen bucks. . . ."

"I can let you have five," I said.

Jelly threw his arms around me and, for a moment, I thought he was going to kiss me. His fat, trembling hands clung to my shirt and his eyes had a worshipful gleam. "Daddy," he said, "you are a doll. A real living doll. You've been a swinging stud ever since Korea."

I remember the Korean Jelly. He'd tip into the tent at four in the morning, treading lightly, his voice high and tremulous, like a

Sometimes he'd ... graceful ballet ...
...guard!" or get... ...mosquito bar...
held. I'd get up... ...quiet so he w...
e other guys. All... score: sev...
...nki...s.
...uldn't be long be... ...ever tried to...
...t h... would alway... ...rd like a ma...
...ub..., "Charlie, n... ...boots, please...
Jell...'s boots, I'd... ...d sit on the fo...
...s bunk. I'd do m... ...lly either gig...
...hea...y, "Yeah ma... ...sten to the th...
...ars, cursing up... ...d, and the p...
...wn the hill, sta... ...rkets befor...
...hea...y frontline C... ...e dusty ro...
...pad...led along ba... ...ere moving...
...d sand. Moonligh... ...muslin clothe...
...te. I was like wh... ...osts.
...y Je...ly and I wou... ...le of hours la...
...ks cursing in th... ...ous woman's...
...his eyes angrily... ...king the mo...
...rom the hu... ...s, moan: "I do...
...no...ing. I think I'... Then he woul...
...he silent, moonf... ...oy to go in...
...s dr...gs and his de... ...e back.
...emory of the Uni... ...ins for me wi...
...sp...it in which I t... g. I really enjo...
...old...rainy morn... ...ck, the infilt...
...you...ic. There we... ...n through tra...
...ey were afraid of... ...r guys who...
...ecause it seemed... ...s the right th...
...ten were guys, a... ...reat majority.
...fuck...ed off during... ...ls of basic tra...
...s we...re young—1... 2... ...rom home fo...
...There were days... ...things happ...
...my...outdid itself... ...tales of tough...
...rd all our lives.
...ce soldiers we tal... ...be fighting in K...
...training I waite... ...seas orders, w...
The mess serge... ...my buddy an...

and we were farmed out as cooks, though I had never fried an egg in my life. Then one weekend, I got on a roaring drunk and went AWOL. Upon my return I was shipped out to another company filled with green trainees and manned by a company predominantly of white southerners.

My color, as always because of GI records, had preceded me. I came into the new barracks and was unpacking my duffle bag when the platoon sergeant walked in. We exchanged a few short comments. The trainees had gathered around us like a group of excited fans in the last round.

Then the platoon sergeant said, "You think you are a smart nigger, doncha?"

I looked up at him and said: "No. I don't think I'm smart. But I do think I'm intelligent."

There was nothing much left for the man to do but walk away. But after that, pressure was put on me from all sides, in a hundred ways, and my nightly prayer was to be sent overseas. I went AWOL about three times during this assignment, because I had heard a rumor that if you took off you would be sent to Korea without orders. The last time I was picked up AWOL I was marched to the stockade with a guard punching a loaded carbine into my back. Later, after my court-martial, I heard that the officers of my company celebrated the fact that they had put me away for six months.

The second day I was in the stockade, I received permission from the chaplain to visit the library. My court-martial had been swift. I was certain that they had put the screws on me. I read up on court-martial procedure and discovered that within seventy-two hours after he has been sentenced a soldier may have the proceedings reviewed.

The reviewing colonel was very understanding. I had had a good record and he was going to suspend the six-month sentence. How could a nice, intelligent young man like me get into such trouble?

But what about overseas, I wanted to know? There was plenty of time, the colonel said.

I walked into the mess hall that noon and a silence fell. I had conquered the company. After that, I had no more trouble. I spent a year at Fort Leonard Wood, only one hundred and twenty miles from home.

favors and a promotion, which I promptly lost because of the platoon sergeant. The platoon sergeant was a southern white, had spent ten years in a federal prison, and could not read or write. He disliked Headquarters tent of his platoon and he disliked Negroes.

But there were many things to turn my mind away from company politics. The Korean people I ran across were wonderful, and I like to believe that my money and the country my uniform represented had nothing to do with the way they felt towards me. The ROK soldiers, the elite of the Korean army (the KATUSAS were the peasants) were better dressed than most of us GIs. (I'll not soon forget trying to evade my houseboy's question as to why I didn't have new boots. He had taken my boots to the village shoemaker to try to have them repaired even though they were ready for the trash barrel.) On the Sunday afternoon when the ROK soldiers received word that they were no longer attached to American military units, they all got very drunk and tore up tents and equipment, shooting wildly with their weapons.

The Korean children used to line up, hungry-eyed, at the fence, to watch all our rich food being dumped into the garbage cans. I remember being invited to a Korean home and, after the tea ceremony, each member of the family came over to me shyly and rubbed their hands through my hair.

In September of 1953, Korea was shaking on her post-war legs in the changing world of East and West. The uncertain peace hovered over everything; at each loud noise our eyes scanned the sky.

I came back home, to Missouri—to Grandma, my friends, with thousands of GIs for whom Korea had been pretty meaningless. It was as if they had never left this country.

Before I went into the army, my feeling about it, about the war in Korea, was that of a boy who loved playing soldier. I looked forward to the United States Army and Korea with glee; it was to be another adventure, another experience, and, when I received my draft notice shortly after my nineteenth birthday, it was like Christmas. I looked forward to fighting, perhaps even to dying.

The night before I left for the army, Grandma and I were sitting on the vine-covered front porch in Missouri. It was a soft, summer night and you could smell the honeysuckle vines which grew up the sides of the porch.

"Sonny, do you still say your prayers?" Grandma asked.

am," I replied quickly a a cigarette.

ot lying to you old a re you?"

am."

I'll take yo a your Now you go on o and
ds. Go on. W don't o it here like so one
firs , before yo go— h re, Sonny."
and I got d n on and put our elb s in
and bowed o head
prayed first a her s ce a peaceful rn:
ly Father, a yo ed one of your h ble
d on their kn es be F ther, I thank y for
hrough this b sed giving me stre g to
ate to minute. our on this blessed su er

voice rose sl tly. up out of the c r of
w Grandma bbi n together. Sh as
faded, flower inte f the porch swi g, en
s her eyes spa led a ew ears were in m.
t you to have rcy g ndson, that he ay
d come over your ore it's too late. F er,
us, I want yo to th r strong arms nd
off to war G de hi e's only a child de
hin home sa y to him and all th er
women in wicke L."
hands were eat my nails hard i t he
hands as I co tinue to Grandma's w
Father, there so l le Children are n
of sin, and I fore w t, they are gr n.
y from home nd rch. They stu le
ys of life. Ble d Je s ur light shine t at y
it and come u o y it is too late a d at
everlasting. sk th ame, throug us
d. Amen."

aused briefly I sa turn, Sonny."
head and sta d ou dark night. There as
here. Darkne Fi tre t lights bea g,
es, and again he sk ouses.
Sonny," G ndm ed. Then she u d.
y child, have a fo to pray?"

I did not say anything. I looked at Grandma and blessed the darkness so I would not have to meet her tear-filled eyes.

"Sonny," Grandma said. "Pray."

I bowed my head again and opened my mouth. The words would not come. I looked up at the porch ceiling. It seemed as if the ceiling was between me and God.

"Well," Grandma said finally, rising, "You might as well get up. I'll pray for you and you try to pray yourself and then it will be all right. If you *believe*, it will be all right."

I got up and kissed Grandma on the forehead. "Goodnight, Grandma," I said.

"Goodnight, Sonny. Don't stay out too late. You'll have to get up early. . . ."

I heard her cry for the first time in my life as I walked off the porch.

I am glad for Grandma that I returned safe from Korea. I was all that she had in this world and I knew what the loss of me would mean to her.

Korea did not turn out to be my personal salvation as a man, nor a field of glorious exploits and adventures. It was simply and deeply my first rude lesson that most men and women suffer unbearably.

...FROM the fi...-flo... is very fine. Th... ...e...ky black, sta... a balmy seventy-nine... ...Empire State bu...ing ...s of lights bea...ing... rainbow-hued... ...search light...Pla... ...otel's blue-whit... ...al, Tip Top Pa...ling... z. Bellowing ab... ...radio plays res... ...aching churn an... ...y of the jukebo...bu... ...age truck.

...sailors pass,... ...ounce in their t... ...six-foot, grayh...re... ...ks by like a wh... ...horse. The A...zon... ...s one of the sail... ...tily. They mo... ...treet. ...on view is l...le... ...Dump with... ...eeks wo...king the... ...ift I see her eac... ...f the BMT su...ay... ...nister in a br... ...der the folds o... ...coat. She solicit... ...d unknown... ...ow she has bee... ...seven years. Sh... ...od, sweet-voic... ...n, all of who... ...ble con game. T... ...is a strict and... ...run on the lin... ...Not just anyone can... ...ei meetings ar... ...Harlart over... ...nce a week, be...
p.m.

L. C., the Tip Top attendant, has just bought a Pepsi Cola from the machine in the garage, and is staring intently at a seven-year-old boy who is walking hand and hand with his parents, ogling that mirage, Rockefeller Center.

I wonder about Tip Top. There is an open doorway between Pizza House and Tip Top Parking. It is deep and dark, almost the width of my narrow room. Men enter this dark, brooding tomb to urinate or to take long nips from a hip-pocket pint. The brilliant neon signs and streetlights create only a gray haze there; it's a kind of island in evening fog. If you are not too particular and don't mind standing up, it is a fine place to have sex, and quite a number of people do just that. The people passing are locked in a dream world, their eyes focused elsewhere. The island is a safe and secret place.

For example: A Negro night-cleaning woman passes the doorway, weighed down with two large packages wrapped carelessly with white tissue paper, like two giant white roses. The Negro woman has the left foot up, right foot down, flat-footed stride of a duck. She seems very tired and looks neither to the right nor left. The knowledge of more work at home clings to her body like sweat. More shirts to iron? Is Junior off the streets? Tomorrow is Saturday, but she cannot afford to sleep late.

As she passed the doorway, the man within stands back from the woman. He stretches out his long arms and fondles the woman's breasts. He is smiling, talking, very sure of himself. I can't see the woman's face, but she is short.

Four young men amble by. They are tourists: All of them wear colorful, short-sleeved summer shirts and blue jeans. There are deep cuffs in their blue jeans. Suddenly, one of the young men raises his arm and points at the tall buildings.

Now the man in the open doorway has his body pointed tight against the woman. His hands are clasped on her buttocks like a vise. The woman doesn't move. The man lowers his head and plants a kiss on her forehead.

Ah! The woman has sprung to life. Her skirt is pushed up around her hips. I can see where her stockings end. The man is in her but his trousers are not down. The woman flings her arms around the man, but her movements are delicate, as if the hormones in her body were frozen.

TONIGHT I CAUGHT the A train, went up to Harlem. Kenya, the Iron Curtain, I thought. When I first got off the train at 125th Street, there seemed to be nothing foreign or menacing about the Saturday night street. But after a while, I felt a certain violence hovering in the air, as if a great symphony of dark emotions was keyed, waiting for the maestro's exploding baton. The great black mass is restless. If you doubt this sense of imminent violence, watch the few uneasy whites who live in Washington Heights, upper Broadway, and the Bronx.

As I walk down 125th Street, I see young men, sharp as diamonds in suits that they can't afford, leaning against flashy cars that don't belong to them, or stepping smartly as if on their way to a very high-class hell. 125th Street is Forty-second Street, Broadway, Times Square, Fifth Avenue all combined in a jungle of buildings. It is a prayer meeting with a hand-clapping, tambourine "Yes Lawd." It's Blumstein's Department Store, the Harlemite's Macy's. It's the Apollo, with the only live stage show in Manhattan. It's the smart bars catering to Big Time wheeling and dealing Negroes and downtown whites, who want a swinging Harlem night.

I turned down a side street where children were playing hide-and-seek, with families gathered on the stoops, or leaning out of brightly lighted windows. Here the sense of violence was in abeyance. It was Saturday night and there was a happy peace

flowing as easily as a mother talking to a sick child. The woman sang the verse and then the rest of the congregation took up the chorus and the sweating fat man showed that the organ was meant not only for cathedrals.

I found myself singing in a small voice. Something stirred inside me. Perhaps it was remembering Wednesday prayer meeting and Grandma and Grandpa. Perhaps it was just a corny emotion; I don't know. I only know that something stirred, touched me, and for a few minutes, sitting in that whitewashed-walled, storefront church, listening to that beautiful voice, I had a feeling that all was not lost. Somewhere there was such a thing as peace of mind and goodness.

I didn't, couldn't, stay long; too many things would start playing hell with my mind. I went up, shook the pastor's hand, and gave him a dollar. He smiled and said, "God bless you, son," and then I left.

It was almost midnight now. Everything was alive on 125th Street. This was Saturday night, the time when the Negroes let their hair down, relax, get drunk, fight and grumble about Mr. White Man and the price of pork and eggs and the troubles of their cousins down south, knowing that, come Monday morning, it will all be the same.

I went into a bar, had a couple of two-for-one drinks, and then a couple more, and headed for the subway. The drinks were terrible and bucked uneasily in my stomach. As I was going down the steps a Jew in a pre-Warsaw suit was coming up, mopping his lined red face. He looked up at me and smiled: "Kinda hot tonight, ain't it, boy?"

"Yes, Lawd," I said, and suddenly and uncontrollably vomited all the way down the subway steps.

I DRIFTED THROU... ...ot days and nigh... ...
the time, despor...le ...working itself o... ...
miser with an e... ...um... Summer'... ...
mer ever end? I...ok... ...tu...e of me abov... ...he
baby in the whi... ...sta...ding in the... ...
one-and-a-half... ...il poised, ale...t... ...
The large, soft... ...ki...g and lock... ...
would grow, be... ...iv..., and later... ...
tance from life.

    I remember... ...nt, "This worl... ...
think: You are... ...h of the tree... ...
Faulkner, excep... ...is Negro. For... ...
line, nothing to... ...b... my own de... ...
fear. But this, th... ...of the present; ... ...
me before I die... ...po...sibly happen... ...
happened?

In the fall of 19... ...m about Gran... ...
a bicycle and ha... ...e...ne-room, r...d... ...
where I had go... ...rs. Grandma w... ...
dress and a larg... ...d straw hat. It... ...
and Grandma w... ...e a... if we shared... ...
I woke up in a... ...dream haunted... ...

most recent letters, written in her neat small script, had not been cheerful, which was unlike her, for even when ill or depressed, she feigned an air of happiness.

I decided to go home.

I remember walking through the courthouse square as the clock tolled six a.m. and broke the small-town quiet. The street was deserted. I knew, without looking up toward the November hills, where the landscape of cottages and big Victorian houses rose to meet a soft dawn, that there would be no movement, no lights in the windows. But somewhere in the brown hills a rooster crowed, and the chill morning air revealed a column of smoke; an early riser burning leaves.

I crossed the gravelled square with its moldy, bronze statue of Captain Zimmerman, the town's founder. The old-fashioned bandstand had a fresh coat of blue-green paint and looked as if it had been abandoned by a touring tent show. (The Toby Ward tent shows of my childhood; the Midwest's summer Broadway.) The slat and iron benches had not changed. They formed a forlorn semicircle. I sat down wearily on one, which was damp with early morning frost, and I looked out across the wide muddy Missouri. My eyes followed the flat river-bottom lands and the thrush-brown jungle of trees, the sparsely populated farms with blue lines of smoke rising from the chimneys, the windmills turning gently in the river wind.

Home.

I was born here, two miles from town in a little valley surrounded by sloping dogwood and blackberry-covered ridges. Now the house where I was born is gone and there are only the wild orange tiger lilies. Cows graze in that cup of a valley. The red-brick schoolhouse and Bette Sue Estill, the little girl with the laughing black eyes, and Grandpa fishing and hunting rabbits when the cornfields were covered with sheets of frozen snow. The Red Dog Café, the Royal movie house, and the Hughes Chapel Methodist Church (named after a great-great-uncle who was a famous Missouri Negro preacher). The whites moved further out from town and the Negroes moved into the town together with the church.

Sitting in the open space of the courthouse square, I found myself suddenly murmuring a solemn, desperate "Oh Jesus." My

...of a tomcat... nothing but... fatigued, play... the town. ...Grandma, ...recognition. ...like—silent, ...minds, a pa... here across ...was my father... ...box, and the... ...time when... my world, ...had lost wh... ...days, ...of a sm... ...who had ...pilgrimage with... ...ing place. ...the bench slow... ...ched lazily ...grin for Capta... Good morn- ...welcoming th... ...the tranquil fi... with two heav... ...everything... down Mai... ...sun was up, a... And there ...song of my... ...souri River ...Mississippi a hu... St. Louis. ...being ha... ...iskly, long ...fresh green la... ...Cooper Street, h... a mound o... ...rd. A porch circl... crazy horse ...tten vines cove... a cape. Th... ...cond floor were... ...es travelle... ...Yellowed la... the living ...the sill supp... otted plan... ...aded lamp. ...ged and I... ...teps slowly ...out of the porc... ...ily, and dis... ...then smiled, a... ...ing hand t...

...ound from with... pped again ...my hands... ...ides. Final... ...oft voice: "A l... ...and she sto... a sense o... ...heavy as a log... ...ed. I b... ...ck the tears.

"Sonny!"

"Grandma!"

We embraced, falling into each other's arms as if the ground under the sagging porch were giving way.

I held Grandma gently in my arms. She was seventy-nine years old. She had been a full-bodied woman, but I could feel the change in her. She was thin now, no more than a bundle of dried sticks. The round face was not even a mask of what it had been. Her cheeks had caved in and there were only her proud bones beneath a thin layer of wrinkled brown flesh. The waist-length hair, before always crowned in tight braids, had almost all gone. What was left was plastered against her skull like a baby's knitted cap. Her eyes were the same: warm, brown, laughing. They peered up at me questioningly.

"Grandma, Grandma," I crooned, rocking her in my arms, hoping she did not note a change on my smiling face.

"Surprised?" I asked, knowing there was nothing I could hide from her.

"Glory be . . . I can hardly get my breath." Grandma looked at me tenderly, there were tears in her eyes. Her voice was happy and lilting, like that of a young girl. "And you didn't even write to let me know you were coming. Shame on you."

We were not only connected by blood; we were friends. Whatever had happened to us, whatever thoughts crossed our minds that early November morning, could not destroy the love we bore each other.

"Let's go inside," Grandma said. I picked up my bags and followed Grandma inside, kicking the door shut.

The living room was not the cool, flowered room of sleepy summer afternoons or the warm crackling room of winter. I could not believe that I had played in this room as a child. Giant red roses in the grimy wallpaper overpowered the room. Hunks of plaster peeped through the wallpaper and paint peeled from the ceiling in fancy paper scallops. A web of dust framed the portrait of Grandpa, which hung above the closed-up fireplace. A horsehair sofa littered with shiny silk pillows was shoved against a wall and near it sat an oil burner, covered with dust. Two carved rosewood tables and four moth-eaten olive chairs occupied the space opposite the fireplace. A hard, rock-maple chair, as perky looking

as ever... the...lace-covered tab... ...of the
bay wind...y. ...traveling at the ed...
Fro... ...ows Grandm...s... ...bed
which... be... ...co t of horrible... ...The
scene of... ...medici e and... ...oom
like a sic...
Fro...e...of...y...ye,...saw... ...the
edge of... ...Sh...resembled... ...Her
thin, bl...d... umbled on...he nig...
"I hav...P...ll... she sai,,"an... ...me
all sorts o...ills...
"You... ...e," I said... ...my
jacket an...la... sh...es...
Gran...a...ve...ef my face. "...
"Sa...e...ld g...ok...l.
Her l...gh...s...tr...ned...But...h... ...and
caugh...he...re...ly...our years bef re... dis-
charge, s...a...y...t...ch food all w... ...and
me. "The... ...t...she...sed to...
I car...f...y...ny...ye...and sat do...n...ofa.
I wanted t...lee...m...e...s, b...t a w...le...
"You...k...m...How'd you...
"You...ow...g or buses," I...fire
engines.
"My...C...nma...arve d...I... ...are
you hungr...Y...s...ething in the...i...
"Thi...ll...u...f...ea," I said...
"I'm g...g...na..." Grand...a... ...tch
myself."
"You'r...ti...e...ix...en...and...ave a...
"Co...e...in...a kiss.
I wen... ...e...ed...er lightly on...e... ...ng
hands so...g...t...ce...nd the fingers...ed... ...ny
face, an...h... ...ves met nine a...
"I've w...ed,...y...f...this day...S ll...e... ...?"
"Still...h...a... ...us...re...up, feebly
"And...une...ea...sweet b essed...
The f...a... ...s...s vept the ro...m... ...I
closed...he...e...s...y, eaving be...m...G... ...dy
stretched o...o... ...p ay ng fo...me.

\* \* \*

The languor of autumn diminished as the nights grew cold. The small-town life slowed down. There was little rain and the old people said that that was a sure sign of a cold, long winter. I loved those new days. I slept well and was up at dawn, chopping wood for the old woodburning stove that Grandma had refused to give up. I made breakfast for Grandma and then would get the morning paper, do some chores around the house, and some also for the neighbors, which made them buzz around me as if I were a saint.

I read a lot that winter, going to the library three times a week. I tried to avoid the kids I had grown up with. They all worked eight-to-five shifts and were carving out their future in this small-town Negro world. And in this quiet world for the first time in years, I relaxed; I drank very little and did not feel the need for sex. Gone was the fevered air of New York, gone the hipped-up, Freudian complications. These small-town folk had problems like people anywhere, but they faced them by looking them square in the eye, accepting them as they accepted changes in the weather.

I remember the first of December, 1958, in that Missouri town on the banks of the river. Snow fell softly through the bare trees and onto the old buildings and houses. Peace. There was almost no sound in the street night or day except for the laughing voices of children returning from school at three in the afternoon or the grinding whirr of a stalled car. Grandma had taken to bed and old Doctor Bess would creep in with his black bag and joke with Grandma and give out white, pink, orange, and yellow pills. Then he would talk with me. He had gone to Columbia in 1905 and we discussed the changes in New York City. Ruby came almost daily; she had married again but was still her same, solid, cold self. I never saw my father, although he lived only three blocks away.

The snow lasted well into the middle of December. Grandma was permanently bedridden, and had developed bedsores. Like most old people, she moved into what is called a second childhood, had lapses of memory. My own mind was on the edge of a cliff during those days; fear had settled inside me. Grandma and I were sometimes cross with each other, but then our eyes would meet.

I remember that clear winter Saturday, blue sky, white sun. The snow was melting and water dripped from the eaves of the house. I saw icicles drop noiselessly from the naked trees and a few birds chirp on the bare branches. I remember the little boy who lived down the street dragging his sled on the sidewalk, the screeching sound of iron on concrete in the winter sun run and the afternoon shadow like fine lacework.

I was sitting in the rocking chair with a black coat and a cigarette, rocking peacefully. Grandma sat up in the bed and said in a slow grave voice: "Sonny, ain't that Mrs. Carter out at her fence? What is she doing out there with a baby in this weather? Why, it ain't only a diaper."

There was nothing out there but a wooden mill and water dripping from a green hedge. The afternoon wore on and I became frightened and called Ruby. Soon the house was filled with neighbor women, church and sewing-circle friends of Grandma's. They all stood around quietly with their hands under their aprons. Doctor Bess arrived and Grandma began reminiscing about people that only the silent old women remembered. Doctor Bess put a hypo and pricked her body here and there. Water ran from her like from a fountain and stopped. Ruby and I changed the sheets again and again. Grandma just lay there, moving her lips with closed eyes. Toward midnight as I put a wet cloth to her lips I saw rose from my stomach and prayed: "Oh, dear Jesus, if I die please let there be nobody in the house but me."

But she did not die. I forced Ruby home toward morning. The little boy who lived down the street brought the Sunday paper. I sat in the rocking chair reading the paper, and Grandma lay hearing the church bell ring for morning worship and thinking "Grandma is very quiet. She's been sleeping a long time. I had better put a wet cloth to her mouth like Doctor Bess said."

I went over to her and applied the wet cloth and she didn't move. I went into the kitchen and made a cup of tea, returned to the living room, and sat down in the rocker. I smoked a half-dozen cigarettes and then went over to the bed. I felt Grandma's forehead. Then I lifted up her right arm which fell back down to the bed with a life of its own and then I fell on my knees beside the bed and cried.

Memory withdraws. There is now only this cluttered, cooking room on West Hundredth Street, in the heart of Manhattan, here, there, again, and now, the Why of my life — the question I crible depression as I sit here watching darkness settle in the corners of this room. Aware of the muted, miscellaneous noises that drift up from the street, I am also aware of the loss of something. It is strange that I had never felt the suffocation of this small room before; as if shadows, objects, furniture were rising toward the ceiling and would explode into what had once been my life. Thinking of all I've ever done and not done. Thinking and feeling this terrible loss.

Where did it all begin? A small town on the banks of the Missouri River. Trees and the red-brick school. Grandpa and Grandma, dead. Grandma. Ruby and all the little girls with ribbons in their hair, and all the people I later met taking the long road through hell.

...L MY DELIVERI... ...is late afternoo...
...y block is com... te... ...up of them ha...
...e end of the st... t. ...t I call upper-n...
...t. The women... fi... ...not practice th...
...ne, and their... ld... ...clean as if eac...
...s. The men all... au... ...ual clothes. On...
...s a mink stole... a... ...st at least $75...
...eak to the gyps... w... ...uilding next to...
...One day, a fe... w... ...rd loud curses...
...e window. The... o... ...ho live next d...
...n the steps o... h... ...ith a middle-...
...n brown hair, b... w... ...hoes, in their r...
...One of the yo... g... ...him have a go...
..., yelling, "H... e... ...r! That's wha...
...h did!"
...A crowd quick... g... ...al of the sages...
...ing came over... d... ...he young gyps...
...gypsy queen,... a... ...unknown ton...
...te, flashing he... o... ...nd glued to he...
...y pocket.
...The argument... w... ...es and the mid...
...in brown fin... y... ...d he headed r...
...n Avenue, wipi... h... ...h his hand. The...

gypsy men went and sat in their car, which was parked across the street. The rest of the clan trooped back into the house, except for Mama, who remained on the stoop, hands on her hips, a cigarette in the corner of her mouth. She had her sharp eyes fixed in the direction of Sixth Avenue.

The crowd of onlookers did not disperse. They were waiting for the second act of the drama. Grinning, discussing the incident, they continued to wait, sure that something more was going to happen. The gypsy queen thinks something might happen too, which is the reason she sent the young men to the car. If the cops or detectives arrive, they can drive off without being noticed. If the middle-aged man had called the police, Mama would have to deal with them.

The owner of the *Steak de Paris* was worried too. He paced up and down in front of his restaurant, arms folded. The gypsies are fine local color for his customers, but fights and cops are another story.

An hour went by, and finally Mama, giving her long braids a toss, sauntered back into her house like a defiant queen. And after the gypsy Mama had returned to her headquarters, a squad car drove by very slowly and I saw a cop point at the gypsies' house. But the squad car did not stop.

Now the question is, what caused a medium-sized, middle-aged man with thin brown hair to beat up a young woman who was telling his fortune? Whatever the reason, it must be a good one because now the gypsies have opened a smaller place almost directly across the street. The gypsy girls sit out in front on chrome-plated kitchen chairs and wooden soda crates and hustle fortunes. All the people passing our block believe that we have an open-air whore house.

It is now evening. I decide to take a shower. Returning from the hall bathroom, I hear many footsteps on the stairs, coming toward the top floor. It is the police.

A sergeant comes up. I am carefully holding a towel around me, the soap and washcloth clutched in my right hand.

"This is all residential here, isn't it?" the sergeant asks.

"Yes," I say.

The police sergeant's sharp eyes take in the corridor and he spots [...] outside the door. "I[...]

"N[...]," I say, showing him [...]

"O[...]," the police sergea[...] back down [...] is [...] "Okay. This is [...]. Residentia[...]

I g[...] ny apartment and have a[...] living room, [...] living gallery of por[...] of the Elmwo[...] look down at the str[...] of about [...] fi[...] people peering up at [...] ecting a red[...] and qu[...] suddenly to a[...] are blocki[...] traffic. But wha[...] I shake [...] laugh, close my shu[...]

Hu[...] footsteps on the stairs. A[...] door. The po[...] 

"A[...] su[...] this building is a[...] police sergea[...] "W[...] kind of business is [...]

"W[...] do you me[...]

"W[...] ve ot his alarm down a[...] police sergea[...] the[...] u[...] like those po[...] ision). "Mind [...] I [...] and look at your pla[...]"

"W[...]" [...] leefully.

Th[...] serge[...] takes one sho[...] liv-ing ro[...] a[...] to le[...].

"T[...] no [...] it[...] s[...]ady business[...] lding," I say. "[...] f[...] alarm. And don't c[...] y door again o[...] I'll[...] you [...] ed for disturb[...] g[...]

Th[...] look dumbfounded. "[...]

"T[...] at[...] sa[...] Usually you kn[...] ou are going[...] you came into th[...] ke the door d[...] be th[...]e looking fo[...] knew damn[...] at[...] the bookies we[...] ll go back t[...] rs now and say no[...] in my buildin[...]

"I[...] to [...] ave disturbed you," [...] says, and e[...]

Fe[...] ty, er[...] self-righteous, [...] and dream[...] the door and[...] that he want[...] an[...] wer but came ch[...] ment follow[...] olicemen. I pro[...] I gave in and started yelling, "Welcome! Come on in!" At last there were about forty policemen in my living room. They formed lines on each side of the room and I walked between the lines of policemen, naked, with my hands clasped behind my back, lecturing on the crime of disturbing innocent citizens' peace.

I knew the police in Sedalia, Missouri—remember?—and I don't like them.

MAXINE's Vi gi a C al ur is iff temp il
grandmother i ess b rn on fter I ni c
Maxine and t k t th Staten Island
Maxine said, w hr a ey , "Cha e y
neglecting me "

It was a pl ea nt e u , c ad ss, wit t
en seventy-fiv deg n and I fough
o the Seventh e u S th erry. Sh
cause I pla ith o r gifts. N
ould get no wh e t a er, is bec us h
real. I don't ay a ul wit a
 equal. Somev ne be t s lte of hild
en adult vor , w og he as frie d S
ed to be a li tle eal r tic ship.

Maxine an ar i ick l voyage
sat on the ar ba e ry passing th
d saying as al ay m go there o
gin telling jo ke un a p dl s which e
en, as the a g w ll e ske fo he v
my arms. he ega i in a au ti g, q
ce. "Doe-r d r a ee When I il
re sharp jab i m n axine fel a le
ietly until th l e ça o Ma hatta

LAURA VEE ARRIVED in the heat of a gray afternoon. The sullen sky gives no promise of rain. The murmurous street voices drift up as if begging for something which escapes them in this elusive city. I am putting down my sixth beer and watching Laura's friend, Jim. He has problems, Laura has said.

Jim has the lanky, awkward grace of a basketball player, a hyperborean face, and unbelievably burnished red-gold hair. He is morosely opening his sixth beer.

Laura is in a gay mood. She has discovered that she is not the only human being with the ability to weep. "Give the lady a beer," she laughed, wiping her ringed hand across her smooth forehead. "I say, how about a cold one?"

"Wouldn't you like something stronger?" Jim asked.

Laura reflects on this. "All right. All right, Jim boy," she said slowly.

Jim went over to the sofa and took a fifth of whiskey from his beach bag. He placed it on the table with the air of a man planning an experiment. I was glad he was not a loud drunk, despite his problems.

"The glasses, Charles," Laura said, giving me a hard stare.

"You know where they are, love juice."

"All right, you kook. But get the ice. You haven't defrosted that thing in a year."

...ra followed me... ...en. "What's ha...

...thing, dear," ... ... "Jim's a little ...
... perhaps you'... ...hat's all."
... you two mal...
...t so loud, 'I a...
... went back to t... Jim was opening ...
... and looked up ... ...f we had invaded ...
... me into ... ...a smiled gaily.
... have a wonde... ...we, Charles?"
...h," ... mumbl... ...my world the w...
...so many meanin... ...have mine s... ... "With the be...
... fucking old m... ...headed old lush.'
... I told myself... ...g to be a very cool ...
... of these ... ... unior gets out of ...

...arles, see if you... ... decent jazz o...
... aid.
... jazz," Jim s... ... is my speed."
...ned on the old... ...ith AM-FM jus...
...dy Day with "... ...".
... is a groove,' ... "Quick girl! G...
... man-killer,' I've... ...drinking and ...
... A wonderful... ...blems do not g...
...them more clea... ...n. I was thinking ...
... said, "Laura... ...and Charles dan...
... not much of a... ...w in quickly.
... much rather... ..., Jim," Laura...
... is a wonderf...
... a slow dance,...
...it's a slow nu...
...it this one out...
...l we dance, Ji... ...sweetly, offering ...
... hand.
... got up and t... ...carefully, diffid...
... am aware of... ...aperone. His da...
... to write home... ...as intense. I wa...
...without really m... ...e floor.

The afternoon waned: three o'clock, a darkened sky, a faint warm breeze. The radio music is smooth now, sentimental, semi-classic in the popular vein. Music for those poignant American Saturday nights, for those quiet American Sunday afternoons, music something like a golden bell, promising that tomorrow will be better. Jazz, good jazz, tells no such lies.

These thoughts cross my mind as I put the whiskey down. Laura and Jim have gone into the bedroom. The whiskey will be of no use to them, so I pour myself another. If I have to be bothered with the tangled lives of others . . . well, let the bastards pay me for it.

"Charles," Laura calls. Her voice sounds tired. "Charles, come here." For some reason I freeze and call out nervously, "What do you want? Cigarettes?"

They are lying on the sturdy narrow bed, naked. Jim is nestled in the curve of Laura's arm, staring up at the ceiling: His eyes are glazed, reflecting, perhaps, his world of dreams. It is not a happy world, judging from his taut face. Laura looks up, sighing, a pleading expression on her face. "Light me a cigarette, will you, Charles?" she said in a polite voice.

I lit the cigarette and gave it to her and stood against the wall with my arms folded, waiting to see what would develop. But, to tell the truth, I'm bored with sex scenes.

"I should be punished," Jim said quietly.

"Why?" I asked.

Jim's voice bordered on a cry. "I can't make it with Laura, I can't make it with anyone, because I think it's dirty! I have all these feelings of guilt. I can't sleep at night."

"In that case, you shouldn't do these things," I said. "Then you could sleep."

Jim got up slowly and began to put on his clothes. "*You* make it with her," he said and went into the living room and closed the door.

I lay down fully clothed beside Laura and took the cigarette from her trembling hand and put it in the ashtray on the bedside table. Then I put my arms around her. She began to cry. There seemed nothing to say or do, so I just held her and let her cry. I could hear Jim typing in the living room.

Finally Laura went to sleep and I went into the living room.

...had gone There ...f paper in the typ...
...over and read i...
This is for Char..., ...e, and went on
...ked-up way, ...bs... ...or a dozen ill-
...and ended with ... X's savagely pu...
...ugh the pape...

...don't know wh... ...es f X's made m...
...thing rose a...t... ...d weight. Wh
...re about Jim a... ...-year-old IBM
...liked good ...oo... ...ve the world,
...no longer believ... ...uldn't make th...
...our problem I ... ...is Laura, or M...
...a. None of the... ...one of them.
...problem, I said.
...and if that w...n... ...tl n the super ca...
...said that I would ... ...move. The H...
...business. Then ... ...a ay of executio...
...d have to give up ... n. his priceless m...

IT IS MORNING. I'm on the second cigarette and the first cup of coffee. It is a time of stocktaking, and what is there to see? A fairly young man with a tired boyish face, saddled with the knowledge of years and nothing gained, lacking a bird dog's sense of direction most of the time, without point or goal. "I am the future," I once wrote in a passionate schoolboy essay. Now, at twenty-nine, I am not expecting much from this world. Fitzgerald and his green light! I remember his rich, mad dream: "Tomorrow we will run faster, stretch out our arms farther." But where will this black boy run? To whom shall he stretch out his arms?

At the moment, I need not think of tomorrow. I've come to a decision. I am getting my possessions in order. Tonight there will be an auction in my pad. Everything will be sold, got rid of. And then I'll go away.

"Darling, it's a shame you have to give up this wonderful studio. There's a most charming little *atelier* near Beekman Place. . . ."

I walked away without a word. Where the hell did she think I'd get the money? Unless . . . Oh no, not that. I touch the bus ticket in my pocket. No Mrs. Lee for me.

Troy and Susan were leaving for an intellectual gathering in the Village. They can't quite forgive me because their child once called me "Nigger," and to conceal the fact have been especially warm and friendly ever since.

Susan flings her arms around me. "Everything will turn out fine, Charles. I know it will. You are *not* to worry!"

Troy squeezes my arm hard. "You could always move in with us. You know we'd like to have you."

I nod and try not to look sad, and see them to the door. They mean well, but they fawn on me too much. There's such a thing as being too Goddamn sincere. I have a double scotch to counteract the champagne and to wash away the dust of Troy and Susan's leaving.

I wondered where Shirley was; she said she'd be over, and then I thought about the other times she'd come here and of how we had quarreled, and of the day—when? a few weeks ago?—we'd gone to Coney Island. And I remembered the time Lena had said, "Why don't you kids get married?" And why not? I asked myself, but I knew we never would.

I was brought out of my reverie by Lady P, trotting by me into the bedroom. At the same moment, Claudia screamed at Laura: "Miss One! That mirror belongs to *me*! And so do the couch and chair. Charlie gave them to me."

Laura stared at Claudia coldly for a moment and then marched over to me. "I thought you said you had *sold* the couch and chair," she said. "Charles, you are a lying son-of-a-bitch. You gave them to that faggot. And you know I wanted the mirror."

"You should have asked sooner," I said weakly.

"How was I to know you'd lie to me?" Laura shot back. "It's such a lovely little mirror and I wanted it. I remember when you bought it at the Salvation Army store."

"Oh shit, Miss One," Claudia said, suddenly bored as only Claudia can be, "you can have it."

Just then Big Daddy came in from the bathroom singing, "I

She kissed me warmly, but she seemed nervous.

"Guess what's in this box?" she said. "Your books. All the books you've lent me. I knew you'd want them. I took a taxi up here."

"What happened to you?" I said. "You were supposed to be here hours ago. Now almost everyone has gone."

"I know."

"Well?"

"Please, Charles," Shirley said softly, taking my hand.

"Fuck it," I said, jerking my hand away.

"I'm not going to marry that doctor," Shirley announced quietly. "I've changed my mind."

I didn't say anything. Suddenly I didn't care. All I wanted to do was sleep, but I knew I wouldn't sleep just yet. Tomorrow I'll sleep on the bus, but now Shirley and I will climb the stairs together, back to my drunken friends upstairs. The party had turned into a free-for-all; I could hear their voices wild above the music, searching for that crazy kick that would still the fears, confusion, and the pain of being alive on this early August morning.

"What's wrong?" Shirley asked. "Charles, what's wrong?"

"Nothing," I said. "Absolutely nothing."

We started up the stairs and then I heard Claudia's voice, as clear as day, scream, "C———!"

# THE WIG

## A MIRROR IMAGE

••••••••••••••••••••••••••••••••

*For Charles Trabue Robb and
in memory of Lowney Turner Handy*

# 1

..........................................

*"Every phenomenon has its
natural causes . . ."*

—JAMES JOYCE

# ONE

I WAS A DESPERATE MAN. Quarterly, I got that crawly feeling in my wafer-thin stomach. During these fasting days, I had the temper of a Greek mountain dog. It was hard to maintain a smile; everyone seemed to jet toward the goal of The Great Society, while I remained in the outhouse, penniless, without "connections." Pretty girls, credit cards, charge accounts, Hart Schaffner & Marx suits, fine shoes, Dobbs hats, XK-E Jaguars, and more pretty girls cluttered my butterscotch-colored dreams. Lord—I'd work like a slave, but how to acquire an acquisitional gimmick? Mercy— something had to fall from the tree of fortune! Tom-toms were signaling to my frustrated brain; the message: I had to make it.

As a consequence, I was seized with a near epileptic fit early one Thursday morning. I stood in the center of my shabby though genteel furnished room, shivering and applauding vigorously. Sweet Jesus!—my King James-shaped head vaulted toward the fungus-covered ceiling pipes where cockroach acrobatics had already begun. The cockroaches seemed extraordinarily lively, as if they too were taking part in the earthshaking revelation. Even the late March sun was soft and sweet as moonlight, and the beautiful streets of Harlem were strangely quiet.

Smiling ecstatically, tears gushing from my Dutch-almond

in the white-tiled room, my heart exploded in my eyes like the sea. My brain whirled.

Do not the auburn-haired gain a new sense of freedom as a blonde (see *Miss Clairol*)? Who can deny the madness of a redesigned nose (see *Miami Beach*)? The first conference of Juvenile Delinquents met in Riis Park and there was absolutely no violence: a resolution was passed to send Seconal, zip guns, airplane glue, and contraceptives to the Red Chinese (see *The Daily News*). The American Medical Association announced indignantly that U. S. abortion and syphilis quotas are far below the world average (see *Channel 2*). Modern gas stations have coin-operated air pumps in the ladies' room so the under-blessed may inflate their skimpy boobs (see *Dorothy Kilgallen*). Undercover homosexuals sneak into the local drugstores and receive plastic though workable instruments plus bonus Daisy trade stamps (see *Compliments of a newfound friend*). Schizo wisdom? Remember, I said to myself, you are living in the greatest age mankind has known. Whereupon, I went to the washbasin, picked up the Giant Economy jar of long-lasting Silky Smooth Hair Relaxer, with the Built-in Sweat-proof Base (*trademark registered*). Carefully, I read the directions. The red, white, and gold label guarantees that the user can go deep-sea diving, emerge from the water, and shake his head triumphantly like any white boy. This miracle with the scent of wild roses looks like vanilla ice cream and is capable of softening in sufficiently Negroid hands.

I took a handful of Silky Smooth and began massaging my scalp. Then, just to be on the safe side, I added Precautionary Oil, thick, odorless, indigenous to the Georgia swamps. Massaging deftly, I remembered that old-fashioned hair aids were mixed with yak dung and lye. They burned the scalp and if the stuff got in your eye you could go blind from it. One thing was certain: you combed out scabs of dried blood for a month. But a compassionate northern senator had the hair aids outlawed. Said he, in ringing historic words: "Mr. Chairman, I offer an amendment to this great Spade tragedy! These people are real Americans and we should outlaw all hair aids that makes them lose their vibrations and éclat." Silky Smooth (using a formula perfected by a Lapp tribe in Karasjok, Norway) posed no problems.

Let the brandy bitch scream her head off, I thought. A Creole from New Orleans, indeed. If there's anyone in this building with Creole blood, it's me.

"I'm dying. Please help a dying widow . . ." the voice wailed from the hall.

I unwillingly turned from the mirror. The Wig was perfection. Four dollars and six cents' worth of sheer art. The sacrifice had been worth it. I was reborn, purified, anointed, beautified.

"I'm just a poor helpless widow . . ."

Would the bitch never shut up? With the majesty of a witch doctor, I went to Nonnie Swift's rescue.

She was sprawled on the rat-gnawed floorboards of the hall, clutching a spray of plastic violets, rhinestone Mother Hubbard robe spread out like a blanket under her aging, part-time-whore's body, which twitched rhythmically. Nonnie's blue-rinse bouffant was a wreck. It formed a sort of African halo. Tears sprang from her sea-green contact lenses. She jerked Victorian-braceleted arms toward the ceiling and whimpered pitifully.

"What's wrong?" I asked.

Nonnie folded her arms across her pancake stomach and moaned.

I knelt down beside her, peered at her contorted rouged face, and got a powerful whiff of brandy.

Like a blind thief's, Nonnie's trembling hands pawed at my chin, nose, forehead, and The Wig.

I wanted to break her goddamned hand. "Don't mess with the moss," I said. "What's wrong with you?"

"I'm in great pain, Les."

I tried to lift her into a sitting position. The lower part of her body seemed anchored to the floorboards.

"Feel it," Nonnie said, belching.

"Feel what?"

"Feel it," Nonnie repeated tersely.

"Don't you ever give up? You're old enough to be my mother."

She screamed again. Cracked lips showed through her American Lady lipstick, which is a deep, deep purple shade.

"Thank you, son," Nonnie sighed.

"Are you stoned?" I asked. I had a feeling she wasn't talking to me.

## CHAPTER 7

I looked down at Nonnie. Perhaps she *was* Creole. "Things are getting better every day," I said.

"Oh. I hope so," Nonnie cried. "Things have got to change, or else I'll go back to my old mansion in the Garden District, where the weeds have grown and the Spanish moss just hangs and hangs, and the wind whistles through it like a mockingbird."

Does that chick read? I asked myself, can she? and decided probably not, she probably saw it and heard it all in the movies.

I had an urge to tell Nonnie she ought to be on the stage or in a zoo. I'd listened to all this fancy jazz for three years. I realize people have to have a little make-believe. It's like Mr. Fishback says: "Son, try it on for size because after you see me there'll be no more changes." Sooner or later, though, you have to step into the spotlight of reality. You've got to do your bit for yourself and society. I was trying for something real, concrete, with my Wig.

So I said to Nonnie, "I'm gonna make the big leap. I'm cutting out."

"You? Where the hell are you going?"

"Just you wait and see," I teased. "I'm gonna shake up this town."

"And just you wait and see," Nonnie mocked. "You curly-headed son of a bitch. You've conked your hair."

"Not conked," I corrected sharply. I wanted to give her a solid blow in the jaw and make her swallow those false teeth. "Just a little water and grease, Miss Swift."

"Conked."

"Do you want me to bash your face in?"

"I'm sorry, sweetcakes," Nonnie said.

"That's more like it. You're always putting the bad mouth on people. No wonder *you* people never get nowhere. You don't help each other. You people should stick together like the gypsies."

"It's a pity, ain't it?"

Although I was fuming mad, I managed to lower my voice and make a plea for sympathy. "I can't help it if I have good hair. You can't blame a man for trying to better his condition, can you? I'm not putting on or acting snotty."

"I didn't wanna hurt your feelings," Nonnie said tearfully. "Honest, Les. You look sort of cute."

"Screw, baby."

"I really mean it. I hope my son has good hair. God knows he'll need something to make it in this world."

"That's a fact," I agreed solemnly. "The Wig's gonna see me through these troubled times."

Nonnie questioned the plastic violets for confirmation. "It gives me a warm feeling to know that I can buy each in my old age," she remarked with great dignity. "My baby boy will be a great something. I'm sure high-school diplomas and college degrees are on the way out, now you can get them through the mail for a dollar ninety-eight, plus postage. Look at the mess all those degrees have gotten us in. By the time he's a grown man success might depend on something else. Might well be a good head of hair."

"That's true," I agreed. Then, blushing, I couldn't help but add: "You know, Nonnie, I feel like a new person. I know my luck is changing. My ship is just around the bend."

"I suppose so," Nonnie said bitchily. "I suppose that's the way you feel when your hair is conked."

I turned and began walking away. Otherwise, I would have strangled Nonnie Swift.

Now, she began to cry, to plead. "Les—Lester Jefferson. Don't leave me flat on my back. Please. I'm all alone. Mrs. Tucker won't help me. You'll have to sub for the doctor."

"Screw."

I had no time for the drunken hag. How could a New Orleans tramp appreciate The Wig? That's the way people are. Always trying to block the road to progress. But let me tell you something: no one, absolutely no one—nothing—is gonna stop this boy. I've taken the first step. All the other steps will fall easy into place.

Who was I talking to? Myself. Feeling at peace with myself and proud of my clear reasoning, I decided to make it up to Miss Sandra Hanover's on the third floor, to what Miss Sandra called her pied-à-terre.

Miss Sandra Hanover was intelligent, understanding. A lady with class.

# T W O

THE DOOR, HUNG with an antique glass-beaded French funeral wreath, was open. Hopefully, I entered and looked over at Miss Sandra Hanover and was chilled to the bone.

Miss Sandra Hanover, ex-Miss Rosie Lamont, ex-Mrs. Roger Wilson, nee Alvin Brown, needed a shave. The thick dark stubble was visible under two layers of female hormone powder. But she had plucked her eyebrows; they *v*'d up toward Chinese-style bangs like two frozen little black snakes. A Crown Princess, working toward a diva's cold perfection, she did not acknowledge my entrance. She looked silly as hell, sitting on a warped English down sofa, wearing a man's white shirt, green polka-dot tie, and blue serge trousers. Her eyes were closed and her Texas-cowboy sadist's boots morse-coded a lament. At home Miss Sandra Hanover normally wore a simple white hostess gown which she'd found in a thrift shop. So freakish, I thought, mustering up a smile.

Coming up, I'd decided not to comment on The Wig, realizing rhetoric would not be effective. The Wig would speak for itself, a prophet's message.

I went over to the warped sofa and said, "What's wrong?"

Miss Sandra Hanover clasped her two-inch fake-gold-fingering hands. Then she opened her bright eyes, but made no reply.

"Did you upset those faggots last night?" I coaxed.

Miss Sandra Hanover blew her nose with a workman's handkerchief. Her face was bright. Then it caused a chalice of tears.

"Oh, Les. It was simply awful. Remember Miss Susan Hayward in *I Wanna Live!* Her voice was so heavy with suffering, that I immediately thought of Jell-O."

"Yeah. But why the waterworks?"

I'm a Brown Princess maskee a disting stare. She bolted over to the junk cabinet and got a personal E.I. cigarette.

Imitating a high-fashion model's bitch stride, Miss Sandra Hanover paraded around the nine-by-ten pied-à-terre, striking grand, filthy Bette Davis poses.

Sucking in her breath, she suddenly stopped and began speaking as if she had rehearsed her monologue diligently:

"Well, I went to this drag party on Central Park West last night. A fishback couldn't chauffeur in the Cadillac's a night light at least. So, your mother had a ball. Ever so grand. I looked like Miss Scarlett O'Hara. Miss Vivien Leigh was simply wonderful, wasn't she? You should have seen how lovely I looked. Flesh-colored satin. I let my servants drag the floor like Miss Rita Hayworth in *Gilda.* I'm making tennis calls galore on Sutton Place South. The sweetest little thing from Arkansas. She had her diamond earrings, like those of Miss Audrey Hepburn, who ate *Breakfast at Tiffany's.* She had this John glaze the foxes. The sweetest little furrier. I didn't even have to do him. I just told him that he really loved his mother. I he wanted to sleep with her when he was four years old."

"Still up to your old tricks." I laughed.

"Now, Lester Jefferson," Miss Sandra Hanover said coyly, "Everybody's got something working for them. I bet you've got something working for you."

Smiling and silent, I went and sat down in a modern Danish chair which looked like a miniature sun lit.

Miss Sandra Hanover cleared her throat. "Remember Miss Gloria Swanson in *Sunset Boulevard?* Coming down that spacious staircase, mad with her own greatness, honey? And all those cornment reporters thinking she was touched in the head? She knew deep down in her own heart that she was a star of the first *multi-tude*! Well, love, that was me last night."

Greedily relishing her victory, Miss Sandra Hanover clucked her tongue, leaned back and struck a *Vogue* pose. Vigorous, in the American style, she wetted liver lips, exhaled, and continued: "Oh, did those faggots want to claw my eyes out! I acted like visiting royalty. Remember Miss Bette Davis in *Elizabeth and Essex*? I sat on that cockroach-infested sofa like it was a throne and didn't even *dance*! I just gave'm my great Miss Lena Horne smile . . ."

Drunk with dreams of glory, Miss Sandra Hanover's voice became a coquette's confidential whisper: "Later, things got out of hand. The lights were turned down low. Sex and pot time. Miss Sammie knocked over the buffet table, which was nothing but cold cuts anyway, and those half-assed juvenile delinquents started fighting. I pressed for the door.

"Three Alice Blue Gowns came running up the stoop. Naturally, they thought I was a woman. I flirted like Miss Ava Gardner in *The Barefoot Contessa*. Then this smart son-of-a-bitch starts feeling me up. You see, I was a nervous wreck dressing for the party. I couldn't find my falsies. I looked high and low for those girls! I had to stick a pair of socks in my bosom. And this smart-ass cop has a flashlight and pulls out my brand-new Argyle socks. Oh! I was fit to be tied. In high drag going to the can at two in the morning. Suffering like Miss Greta Garbo in *Camille,* and before you knew it: daylight . . ."

"And the doll was ready for breakfast in bed," I joked, craning my neck for a glimpse in the oval-shaped mirror above Miss Hanover's crew cut.

She cleared her throat again and slumped back on the sofa. "Breakfast? I couldn't eat a bit. Slop! I felt like Miss Barbara Stanwyck in *Sorry, Wrong Number.* But I did this lovely guard and he brought me two aspirins and a cup of tea."

Miss Hanover fell silent. I couldn't resist another glance at myself in the mirror, dreaming an honest young man's dream: to succeed where my father had failed. Six foot five, two hundred and seventy pounds, the exact color of an off-color Irishman, my father had learned to read and write extremely well at the age of thirty-six. He died while printing the letter Z for me. I was ten,

Dead she wasn't. No one like that ever dies. I got up, found a bottle of Chanel No. 5 and bathed Miss Hanover's forehead and temples with the perfume.

Counting to ten, I stared at Miss Hanover's carefully brushed crew cut. I missed her glamorous false wig. It was true; everyone had something working for them.

Presently, the great actress regained consciousness.

Sighing erotically, she looked up at me. "I must have fainted. Isn't that strange? And you look strange too, love juice."

Swallowing hard, I backed toward the door. "I'd better be going," I said.

"Now, Les," Miss Hanover chided.

"I'll see you later, doll."

The Crown Princess rose quickly. "Come here, honey," she pleaded. "I ain't gonna bite you. My, my. Those beautiful curls. Naked, you'd look like a Greek statue."

"Yeah," I mumbled and bolted out the door and down to my second-floor sanctum. Pleasure, I reflected, was not necessarily progress, and I had a campaign to map out. I had to get my nerves together.

# T H R E E

WHISTLING "Onward, Christian Soldiers," I put the night latch on my door. I wanted no one coming in. I lit a cigarette, flopped down on the landlord's hallelujah prize, a fire-damaged sofa bed, crossed my legs, and exhaled deeply. I smiled lightly, like a young man in a four-color ad. I realized that nothing is perfect, but still, there was a possibility I might now be able to breathe easier. The Wig's sneak preview could be called successful, provided one knew human nature. Nonnie Swift's taunts: pure jealousy. Miss Sandra Hanover: simply a case of lust. I grinned and touched my nose.

Dear Dead Mother and Mother. Why do I have visions of guillotining you? Mother baked lemon pies. Father was a Pullman porter, a heroic man with a cat's gray eyes. Worthy colored serfs, good dry Methodists—they did not believe I had a future. How could they have possibly known? Otherwise, they'd have done something about my nose. No, it's not a Bob Hope nose, no one could slide down it, although it might make a plump backrest. If my parents had been farsighted, I would have gone to bed at night with a clothespin on my nose. At breakfast, Father would have peeped from behind the morning paper and lectured me on my bright future (I've seen those damn ads and motion pictures. I know how fathers act at the breakfast table).

to pay up. In what way I can't say. But there'll be no way out.

Dammit! The doorbell buzzed, a desperate animal-like clawing, funny little noises, like a half-assed drummer trying to keep time.

Upset, I went and flung open the door.

Little Jimmie Wishbone stood there. A dusty felt hat pulled down over his ears. Cracked dark glasses obscured his sultry eyes. The ragged army poncho was dashing and faintly sinister, like a CIA playboy.

"Brroudder! Ain't you cracket up yet?" Little Jimmie shouted. "I thought I'd see you over thar."

I stiffened but gestured warmly. "Come in, man. When you get out?"

"Yestiddy, 'bout two o'clock."

"Good to see you, man."

Grunting like a hot detective, Little Jimmie surveyed the room. He flipped up the newspaper window shade and looked out on the twenty feet of rubbish in the backyard. He jerked open the closet curtains. Satisfied, he pulled a half gallon of Summertime wine and Mr. Charlie's *Lucky Dream Book* from under the poncho and put them on the orange-crate coffee table.

"You're looking good," I said, hoping I didn't sound as if I were fishing for a compliment.

"Am I?" Little Jimmie wanted to know.

Sadly, I watched him ease down on the sofa bed, like a king in exile.

Aged twenty-eight, Little Wishbone was a has-been, a former movie star. *Adios* to fourteen Cadillacs, to an interest in a nationwide cathouse corporation. He had been the silent "fat" owner of seven narcotic nightclubs, had dined at The White House. Honored at a Blue Room homecoming reception after successfully touring the deep South *and* South Africa. At the cold cornbread and molasses breakfast, Congressmen had sung "He's a Jolly Good Nigger." Later, they had presented him with a medal, gold-plated, the size of a silver dollar, carved with the figure of a naked black man swinging from a pecan tree.

I had to hold back tears. Could that have been only two years ago? I wondered. I got a couple of goblets from under the dripping radiator. Mercy—depression multiplies like cockroaches.

We had killed Summertime. Little Jimmie kept his eyes fastened on the empty wine bottle. He looked like an angelic little boy who had been kicked out of his orphanage for failing to take part in group masturbation.

"You look down," I said. "You need some nooky."

Little Jimmie sighed. He looked very tired. "Nooky? Dem white folk messed wit yo boy. Shot all dem currents through me. Y'all took way my libin', I said. And they jest kept shooting electricity. It was even popping out my ears. I took it like a champ. Kinda scared dem, too. I heard one of dem say: 'He's immune. It's the result of perpetual broilization. Nothing will ever kill a Nigger like this.' I did my buck dance and the doctor said, 'They got magic in their feet.' Man, I danced into the village. Now they can't figure out why those currents and saltpeter make me so restless. They puzzled. I'm amused. But it's not like my Hollywood days. All my fans and those lights and twenty-seven Cadillacs."

"Fourteen Cadillacs," I corrected.

"Fourteen," Little Jimmie agreed. "But I traded them in every year. Les, I just don't feel right. I just ain't me."

"I know what you mean."

"What am I gonna do?"

"You need another drink."

"Yeah. Some juice. Out there . . ."

"You didn't escape, did you?"

"Where could I escape to?" Little Jimmie exclaimed.

"Nowhere, man," I said, averting my eyes.

"I can't even get unemployment, though I was honorary president of the Screen Guild."

"You could always pick cotton in Jersey," I said.

"Pick cotton?" Little Jimmie sneered. "What would my fans think? I think I'll appeal to the Supreme Court. I figure they owe me an apology. I worked for the government, man. I kept one hundred million colored people contented for years. And in turn, I made the white people happy. Safe. Now I'm no longer useful in the scheme of things. Nobody's got time for Little Jimmie Wishbone."

"What did you expect? Another medal? It's not profitable to have you *Tom* . . . It's a very different scene."

[illegible] what are [illegible]u gonna [illegible] the hell don[illegible] you [illegible]

[illegible] tell [illegible] you th[illegible] doing last summer? [illegible] time I got [illegible] money [illegible] chicken I b[illegible]ugh[illegible] a [illegible]

[illegible] between friends is [illegible] [illegible] scared up a breath [illegible] "I'm gonna [illegible] someth[illegible] [illegible] tried before. Dig [illegible]

[illegible] Jimmie grunted [illegible] "[illegible] at all those [illegible] [illegible]cans the[illegible] import [illegible] and cabbag[illegible]."

[illegible] an American," I [illegible]

[illegible] I've got a [illegible] dollar[illegible]

[illegible] American. That's a [illegible] fact. America [illegible] grease and hard [illegible] --you's [illegible] I'm gonna work [illegible] a bitch. D[illegible] you [illegible]

[illegible] heard you. Now [illegible] to the street [illegible]

# F O U R

LITTLE JIMMIE AND I moved out into the street under a volcanic gray sky. A cold wind made a contradictory hissing like an over-heated radiator, crept under heavy clothing with a shy but deter-mined hand. Nothing could stifle our sense of adventure; Little Jimmie was home again, and I always feel cocksure, Nazi-proud, stepping smartly toward the heart of Harlem—125th Street.

125th Street has grandeur if you know how to look at it. Harlem, the very name a part of New World History, is a ghetto nuovo on the Hudson; it reeks with frustrations and an ounce of job. Lonely, I often leave my airless room on Saturday night, wan-der up and down 125th Street, dreaming of making it, dreaming of love. This is the magical hour. The desperate daytime has, for a time, disappeared. The bitter saliva puddles of the poor are cov-ered with sperm, dropped by slumming whites and their dark friends who wallow in the nightclubs that go on to early morning. These are people who can afford to escape the daytime fear of the city. Envious, I watch their entrances and exits from the clubs. I especially watch the Negroes, who pretend that the black-faced poor do not exist.

I glanced at my misbegotten friend, a silent but bright-eyed Little Jimmie Wishbone. In his heyday, he'd been unique: a real

falling in line. The opportunity for Negroes to *progress* was truly coming. I could hear a tinkling fountain sing: "I'll wash away your black misery—tum-tiddy-diddy-tum-tee-tee." Yes. Wigged and very much aware of the happenings, I knew my ship was just around the bend, even as I had informed Miss Nonnie Swift.

125th Street, with its residential parks, its quaint stinking alleys is a sea of music, Georgian chants, German lieder, Italian arias, Elizabethan ballads. Arabic lullabies, lusty hillbilly tunes. Negro music is banned except for progaganda purposes. "We'll let *them* borrow our music," a Negro politician remarked recently. "We'll *see* what it does for them. We'll see if *they* ride to glory on our music." I remember the Negro politician sailed a week later on a yacht, a sparkling-white yacht, complete with sauna, wine cellar, and a stereo record collection of Negro music second only to the Library of Congress's.

No one's perfect, I was thinking, when Little Jimmie elbowed me.

"I see *they're* still here," he said angrily.

"Of course, Little Jimmie," I said softly, mindful of his mental condition, his swift descent from Fame.

"You're nuts."

"Don't get yourself worked up," I said. "No one's gonna bother you."

"But they're still here," Little Jimmie protested.

"Naturally." I knew all along what had him bugged. It was the police.

New York's finest were on the scene, wearing custom-made Chipp uniforms, 1818 Brooks Brothers shirts, Doctor U space shoes (bought wholesale from a straw basket in Herald Square). A pacifistic honor guard, twelve policemen per block, ambitious nightsticks trimmed with lilies of the valley, WE ARE OUR BROTHER'S KEEPER buttons illuminating sharp-brimmed Fascist helmets—they bow to each fast-moving Harlemite from crummy Lenox to jet-bound Eighth Avenue.

Little Jimmie's fear was disgusting. The policemen were our protectors, knights of the Manhattan world. I wasn't afraid. I was goddam grateful.

"Are you ready?" I asked cheerfully.

"We gotta make it just to Eighth Avenue. It's not like a cross-country race."

"It's the same!" Little Jimmie cried. He pulled the felt hat down over his ears and started off.

I let him have a comfortable lead. Arching my arms, head held high, I bounded off graciously, the son of a desperate, dead runner.

Up ahead, a policeman sharpening a bowie knife snapped to attention as I dashed across Lenox Avenue.

Bowing, the policeman said, "Good morning, sir."

"Morning," I replied, gasping for breath. I'd never been frightened before, believe me. Little Jimmie's gloomy forecast, I told myself. He's a very sick has-been.

And soon I bypassed him, smoothly sprinting toward a photo finish. I galloped across the right side of Eighth Avenue, feeling my ego-oats. I was in good condition for the Spring Run-Nigger-Run track meet (the winner of this meet receives a dull black wrought-iron Davis Cup. There is always savage bribery; each borough president shills and makes a play for his favorite black son). Sunrise, sunset, winter, or summer—it had never been Succoth—the Promised Land, or the ingathering of the harvest for me. But with The Wig it might soon be.

I wiped my sweaty brow and saw three whores standing on the corner, adjusting white kid gloves.

"Little Jimmie," I called. "Look at our reward. Standing tall, sweet, and brown."

Little Jimmie eased up his pained physical-fitness smile. "Call the mojo man. Too bad Caddie number twenty is in the repair shop."

Stalking coolly, we approached the three whores.

I opened. "What you pretty girls doing out in this weather?"

The finely built group spokesman scanned the sky and giggled. "We're waiting on the Junior League pick-up truck. Those fine ladies, always so discriminating, have consented to see us. We're gonna add a little funky color to their jaded lives. Ain't that nice? They're planning a tea benefit for Harlem settlement houses. We're in charge of the entertainment. Ain't that nice?"

"It sure is," Little Jimmie guffawed boyishly.

"An honor," I agreed, eyeing the innocent, lyrically pretty

ance. I ... sh ... ed ... oves
verted ... nd- ... yes.
rema ... fer ... ike ... ni.
to cha ... umpl ...
Sponge a ... clea ... er ... do
e."
"You lo ... ," ... up ... ittle
e.
e rus ... ak ... en; ... his
n the ba ... and ... in ... jest
be. I ... shl ... om ...
e gro ... ch ... glow ... ght
"Little J ... e ... star ...
do de ... said ... eard ... v"
hat w ... se ... vision ... ie
odest ...
e wh ... L ... ed,
ng th ... s tr ... vard ... m
ss me ... mach ... urn ... n
ys du ... S ... noc ...
"When ... no ... pictu ... t-
e gro ... d ... tron ...
"Well," ... gr ... ndly, ... y,
wa ... or ... ester ... at
we'd ... at ... Swit ... ot
ty, yo ...
e gro ... he ... w tr ...
-so e ... e ba ... rls. ...
ière. ... tick ... lpe ..."
olly ... d ou ... tle ... I
sa
o dec ... ai ...
calcul ... he fi ... uilt, ... n
be ... o sho ... you ...
b ...?
le Jim ... he g ... e
a ... boy j ... fres ..."
You and ... ge ... ske ...
s ... in S ...

"I got him in Hong Kong last year."

"I do declare."

I wanted to kill the dirty, wine-drinking son of a bitch. I bowed my beautiful head in shame, silently vowing to see Madame X, the reincarnation of Medusa, the smoldering rage of the Harlem firmament. A few incantations by her, and Little Jimmie's wagon would really be fixed.

"Orientals make the best servants," the spokesman commented.

"That's true," Little Jimmie was quick to agree. In Hollywood, he'd had a Finnish cook and a British gentleman's gentleman.

"We're servantless. Thursday, you know," the spokesman smiled sweetly. "And we're simply delighted to meet you, Mr. Wishbone, in the flesh. I think we should give those Junior League girls a rain check. Another day for dice and cards and chitchat and Bloody Marys. But I'd be delighted if you'd join me in my study for an informal lunch. I'm a follower of Dione Lucas and James Beard, you know. I'll try to whip up something simple. Kale and turnip greens cooked with juicy ham hocks. Yankee pot roast. German potato salad. Green beans soaked in fat back. And my specialty, cornbread and sweet-potato pie."

Little Jimmie made a dapper bow. Lordly he said, "Delighted. One gets tired of frozen frog legs, frozen cornish hen, instant wild rice, and pasteurized caviar."

"Well, just come along with us," Hostess spokesman smiled. "The Deb can stay with your valet and keep him company. 'Bout as close to royalty as she'll ever get."

Swooning, Spongecake said: "I do declare. Such a refreshing change from the round of parties and balls and dinners at the Bath Club where we're always encountering the same crowd."

The worms in my stomach were too hurt to cry over the great luncheon—they were resigned.

I watched spokesman and Spongecake proudly encircle Little Jimmie, saunter down Eighth Avenue.

"And you have twenty-five Caddies," Spongecake marveled.

"Forty-two," Little Jimmie lied. "And I'm getting a Rolls next week."

A loner, always on the outside, I looked at The Deb.

"You sure got pretty hair," she said.

"[illegible] sked, [illegible] lover-boy [illegible]

[illegible] se [illegible] er bo [illegible] battered [illegible] hair is [illegible] ky. Nobody [illegible]

[illegible] and go [illegible] of my lonely [illegible] cally [illegible] We were [illegible]

"[illegible] said. "[illegible]

[illegible] Madam [illegible] too. [illegible] I can go [illegible]

[illegible] ms a [illegible] and fell [illegible]

[illegible] flesh made [illegible] through my [illegible] s. [illegible] sweet desire [illegible] power and [illegible]

"[illegible] The De [illegible] gentlemen [illegible]

[illegible] it was the [illegible] gentleman. [illegible] say that."

"[illegible] a Swedish [illegible] I feel like [illegible] 're a man [illegible] sensitive. I [illegible]

"[illegible] ing," [illegible] rather [illegible]

"[illegible]

"[illegible] Some place [illegible] an open fire, [illegible] music."

"[illegible] tic," The De [illegible] lips brushing [illegible]

"[illegible]

"[illegible] me [illegible] know: [illegible]

"[illegible]," [illegible] "we [illegible]..."

"[illegible]. This [illegible] "You gotta [illegible] I'm simp [illegible] girl."

[illegible] broke [illegible]

"You American females are very strange. In Europe . . ."

"Sweetie, I dig you *and* your Wig. But they'd bar me from the union if I gave it away. The chairman said: 'No finance, no romance.' I hope you understand."

Sadly, I slumped against a litter basket. I'd had The Wig less than four hours and already I felt the black clouds gathering.

"I'll see you around, sweetie," The Deb smiled and walked away.

"Yeah," I mumbled, comforted with the knowledge that I was at least on the right side of Eighth Avenue.

# FIVE

Rejected, dejected, I started walking east on 125th Street. The wind was dying and the sun had come out. Those cool knights, the cops, were dozing or filing their fingernails or reading newspapers. Negroes no longer raced across streets. They had slowed to a sensual stride. It was siesta time in Harlem. Everything was so quiet and peaceful that you wanted to take the mood home in a paper bag and sleep with it.

A candy store's loudspeaker played a Bach sonata—Landowska on the harpsichord. But the only music I heard was "no finance, no romance." The Deb, I sighed, feeling my whole body shake like thunder.

Up ahead loomed a great big fat bank, a foreign bank. Bracing my shoulders, I went into the bank and asked about a porter's job. I might as well try the dream of working my way up. Yes, there was an opening, I was informed by a very polite Negro girl with strawberry-blond hair. First, I had to fill out an application and take a six weeks' course in the art of being human, in the art of being white. The fee for the course would be one-five-o.

I thanked the girl with a weak smile, saying I'd return later in the afternoon or perhaps tomorrow. I'd have to place a long-distance call to Nassau.

was first reported. The Negro youth had committed a sexual out-rage, according to *Confidential Magazine* in its exclusive interview with the host and hostess, who were famous for their collection of Contemporary Stone Art. Their sexual safaris were legendary, too. Inspired by childhood tales of lynchings (ah, the gyrations, the moans, the sweat, the smell of fresh blood, the uncircumcised odor), the couple had explored Latin rice-and-bean delights, European around-the-world-scootee-roots, Near Eastern lamb, flip-flop, and it's-all-in-the-family.

Hoping to avoid the press, which arrived by helicopter, fifty miles from shore, exhausted, jaded, they returned to their native land on a luxury liner but in steerage class, with seventy pieces of Louis Vuitton luggage.

"It was off-season," the hostess had jokingly told reporters. The host added with great dignity: "We are returning to our native land, where fornication is pure and simple. We're returning to the womb of nature." They went into seclusion in their Greenwich Village carriage house until the night of the celebrated "happening," the night that was to reestablish their worldly reputation. The gleaming, white-toothed young Negro with the rough but carefully combed kinky hair (if one ran one's hand through his hair, one trembled and saw Venus and Mars) displayed a rosebud instead of a penis! The effrontery—a Negro and nipped in the bud! Certainly a shock that could drive anyone to murder, only it hadn't been murder, the courts decided. It was only a happening.

Sleepless still, I rolled over and scratched my stomach. I felt weak—a sure sign that happy days were here again and that I'd already opened a new door. As a child I'd always believed I could fly. One night, after sniffing The Big O in someone's bathroom, I *knew* it was possible. Until the countdown. Then I couldn't stand up, I was anchored to the floorboards. But the sensation, the idea of flight, the sensation of being free, that had been wonderful! I touched The Wig. Yes. Security had always eluded me, but it wouldn't much longer. American until the last breath, a true believer in The Great Society, I'd turn the other cheek, cheat, steal, take the fifth amendment, walk bare-assed up Mr. Jones's ladder, and state firmly that I was too human.

Lying in the quiet darkness, I decided to see Little Jimmie in

# 2

· · · · · · · · · · · · · · · · · · · · · · · · ·

*"If I could holler like a mountain jack . . ."*

—FROM *JOE WILLIAMS SINGS*

# S I X

WE KEPT OUR early morning séance with The Duke. He'd come a long way from his handyman-porter days in Chicago. A perfect specimen of the young man on the Amen train to success, the Duke had recently returned from his forty-seventh expedition into the Deep South and he had returned with a fantastic collection of antiques, a rare, historic collection. Sincere culture-prowling club-women were bursting out of their Edith Lances bras, trying to persuade The Duke to let his collection be included on their spring house tours.

The collection was extraordinary. It included the last word in expensive water hoses (nozzles intact, brassy but dented by human skulls); an enormous hunk of chestnut-colored hair from a Georgia policeman's gentle dog (The Duke planned to have this among his contemporary masterpieces); a hand-carved charred cross seven feet long; three dried Florida black snakes in a filigree shadow box; a lace handkerchief, reputed to be one of the oldest in America. These assorted objects were casually arranged in The Duke's mansion on the solid gilt edge of Central Park North and Fifth Avenue.

Little Jimmie and I swanked our way toward the Avenue. I saw people shield their eyes from The Wig.

"Oh, it's a mother-grabber. But I had thirty-five Caddies and I hear The Duke's only got one coupe de ville Caddy and that's almost a year old. I used to trade my Caddies in every four months."

Little Jimmie slowed, deep in past memories.

"Sure," I said, and tugging his arm, I led him gently across the street.

The Duke's soot-caked five-and-a-half-story limestone mansion did lean slightly out over the sidewalk, but, as he once remarked, that was part of its charm. It was a real conversation piece. Who else in Manhattan could boast that half of the fifth floor had fallen into the street by itself? The Duke didn't even have to call the demolition crew, though the Sanitation Department complained like hell when they had to clean up the bodies of three small children, all victims of rickets disease. A joyous Welfare Department sent The Duke a twenty-five-year-old quart of Scotch and officially axed the children from their list. The poor mother, The Duke had told me with tears in his eyes, was twenty-three and very frail and had seven other illegitimate children on welfare, including two sets of twins.

"It's a beauty," Little Jimmy exclaimed as we bounced up the gold-veined marble steps. "But in my Hollywood heyday I had a twenty-car garage. Miss Mary Pickford and Mr. Douglas Fairbanks, Senior, ruled Hollywood in the twenties and *I* ruled Hollywood after the Second World War. That is, until those devils sent me into exile . . . ."

Little Jimmie shed one great tear, his trembling hand grasped the railing of the stoop.

"Now, don't go into that again," I said softly. "You'll get upset and be back in Kings County. Everything's cool. You're gonna reap fame and fortune in another field."

"But I was a star," Little Jimmie protested. "A movie star is the greatest thing in the world. A movie star lives forever."

I nodded and pressed the buzzer. The Wig would live forever, I thought. A monument to progress in the name of my dead parents.

Presently, the double-barred iron door swung open and we went into the bare white entrance hall.

Brandishing a genuine poison bow and arrow, The Duke emerged from behind a sackcloth curtain. Exactly five-feet-five, a

[illegible] version of Maxi[illegible] of M[illegible] he carefully [illegible] *The Natio*[illegible] [illegible] bright [illegible] Turk[illegible] tr[illegible] [illegible] Hong Kong [illegible]
[illegible]

"A[illegible] a little [illegible] life," he joked. "I wa[illegible] [illegible] show."

"W[illegible] made you [illegible]" I asked. "After all [illegible]"

"W[illegible]," The Duke [illegible] know what is. I [illegible] marijuana [illegible] teen."

"I v[illegible]," Little [illegible] said [illegible]y.

"Ho[illegible]," I said, [illegible] mountain air and [illegible] voice, [illegible] for the intell[illegible] "An[illegible] you get high, [illegible] Getting high's gonna se[illegible] [illegible]"

"I know," The Duke [illegible] a garland of [illegible] "Marijuana is h[illegible] like hatred. It's [illegible] major drug [illegible] the government . . ." The D[illegible] [illegible] soft and [illegible] "That will be to[illegible]

"I guess you heard," [illegible]

"Oh. You mean [illegible] . It's great, man."

"[illegible] the experiment [illegible] public poll, you [illegible] get down to [illegible] matter."

[illegible] grinted. "[illegible] like a goddam [illegible] everybody [illegible] There was a ten [illegible] hundred and [illegible] Six people injure[illegible] [illegible]"

"[illegible] I say I was going [illegible] this town?" I la[illegible]

"Well," The Duke no[illegible] agreement. "I don't see [illegible]"

[illegible] ded [illegible] "[illegible] Louis B. Mayer [illegible] here at MGM.' A[illegible] Louis.'

"[illegible]," The D[illegible] quietly. "Nobody co[illegible] ten-foot pole [illegible] your place as [illegible] Mickey Mouse [illegible]y.'"

[illegible] my place [illegible] moviegoer's he[illegible]

tle Jimmie cried. He flung the plastic attaché case to the floor angrily. "It was those secret devils that double-crossed me . . ."

"What secret agents?" I scoffed, forgetting that he was touched in the head.

"How should I know?" Little Jimmie pleaded. "All I know is I'd jest been made an honorary member of the Arm Forces. This was wartime, mind you, but General Motors okayed a custom-built job for me. I was essential to the war effort. I made the people on the home front forget fear and tragedy."

Lies, insanity—I didn't care. "Peace on the home front? What the hell are you talking about? There was tragedy. My father learned to read and write and then died. My mother died grieving over him. That's how things were then. And I suppose you showed your teeth when the white folks said, 'Two more niggers gone.' I remember in the picture called *The Educated Man* there was a line that made the whole country laugh. 'No sur. Me caint weed nor wight to save muh name . . .'"

Little Jimmie came over and tried to console me. "That was just part of the script, Les."

"Then why did you always sign your name with a rubber stamp and put an X beside it?"

"That was a gimmick. I had a good public relations working for me."

"But do you really know how to read and write?" I asked, breaking away from his grasp.

"I know how to read the Gallup Poll, *Variety,* and *The Hollywood Reporter.* I placed first in *Photo Digest Magazine*'s popularity contest five years in a row. And then . . ."

Little Jimmie slumped against the wall and moaned, head hung low, large, ashy hands grasping at something that wasn't there.

The Duke sighed. I felt a quick pain, felt sweat splash down my armpits. I thought of The Wig and my own dazzling future, but that brought little comfort now.

Finally I forced myself to say loud and clear: "Yeah. Just about the time you were gonna get an Academy Award they kicked your ass out of Hollywood."

Little Jimmie raised his head slowly and looked over at me. "You didn't have to say it like that, Les."

[illegible] could I say? It's [illegible]
forms.
[illegible] sweet [illegible] | [illegible] good stuff for [illegible]
[illegible] singers. [illegible] singers. That [illegible]
[illegible] ain't [illegible] | [illegible] Any[illegible]
[illegible] five- or ten-[illegible]

[illegible] couple of joints [illegible] see what [illegible]
Jimmie," [illegible]
[illegible] New [illegible] | [illegible] trying to [illegible]
[illegible] painfully [illegible]
[illegible] by [illegible] | [illegible] said, follow[illegible]
[illegible] room. [illegible]
[illegible] | [illegible] been a [illegible]
[illegible] into a [illegible] | [illegible] moved in, [illegible]
[illegible] dead, [illegible] | [illegible]
[illegible] | [illegible] Function[illegible]
[illegible] under [illegible]
[illegible] | [illegible] the [illegible]
[illegible] as bowl [illegible]
[illegible] seeded, and [illegible]
[illegible] marvelous [illegible]
[illegible] is agreed [illegible]
The [illegible] | [illegible] is private [illegible]
[illegible] | [illegible] seven four [illegible]
[illegible] site a modern [illegible] did not want [illegible]
significance [illegible] | [illegible] of the Na[illegible]
Civil War, [illegible] | [illegible]
[illegible] | [illegible] family in Jew[illegible]
cross.
[illegible] | [illegible] your service. [illegible]
[illegible] down [illegible] | [illegible] to [illegible]

[illegible] made [illegible] | [illegible] Muddy [illegible]
[illegible] of The [illegible] | [illegible] yesterdays. [illegible]
[illegible] finest. [illegible] | [illegible] the Jimmie [illegible]
[illegible] of pot. [illegible]
[illegible] hand out [illegible] | [illegible] up, [illegible]

inhaled deeply, and thought: Happy days. Little Jimmie and I will be rock 'n' roll sensations. Plus, I have The Wig; plus, there is still potency in the Little Jimmie Wishbone name. Plus, pot.

Feeling the pot and my bravado load, I went to the drug bar and flipped another joint into my golden lips and then looked over at Little Jimmie.

"Another pipe, man?"

Holding the pot in his head, riffling sheet music, Little Jimmie nodded gravely and I refilled his pipe.

Dry-heaving, The Duke clamped his hands over his mouth and turned toward the wall.

Two minutes later, he swung back around, breathing hard. "Fill my sax, Les. We'll make a session."

The Duke, a frustrated musician, always smoked pot out of a baby saxophone. A cute gimmick, like those coffeehouse musicians before Lily Law ended that scene. Smoke drifting out of the saxophone, a motif of cool music.

I filled the sax and joined The Duke, who now sat Indian fashion on the floor.

Three (pot-smoking) Wise Men, we silently savored the joy of marijuana, unmoved by the 10 A.M. foghorns signaling the first quarterly hour of radioactive dust.

The Duke elbowed me. "Are you feeling it?" he grinned.

"I am getting together," I replied. The image of The Deb floated into my mind. Boiling with inspiration, I added: "We could start off with a rock 'n' roll love song.

You upset me like the subway at night
Do, do, do uh a do . . . do
We'll hold hands in the first car
You and I and Oh . . .
Do, do, do, uh a do the policeman.
Do, do, do, uh a do, do

"What's the rest of it?" Little Jimmie asked.

"That's all. We jest keep repeating. Then let the sax and piano pick it up and, baby, we have at least two minutes. A record. A hit on our hands. By the time we make our first personal appearance on a TV show, we'll think of something freakish. You've gotta

# SEVEN

AFTER CLANSMEN GOOD-BYES, we were mellow. I wanna tell you: every muscle and vein in our bodies relaxed. We moved out onto the Avenue like crack athletes, briefly spotlighted by the fickle March sun. The Avenue was deserted and quiet except for the long-drawn-out cries of a hungry child. A rare cry. Normally, the Avenue's children were well fed, healthy, and happy.

"Terrible. Ain't it?" I said, looking up and down the Avenue.

A wave of old-star glory had washed over Little Jimmie. "It'll all be over soon. Remember when I was a star? Butter and biscuits and Smithfield ham every day. I was one of the big wheels in the machine. It'll be like the old days after we cut our first side."

"We can't miss," I said. "We've got too much going for us."

In an extravagant mood, I hailed a taxi, a sinister yellow taxi, festooned with leather straps and Bessemer steel rods. What looked like black blood caked the rear fender. The driver was a small pale man with an open face.

"Good morning," he said in a quavery voice. "I am at your service."

"Paradise," I snarled, easing into the taxi.

"That's Broadway and Fifty-second street," Little Jimmie said. "The musical capital of the world. We're part of the action."

[illegible] e," he bellowed [illegible]
[illegible] changed [illegible] es an [illegible]

[illegible] wrong with the [illegible]
[illegible] he exclaimed. [illegible]
[illegible] driver's face. [illegible]
[illegible] is the greatest [illegible] I am [illegible]
[illegible] distance. You [illegible] I should [illegible]
[illegible] steps [illegible]

"Get his stow [illegible]
[illegible] swallowed hard [illegible] "Yes, [illegible]

[illegible] along smoothly [illegible] down [illegible]
[illegible] Upper Avenue's [illegible] The [illegible]
[illegible] looked at [illegible]
[illegible] workers from [illegible]
[illegible] 2nd and Fifth [illegible]
[illegible] energetically [illegible]
[illegible] infants [illegible] cops [illegible]
[illegible] nursemaids [illegible]
[illegible] machine [illegible]
[illegible] buildings they [illegible]
[illegible] voices [illegible]
[illegible] from [illegible]
[illegible] ikans [illegible]
[illegible] I thought [illegible]
[illegible] my Del [illegible]
[illegible] Jefferson [illegible] ass [illegible]
[illegible] the Mercer [illegible] It [illegible]
[illegible] did [illegible] it [illegible]
[illegible] other, I thro[illegible] , I [illegible]
[illegible] our way." [illegible]

[illegible] teeth caught [illegible]
[illegible] Little Jimmie [illegible]

"Guess he's got thin blood."

"He's a skinny little son of a bitch."

"It's a wonder the wind doesn't blow his ass away."

Little Jimmie chuckled, and leaned back in the seat like a king.

"I ain't cold," the pleasant-faced driver cried. "I'm scared to death. I know you gonna take my leather straps and chains and beat me up. I know you gonna make black-and-blue marks all over me and take my money. Ain't that right? Ain't that right?"

Sighing, Little Jimmie said, "Is he trying to get in on the act?"

"No, man. He's a masochist. Dig?"

"Come on," the driver shouted. "Beat me and get it over with. I can't stand the waiting."

"Don't blow your cool," I warned him.

"Ain't that right, ain't that right?" Little Jimmie laughed.

"Sounds like the title of our second solid-gold hit record."

Just then the taxi driver picked up speed, raced down Fifth Avenue to 62nd Street, where he slammed on the brakes quickly.

"All right," he sneered. "Shut your trap. I've had enough from you jokers."

"Dig this mother," I said.

"What was that?" the driver snapped.

"Lay off, man," Little Jimmie said.

The taxi zoomed through a blinking red light and came to the fountain fronting the Plaza.

"Boys," the pale taxi driver began clearly, "you ain't on home ground now. You had your chance. So now don't you blow your cool. This is my turf. We're *downtown*."

"I know, I know," I sighed.

"Yeah," Little Jimmie put in, "but we're the two new BB's from tin-pan alley. You wouldn't wanna do nothing that would fuck up the economy and cause an international incident, would you?"

"Jesus," the taxi driver exclaimed. "Wait until I tell the kids and my old lady. Jesus. You could have had a police escort all the way downtown. Get you away from the Harlem riffraff. I knew all along that you two gentlemen were something special. The riffraff is causing all the trouble. Making it bad for you colored people."

"I know, I know," I sighed again as we swung on to Central

I pressed the elevator button. "How do you feel?"

"Like being born again. I know how you feel too, on the first wave of fame."

The wide doors of the elevator swung outward like the doors of a saloon. Little Jimmie braced sloping shoulders and pushed past me.

"Let's go, boy," he said.

A sudden thought hit me. "We don't have a manager," I said.

"It doesn't matter at this stage of the game. Press the button. Eighty-eight. I'll do the talking. You know I'm an old hand at this type of thing. But in the past, people always came to me. Either to my Beverly Hills mansion or to my Manhattan penthouse. But we'll manage."

The elevator closed silently. We stood stiff and proud, our hot eyes focused on the walls of the elevator. The walls were eye-catching: mahogany, with carved musical scales and American dollar signs.

"Lucre, my ghost," Little Jimmie sighed.

"You're a swinging stud."

"Nothing to it, boy. I know what's happening. I've had too many gigs."

Exiting from the elevator, I prayed for ten thousand one-night stands, for a million six-week holdovers. Balloon images of The Deb burst inside my excited beautiful head. I was happy like a man when a particularly painful wound begins to heal. I was no longer jockeying for position: I was *in* position. I followed Little Jimmie through the great bronze doors of Paradise Records.

The receptionist was licking stamps, and a sequined sign on the desk said: MISS BELLADONNA.

"Yes?" Miss Belladonna said in a hoarse voice, without looking up.

"We're the two new BB's and we want a hearing," Little Jimmie said with great dignity.

"Yeah?"

"Yes, young lady."

Miss Belladonna yawned. "Well . . ."

Impatient, Little Jimmie drummed his fingers on the kidney-shaped glass desk.

"We have the networks and the press by the balls," Mr. Pingouin said, smiling shyly.

"I should say we have," Miss Belladonna said. She seized the hand mike. "Mr. Sunflower Ashley-Smithe. Front and center!"

Silence, a rich soft silence, enfolded the nonchalant future recording stars, the jaundiced receptionist, and the owl-eyed first assistant vice-president.

Presently, doleful Muzak came on with Napoleon's Funeral March. Little Jimmie stood at attention, Miss Belladonna seemed to doze, Mr. Pingouin bowed his head, and I counted to one hundred.

Then Mr. Sunflower Ashley-Smithe entered to the strains of "Home on the Range."

There was nothing unusual about Mr. Sunflower Ashley-Smithe. A thoroughbred American Negro, the color of bittersweet chocolate—chocolate that looked as if it had weathered many seasons of dust, rain, and darkness, chocolate that had not been eaten, but simply left to dehydrate. He was more than six feet tall, I guessed. And when he smiled at us, I knew my ship was docking at last.

"Gentlemen," he said and bowed sedately. "I know ours will be a perfect relationship. Now, will you please join me in the inner room."

"It's our pleasure," Little Jimmie bowed back.

"Oh! Goodness," Miss Belladonna squealed. "This is so exciting. It always is."

"Have a happy session," Mr. Pingouin said, "and please remember that you are in the hands of Paradise."

Despite an abundance of expensive flowering plants, the inner room had the serene masculinity of a GI sleeping bag. Facing the window wall were two baby-grand pianos with smooth brass finishes. Large lounge chairs formed a fat lime-green circle centered on a stainless-steel coffee table. It was a large pleasant room, ideal for music.

"Gentlemen," Mr. Sunflower Ashley-Smithe said, extending the pale pink palm of his dark hand, "please be seated. Everything is very informal here at Paradise. That is the key to our worldwide success."

Finger popping, Little Jimmie agreed. "That's the method. When I was making my last trilogy of flicks about homesteaders . . . Wow!

board expertly. "Wonderful. Your choice of an opener is great."

Little Jimmie cleared his throat and peered at the sheet music closely. "Now, I'll take the verse and you take the chorus, Les. Let's rip a gut. This must be spontaneous."

The musical genius of the century laughed vigorously. "Let's see if you're colored."

Camaraderie like sunlight filled the inner room. I really felt as if I *could* bust a gut. I wasn't embarking on a Madison Avenue or a Wall Street career. No, this gig was glamour, Broadway, night lights. Champagne supper clubs, call girls, paying off bellboys and the police. A million hysterical teenagers screaming, clamoring for your autograph, a strand of your curly hair, a snotty Kleenex, a toothpick, a bad cavity filling, a pawnshop diamond ring, and all because few parents are child-oriented. And now *I* was a part of the racket!

"Lester," Little Jimmie said sharply.

"I'm with you, baby."

"Ready?" Mr. Ashley-Smithe asked.

I watched Little Jimmie flex his muscles, clench his fist, and breathe deeply. So deep I could see the outline of his soul on his sweating face.

And then he began to sing as if he were alone in a splendid garden on a cool summer morning. Looking at his contorted face, I thought: what a magnificent actor. A Harlem-born great actor.

Mr. Ashley-Smithe was impressed too. He clasped his hands and closed his eyes.

"The rebirth of my hero," he whispered.

Gesturing, alone in the garden, Little Jimmie's voice filled the inner room.

*Harlem nights are gloomy and long*
*A cold, cold landscape*
*Darkness, darkness.*
*Will I ever lift up my voice . . .*
*And sing,* I falsettoed right on key.

"You curly-headed son of a bitch," Little Jimmie yelled, "you didn't bust a gut!"

"What?" I faltered.

# EIGHT

NO LAUGHTER WELDED my shocked dark heart. I marched swiftly out of the inner room, past Miss Belladonna, who seeing my face screamed, "Goodness!"

Waiting impatiently for the elevator, I wanted to scream myself. The Wayward Four rocked, rolled, wallowed through the loud-speaker Muzak. *"Play-a simple melody, play-a simple melody,"* they sang. Off-key, no doubt spitting their puberty juice. "A racket," Sunflower Ashley-Smithe had said. Well, I wanted no part of it. Right then and there, I told myself, it had been an impulsive, foolish mistake. I was destined for a higher calling. Perhaps not Madison Avenue or Wall Street. No. A real man-sized job. A porter, a bus boy, a shoeshine boy, a swing on my father's old Pullman run. Young Abe by the twenty-watt bulb. Sweating, toiling, studying the map of The Great Society. One is not defeated until one is defeated. Hadn't the drugstore prophet said, "You may become whatever you desire?" Perhaps I'd even become a politician or a preacher—those wingless guards against tyranny and misery.

The saloon doors of the elevator opened. Piously, I entered. Muzak thundered with a gospel group singing:

*This little Light of mine . . .*
*I'm gonna let it shine . . .*

# N I N E

THE SUN WAS very bright the following morning; there was something almost nice about the polluted air. I had my glass of lukewarm tap water, said my Christian prayers, recited a personal Koran, and kissed the rat-gnawed floorboards of my room. (Nonbelievers, please take note: I was definitely insane, an ambitious lunatic.) I had spent a sleepless night plotting and thinking. Impersonation is an act of courage, as well as an act of skill, for the impersonator must be coldhearted, aware of his limitations. I, however, suddenly realized I *had* no limitations. I felt good. The sun was shining. Bathed in its warm rays, I became Apollo's Saturday morning son. My new image had crystallized. An aristocratic image, I might add. The new image was based on The Wig, and was to be implemented by the forethought of Mr. Fishback. It took me a little while to accept the fact that I was going to act upon it, but I did.

Here is the timetable: 10 A.M., perspiring. 10:15, borrowed two cigarettes from Nonnie Swift. Three minutes of cheers; Nonnie had been barred from the Harlem Sewing Circle because of her Creole past. Quarter of eleven, a last status sip of lukewarm water. At two minutes to eleven I snatched Mr. Fishback's Christmas gift from under the sofa bed: an all-purpose, fake, forged Credit Card, guaranteed at five hundred hospitals in all fifty states. Honored

[illegible] the trouse[illegible] [illegible]
[illegible], and [illegible]
[illegible] Jack's [illegible] I[illegible]
[illegible] I found [illegible]
[illegible] Cond [illegible]
[illegible] ville [illegible] dele[illegible]
[illegible] with Fath[illegible] *to [illegible]*
[illegible] marriage[illegible]
[illegible] Like [illegible]
[illegible] I di[illegible] [illegible] They'[illegible]
[illegible] high, [illegible]
[illegible] rough [illegible]
[illegible] of the [illegible]
[illegible] of cou[illegible]
[illegible] in the [illegible]
[illegible] Mac," I s[illegible]
[illegible] an salut[illegible]
[illegible] the [illegible] *y* [illegible]
[illegible]
[illegible] "I [illegible]
[illegible]
[illegible] n wou[illegible]
[illegible] sir. Wh[illegible] the [illegible]
[illegible] made [illegible] adjec[illegible]
[illegible] d gran[illegible]
[illegible] valu[illegible]
[illegible] years in [illegible] "Th[illegible] you sir."
[illegible] urnam[illegible]
[illegible] O'Reill[illegible]
[illegible] re[illegible] "
[illegible] you, sir?"
[illegible] valued [illegible]
[illegible]
[illegible] e did [illegible]
[illegible] ancien[illegible]
[illegible] I felt [illegible]

carpet, a sensation not altogether pleasant, but I was determined to maintain my bored-rich-boy expression. I pressed a well-scrubbed finger against the doorbell and waited.

Tom Lacy opened the penthouse door. Tomming a wee bit, he bowed and rolled his eyes. He seemed not to recognize me. Was The Wig that effective?

"Ain't nobody home. They is in the country," he said. "Won't be back till late Monday morning."

"You're the man I wanna see."

Moaning, Tom Lacy looked away. "Mister, I ain't done nothing and I ain't buying nothing. Good day."

"Just one moment, please."

"Mister," Tom whined, "I done told you already. I ain't buying nothing. I gits plenty of good used clothing from the boss, and the mistress throws a few hand-me-downs to the old lady. I got plenty of insurance and a wristwatch that runs jest fine. I'm scared of cars. And as you can see, skin lightener will do me no good and I'm dead set against hair grease and don't try to sell me no back lot in Westchester, cause I ain't buying. But come back Monday. They'll be back then."

Yesterday at Paradise Records, Ltd., in a moment of panic, I tried like hell to bust a gut. Now staring hard at Tom Lacy, staring at his sweaty immobile face, I tried not to bust a gut.

Slightly envious of his brilliant impersonation, I said, "Shit."

"Mister. I didn't mean to offend you. I jest don't need nothing. I is way up to my ears in debt already."

"Okay, Tom. Can the cat. It's me. Your boy Les. Ask me in and fix a drink."

Tom Lacy stared hard at me. Gritting his alabaster-coated false teeth, he let the placid mask of his face change to that of a natural killer.

Just to be on the safe side, I took several steps backward.

"I ain't in the mood for no jokes. I had to work my ass off to get them bastards to the country."

"Man, you just ain't with the happenings. You're non-progressive."

"Youyouyou . . ." Tom Lacy shouted.

"Control yourself," I said. "You're sweating too hard and might catch a cold."

"Shut up," my grieving friend commanded. "Don't interrupt. I'm trying to talk to you like a father. Yes, trials and tribulations. You were such a good boy. Your dear parents taught you to read and write. You had good manners and went to Sunday School. And you've got a sturdy head on your shoulders. I was always proud when I never found your name on the sports page of the *Daily News* listed among them juvenile delinquents."

"Tom. You're breaking my goddam heart."

"WHAT HAVE YOU DONE TO YOUR BEAUTIFUL HAIR?"

"Nothing," I said.

"Infidel!" Tom Lacy accused in a shaking voice and lunged at me again.

I jumped back quickly. "Listen to me. Please. I'm doing this for the sit-ins. Did you hear me? I'm doing this for the sit-ins."

"The sit-ins?" Tom Lacy's dawning smile was absolutely saintly. "Great day in the morning!"

"Yeah," I grinned. "What a morning."

"Man, you had me scared to death," Tom said.

"I was a little uneasy myself."

Tom wiped his sweaty brow. What would the hero like to drink? Champagne? A little Château Haut-Brion? Or could he whip me up a quick snack? Rossini steak? Creamed eggs in ramekins, slightly gratiné, floating in caviar?

"No. Double vodka on the rocks. Gotta work a picket line this afternoon."

"Okay, sport," Tom smiled. "I *knew* you'd never betray us!"

Settling back in a down-stuffed chair, I said, "How could I possibly betray you?"

"Your parents would be proud of you."

"How's the chart coming along?"

Tom frowned sadly. "Not too good, Les. According to this morning's *Times,* only a hundred and seventeen died."

"That isn't too bad," I said, accepting the vodka.

"There have been better days," Tom said, pulling up a comfortable chair, a kind of Chinese rocking chair.

"Of course," I agreed. "Still, you can't complain. Anyway, Easter is coming, and after that it will be vacation time all over America."

"I know. But I like New Year's Eve better."

"We're very modest."

"If I were you, I wouldn't worry," Tom told me. "Family trees don't mean much these days."

"I'm sure happy to hear that."

Rocking, Tom looked as warm and shrewd as Harry Golden. "Yes. We're making progress. Finally things are looking up."

"You're right," I said. "Now the Puerto Ricans are getting shit from the fan."

Tom Lacy had a faraway look in his eyes, and they were misty. "No. It won't be long now."

A tugboat droned on the East River. I don't know why, but I suddenly thought of Abe Lincoln, and Thomas Jefferson too, and all the people who had made me believe in them. I leaned forward in my chair, dead serious, and listened to my godfather's wisdom.

My godfather shook his weary head. "Lord. I can hardly wait to act like a natural man. I've had to Tom so much that it's hard for me to knock it off. I even shuffle and keep my eyes on the floor when I'm talking to my own wife."

"I know what you mean. When I'm in a restaurant and leave a tip, I feel as if I'd committed a sin."

"That's a fact," Tom agreed. "It's like giving myself a tip somehow."

"By the way, godfather. Could you let me hold fifty?"

"What?"

"Fifty dollars."

"I ain't got no money," my godfather whined. "It takes every cent I get for those charts. I have to subscribe to every daily and weekly newspaper in the country."

"Have I ever failed to come through? Who went downtown with his little red wagon and got all those old newspapers when you were in bed with the flu last winter?"

"What you need it for?"

"Haven't I got to eat in all those segregated restaurants?"

"You're right," Tom Lacy agreed, reaching for his wallet. "Are you sure fifty will be enough?"

Strutting down Sutton, I perhaps looked like a happy citizen of Manhattan but my real roots were deep in the countryside that

Life is worthwhile, for it is full of dreams and peace, gentleness and ecstasy, and faith that burns like a clear white flame on a grim dark altar.

I got the fifty from my suit-coat pocket and gave it to the man—not because I was frightened or generous or worried about sleepless nights—I gave the man the fifty because he *looked* like a slave. I knew he was a slave. I have a genius for detecting slaves.

"Thank you and may God bless you," the slave said.

"You'd better get something to eat and a room," I said.

Then I turned off Sutton Place South and walked up 54th Street and up First Avenue toward home, toward Harlem.

# T E N

IT WAS SATURDAY NIGHT. The sky was starscaped, and homespun rib-tickling brotherly love had settled over the city. You felt it even at the frontier gate, above 96th Street, leading to the Badlands of Harlem. The air was different too, with a strange smell rather like mildewed bread. And I, too, managed to be happy (courtesy of Mr. Fishback's Christmas gift): at the end of the evening, The Deb had come home with me.

Now while Saturday night turned into cold Sunday, I copulated like crazy. My groin ached.

"You're too much," I said.

"Whee!" The Deb somersaulted and wiggled her toes. "You've made me extremely happy, Mr. Jefferson."

"Do Debs really like that?"

The gyrating Deb moaned.

I wiped my forehead, watching The Deb's rhythmic buttocks. "Wanna be a slave, baby?"

"Yes. Come on, lover. It really moves me."

"Take it easy, little woman."

"Please. It drives me out of my gardenia-picking mind."

"I've had enough," I sighed.

"Don't you wanna make me happy?"

breezed uptown in a Duesenberg from Buckingham livery. Jesus, woman."

"That's all very true," The Deb said, "but you didn't give me any money to get my hair fixed."

"Tomorrow, love. You'd only get it messed up in bed."

"You don't want me to have my hair fixed," The Deb protested.

"That's no way to talk. Tomorrow, love. Tomorrow I'll see personally that you get the works at Helena Rubinstein."

The Deb sulked. Her body was rigid on the sofa bed. "You foreigners are just like white people. You don't like to see Negroes with good hair. You're not just satisfied with getting your rocks off . . . you like to get an extra kick. By running your hand through kinky hair!"

"You don't understand," I said weakly.

"Oh, but I do! I got your number, sweetcakes."

"But you've got such wonderful hair. So natural. You want to be different, don't you?"

"I am different," The Deb informed me.

"Not if you have curly hair like me."

The Deb looked hard at me. "When I get my hair fixed tomorrow I will be like you. Almost, anyway. And pretty soon us colored people will be as white as Americans. They gonna make some pills that will turn you white overnight. Won't that be a bitch? *Everybody* will be up shit's creek then."

"You'll take all the excitement and drama out of being Negro," I laughed.

"Have you ever wanted to be a Negro? I'm not talking about daydreaming of being a Negro. I mean, have you really considered it?"

"No. I'm afraid not."

"Then why have you got that suntan?" The Deb asked.

"I suppose for the same reason that you want curly hair."

"According to the Bill of Rights, which I read in grade school, being black is a sin in this country. But I never heard of curly hair being a sin."

"You're right," I said. "Now come on and give daddy a kiss."

"You know what you can do for me."

"Are you gonna be discriminating, after all I've done for you?"

never known, I tried to ram my tongue down The Deb's throat.

She squirmed under my power and I understood the lust of the conquistadors.

"Daddy," she begged, "turn on the other side of 'Rocking With It.'"

"In a minute, cupcake."

"I'm gonna scream!"

"Scream," I laughed. "Scream your fucking head off. I've got you covered."

# E L E V E N

MORNING CAME as I knew it would: gray with rain. Cooing pigeons and doves. The smell of bacon grease and burnt toast and powerful black Negro coffee, spiced with potents which would enable you to face The White Man come Monday morning. The sound of Mrs. Tucker's Carolina litany could be heard through the wall. A typical Sunday morning.

Grateful, I reached up and touched something unfamiliar: The Wig, silky and very much together. Then I began to doze, until I felt The Deb's lips against my neck.

"Les, honey," she yawned. "Be a good boy. Don't be a finky-foo."

"No," I mumbled. "Not the first goddam thing in the morning."

"I hate you!"

"Go back to sleep. It's early."

"Oh. You'll be sorry."

"Knock it off, cupcake."

"I hate you!"

I had to quiet the bitch. So I pinched one buttock and commanded: "Sleep or else I knock you out of bed."

"No, you won't," The Deb sneered. "I'm getting up. I'm cut-

[illegible] hours we [illegible]

[illegible] kno[illegible] she [illegible] de?" Deb asked.

[illegible] now [illegible] to [illegible] se an [illegible] one [illegible] ti[illegible]," she s[illegible] a simp[illegible] like [illegible] on the record pla[illegible] music, [illegible] ly [illegible]." [illegible] head [illegible] she [illegible] s[illegible] there w[illegible] heat [illegible] pigeon [illegible]

[illegible] ng had [illegible] The D[illegible] ing, Wi[illegible]

[illegible] led, I [illegible] A[illegible] fi[illegible] out."

[illegible] dress, [illegible] the ro[illegible] m, for th[illegible] ing [illegible] overs' [illegible] day n[illegible] be[illegible] Deb [illegible] Ha[illegible] you w[illegible] with m[illegible] out. Al[illegible] posses[illegible] no one [illegible] ting out. [illegible]

[illegible] ad ha[illegible] ly [illegible] my th[illegible] overfl[illegible], I [illegible] tly. The[illegible] hing he[illegible] so [illegible] mig[illegible] crown [illegible] y [illegible] at I w[illegible] F. I'd ha[illegible] center [illegible] h[illegible] ve with [illegible] e thos[illegible] ion and [illegible] tched the [illegible] e food [illegible] ut head [illegible] get s[illegible] its mo[illegible] on, I [illegible] g the do[illegible] the he[illegible] w[illegible] to go [illegible] ast on[illegible] the ra[illegible] ook th[illegible] don't [illegible] about [illegible] me. W[illegible] a [illegible] er? N[illegible] this scr[illegible] al pict[illegible] of being someone else, and a part of the picture was that my luck would change. But had it? No, life still seemed to have me by the balls, stuffing poison enemas up my ass.

"Oh, well, tomorrow's Monday," I said aloud to the cockroaches on the ceiling pipes.

Then, like the first trumpet of morning, piercingly alive, like the cello of death, Nonnie Swift screamed.

"No," I sighed. In a gesture of rejection, I crossed my hands over my penis.

"Help," Nonnie cried. "I mean it this time."

"That's what the would-be suicide said when he slipped accidently off the bridge," I thought happily.

"Help! Help!"

The voice was coming closer. A mad bat with a human voice was running amok in the hall.

A rattling rap on the door.

"Les!"

I felt as if the skin were peeling off my face.

"Do you want me to break the door down?" Nonnie shouted. "I know you're in there. I always thought you were a gentleman like those cotton planters who used to court me down in New Orleans. I never thought you'd let the rats eat me up!"

I wanna tell you: pins and needles pricked my body. Rising slowly to a lotus position, I felt the glow from The Wig. My Imperial lips quivered. Tremors shook my brain. Starry brain pellets finally exploded.

Rats. *Rats!* The Magic Word.

I jumped out of bed, slid into my pants, ran to the closet, and grabbed my spear gun.

Barechested, barefooted, I was sort of an urban Tarzan, a knight without a charger.

"Where are the rats?" I shouted, storming out the door.

"My hero," Nonnie sang. Her face set like stone. "They're in my room. Where the hell do you think they're at?"

"Lead the way, woman."

"Follow me," Nonnie said.

And I followed, hot with excitement, clutching my spear gun, ready for the kill. One hundred rat skins would make a fine fur coat for The Deb.

# TWELVE

ONE MAGNIFICENT RAT, premium blue-gray, and at least twenty-five inches long, walked boldly into the center of Nonnie Swift's cluttered living room, its near-metallic claws making a kind of snare drum beat on the parquet floor.

"I started to call the ASPCA," Nonnie whispered.

"I'll handle this mother," I said.

"Please be careful."

"Sure thing." An old proverb crossed my mind: Bravery is a luxury; avoid it at all cost. "Take the gun," I said to Nonnie.

"Oh! Les . . ."

"Take it."

A terrified Nonnie reached for the spear gun. "I'm praying as fast as I can, Lester Jefferson."

"This is gonna be child's play," I said. "Hell. I thought he'd come on like a tiger," and just then, before I could get into a quarterback position, the rat bit my left big toe.

"The sneaky son of a bitch," I yelled, hopping on one foot.

"Are you wounded?" Nonnie cried.

"No. I got tough feet."

The rat moved back. He had a meek Quaker expression and the largest yellow-green eyes I've ever seen on a rat.

"That's the spirit," Nonnie said. "I'll get the coal shovel and bang against the wall. Then I'll close my eyes. I don't want my baby to be born with the sign of a rat on him."

Waiting for Nonnie's overture, I stood up and stretched. The blood had caked on my hands, making them itchy.

"This is gonna be more fun than a parade," Nonnie said. She spat on the coal shovel for luck.

"I'm ready when you are," I said, bracing my shoulders and sucking in my belly.

"Here we go," Nonnie cried, and banged the shovel against the wall three sharp whacks.

Lord! Eight rats bred from the best American bloodlines (and one queer little mouse) jumped from holes in the *chinoiserie* panels. Nonnie had her eyes tight shut and was humming "Reach Out for Me." Or were the rats humming? I couldn't quite tell.

Fearless, I didn't move an inch. Images of heroes marched through my Wigged head. I would hold the line. I would prove that America was still a land of heroes.

Widespread strong hands on taut hips, fuming, ready for action—I stomped my feet angrily. If I'd had a cape, I'd have waved it.

The rats advanced with ferocious cunning.

Perhaps for half a second, I trembled—slightly.

With heavy heart and nothing else, Nonnie Swift prayed. Through the thin wall, I heard Mrs. Tucker wheeze a doubtful, "Amen."

Then, suddenly feeling a more than human strength (every muscle in my body rippled), I shouted, "All right, ya dirty rats!"

My voice shook the room. Nonnie moaned, "Mercy on us." I could hear Mrs. Tucker's harvest hands applauding on the other side of the wall. The rats had stopped humming but continued to advance.

And I went to meet them, quiet as Seconal (this was not the moment for histrionics)—it would have been foolhardy of me to croon, "Rasputin, old buddy."

Arms outstretched, the latest thing in human crosses, I tilted my chin, lifted my left leg, and paused.

They came on at a slow pace, counting time. The mouse shrewdly remained near the wastebasket, just under the lavabo.

nie. She was backed against the door, mesmerized with admiration.

When I turned to face the enemy again, two rats were retreating.

Pursuing as fast as I could, I slipped on the waxed floor and fell smack on the remaining three. But I fell easily and was careful not to damage the fur.

I lay there briefly, rolled over, and scouted for the deserters. Two were making a beeline for the wastebasket, which was brass and steel and filled with empty Fundador bottles.

I was decent. I waited until they thought they were safe, only to discover that they were actually ice-skating on the brandy bottles.

I knelt down and called, "Rasputin, Rasputin." They raised their exquisite heads and I put my hands in the wastebasket, grabbed both by the neck—I squeezed, squeezed until the fur around their neck flattened. It was easy.

"You can open your eyes, Nonnie," I said in a tired voice.

"A Good Man Is Hard to Find," the gal from Storyville sang.

I was tired. I made a V-for-victory sign, winked, and started skinning rats.

Someone knocked at the door.

Nonnie was excited. "Oh, Les. The welcoming committee has formed already!"

"Wanna sub for me, cupcake."

"Delighted."

Another knock. "It's Mrs. Tucker, your next-door neighbor, and I couldn't help but hear what was going on . . ."

"There ain't no action in this joint, bitch," said Nonnie.

"I just wanted to offer my heartfelt congratulations to young Master Jefferson."

"Is that all you wanna offer him?" said Nonnie bitchily.

"Now that's no way to talk, Miss Swift, and you a Southern-bred lady."

"You're licking your old salty gums," Nonnie taunted. "You smell fresh blood. If you're hungry, go back to yo' plantation in Carolina."

"I will in due time, thank you." Mrs. Tucker withdrew in a huff.

"Go! Go!" Nonnie said, and turned abruptly and walked over

# THIRTEEN

THREE HOURS LATER, I found myself with a slightly crushed Christian Dior box, jumping the sidewalk puddles, in which I saw the reflected solidity of Victorian brownstones. Despite the chilly drizzle, children seemed to be enjoying themselves on the fire escapes: laughing, singing, catching raindrops, telling dirty stories.

I walked along, blinking at the reflections in the pools, thinking of the children against the background of the harsh Harlem streets (but magical, all the same, stuffed with riches), and looking up now and then at the wet gray sky, only to be knocked out of my reveries by the sound of music.

It was blues, blues so real the'd make you hollow at five o'clock in the morning, no matter if you were alone or in the arms of your lover. These blues were coming out of a three-for-one bar and grill. I stopped for a moment and listened to Jimmie Witherspoon grind out "See-See Rider" on the jukebox. Through the steamy face of the grill, I saw hands working with the dexterity of an organ grinder, turning banquet-size slabs of barbecue spareribs on a spit. I could smell the spareribs, too. The crawlers in my stomach performed (Mr. Fishback's Credit Card carried no weight in three-for-one bar and grills), so I moved on down the street, past select pawnshops, fourth-hand boutiques, liquor stores. In a

[illegible] phone [illegible] of young [illegible]
[illegible]
[illegible] was [illegible]
[illegible] father [illegible]
[illegible] did [illegible]
[illegible]
[illegible] to hear [illegible] was not [illegible]
[illegible] where [illegible]
[illegible]
[illegible] Zo[illegible]
[illegible]
[illegible]
[illegible]
[illegible] committed [illegible]
[illegible]

[illegible] the [illegible] ized the [illegible]
[illegible] Ru[illegible]
[illegible] under the [illegible]
[illegible] Fishba[illegible] from [illegible]
[illegible] of [illegible]
[illegible] Christian [illegible]
[illegible]

[illegible] ceiling [illegible]
[illegible]
[illegible] ted [illegible] opposite the [illegible]
[illegible]
[illegible] you [illegible]
[illegible] up. H[illegible]
[illegible]?

[illegible] and [illegible] paper [illegible]
[illegible]

[illegible] The [illegible]
[illegible] ted. "[illegible]
[illegible] the [illegible]."
[illegible] don't [illegible] not [illegible]."
[illegible], walked away [illegible]
[illegible]

The strains of "Muslim Da-Da, Mu-Mu" (the Faust of rock 'n' roll) drifted from The Deb's pad, but nothing could blanket my schoolboy joy as I knocked on the solid door.

The doorknob fell off. Rolled, spun like a top. I watched until it stopped and then turned, certain The Deb would be spying through the peephole.

"Oh. It's you," were her first words when she opened the door. She wore a yellow robe. "Come on in *if* you gonna."

"Thanks," I said nervously.

"You almost missed me. I was just getting ready to go to Radio City Music Hall. In a taxi, so as not to miss the newsreel."

"I thought perhaps we'd go to some quiet bistro . . ."

"You got any money?"

"Why must you *always* think of money?"

The Deb stared at me briefly. "You're a card," she said. "Did you know that?"

"Now, cupcake . . . Look. Here is a little something I thought you might like." I held the box out.

"Oh. A present. What is it . . . no, let me guess. The definite, collected rock 'n' roll records?"

"Guess again."

"It wouldn't be a blond Macy's wig, would it?"

"Women," I sighed. The most fascinating, hypnotic—the strangest creatures on the face of the earth.

"Give it to," The Deb said and lunged at the box.

"Easy, baby," I said, brushing her hand aside. I tossed the Dior box casually on her rumpled bed and sat down on a sick chair which was vomiting straw.

The Deb's hands tore the box open. I yawned.

"Oh! Oh Oh! Oh!"

Hot-eyed, I watched The Deb fling open her yellow robe and press the pelts against her naked body.

"Mr. Jefferson, you are *the* most thoughtful man!"

"Just a little token of my esteem."

The Deb switched over and gave me a wet smacking kiss on the forehead. It was a sugar-daddy kiss, but I was grateful to be in her alluring old-rose presence. Dimpled nipples brushed my chin; the scent of her body was fresh as dew. My hands prepared for travel.

[illegible] in Jefferson [illegible]

[illegible] The [illegible] "To [illegible]

[illegible] gentleman [illegible] country [illegible]

[illegible]

[illegible] supposed. [illegible]

[illegible] I'll just [illegible]

[illegible] landlord [illegible]

[illegible] walk [illegible]

[illegible] after [illegible] It's [illegible]

[illegible] eating [illegible]

[illegible]

[illegible] new [illegible]

[illegible] she [illegible]

[illegible]

[illegible] sensible [illegible]

[illegible]

[illegible] and [illegible]

[illegible] pro[illegible]

[illegible] inform[illegible]

carrying a covered stretcher. The frame of the stretcher gleamed under the street light.

Nonnie and Miss Sandra Hanover were coming down the stoop. Miss Sandra Hanover was out of costume. She wore blue jeans and a man's raincoat.

"It's old Miz Tucker, Les. Poor old thing passed away about an hour ago."

"Yes," Nonnie said. "Thoughtless bitch. She had to kick off and me in the condition I'm in."

"That's too bad," I said.

"We're going to the funeral home and make arrangements," Miss Hanover said. "She's got no family, so we're shipping her back to her white folks in Carolina."

"Yes," Nonnie said vigorously. "That was her last wish. To have her remains sprinkled on the plantation's blue grass. She'll make excellent fertilizer, I'm sure."

"Where's Mr. Fishback?" I asked.

"Go up and look in your room," Nonnie said. "He stopped by after you so rudely walked out on me this afternoon. I saw you steal that fancy box off the garbage truck."

Fuming, I rushed up the stairs.

Two messages were stuck under my door. One was from Little Jimmie Wishbone and read:

URGENT. Must talk with you. Please call me at this number.

But there was no telephone number on the matchbox cover. I picked up Mr. Fishback's note. It was written on Mr. Fishback's usual fancy paper, a pale gray, with a border of asphodels and black bleeding hearts. It read:

Lester Jefferson, this will come as a surprise STOP I am leaving for the deep-sea diver's club STOP on Eleuthera Island which is in the Bahamas STOP From there I will go by chartered plane to Toledo, Spain STOP Will return in good time STOP

"—F— —," I said. Hump Mr. Fishback. But what did he mean: "Return in good time"?

# FOURTEEN

THE FOLLOWING MORNING was, naturally, Monday, warm, windless, with a calendar-blue sky. I was up at the crack of dawn. I shaved, took a bath, borrowed a cup of day-old coffee grounds from Nonnie Swift from which I brewed a fine pot of java. Sitting at the kitchen table over coffee and cigarettes (it pays to rise early: first one in the john, where I found a pack of unopened filter-tip cigarettes), I began reading a small leatherette-bound volume, *The New York Times Directory of Employment Agencies*. "Whatever the job, depend on a private employment agent to help you find it," it said. "You'll find more employment-agency jobs in *The New York Times*"—a statement I was extremely glad to hear, for I was in desperate need of a job.

Before the first cup of java had cooled, I started to read a listing of the employment agencies.

CAREER BLAZERS—FLAME THROWERS & EXTINGUISHERS AGENCY
We Are Looking For Young Men On The Way Up!
We will find you any type of job that can be performed by a human being and not by computers. The fact that it sounds so ridiculous is what makes it so appealing and a step forward! Your very own human future! It wasn't too long ago that the idea of having humans in every major industry was thought to be a little "ridiculous." But now these dreams are realities. We must all look for new worlds to conquer.

your medical expenses in confidence. We enjoy our employees and are liberal with them. Good salary plus low-cost lunch.

EXPORT EMPLOYEE SEEKERS

The Opportunity Of The Year!

If you could write your own ticket you'd probably leave out some of the things offered by our client. No children. Multi-million-dollar credit benefits. Tax-free and sugar white. Brains and fortitude—not required. Do you live in a slum area? Do you have the ability to sell? Fantastic response to our Negro sale. Acclaimed by top authorities.

If you think you qualify for this remarkable opportunity, please come to the East Side Air Terminal. Car necessary. Full transportation and monitoring. Paris. San Francisco. Hawaii. Take your pick. Our client asks us for men with vibrations. Men with a desire to succeed before 30! Men who are extremely active in extracurricular activities. Do you have the ability to reach top men and test, gas, debug, and interview? We are seeking safety maintenance men. Civil. Designing. No hand devices. This is a position entailing use of radar—malfunction performances as applied to manned space vehicles. No transients need apply. Our chief will be in New York. Liquidation is necessary.

ACT NOW!

When applying, please bring separation papers.

I closed *The New York Times Directory of Employment Agencies,* although there were still forty-six more pages of listings, lit a cigarette, and leaned back in my chair, thinking. You Are Not Defeated Until You Are Defeated, I thought. You must maintain a Healthy Outlook when seeking a job, I added.

So I threw the employment directory out of the window and made up my mind to see The King of Southern-Fried Chicken. I would become a chicken man. It wasn't work in the real sense of the word. The pay was $90 for five and a half days, plus all the chicken you could eat on your day off. Not many young men lasted long with the Fried Chicken King, but I'd stick it out until I could do better. At least, I consoled myself, the feathers were electrified.

For the truly ambitious, time truly flies. One hour later, I was crawling through the streets of Harlem on my hands and knees, wearing a snow-white, full-feathered chicken costume. The costume was very warm. The feathers were electrified to keep people from trying to pluck them out or kicking the wearer in the tail. So effective was the costume that I didn't even have to stop for traffic signals; traffic screeched to a halt for me. And, as I said, the pay

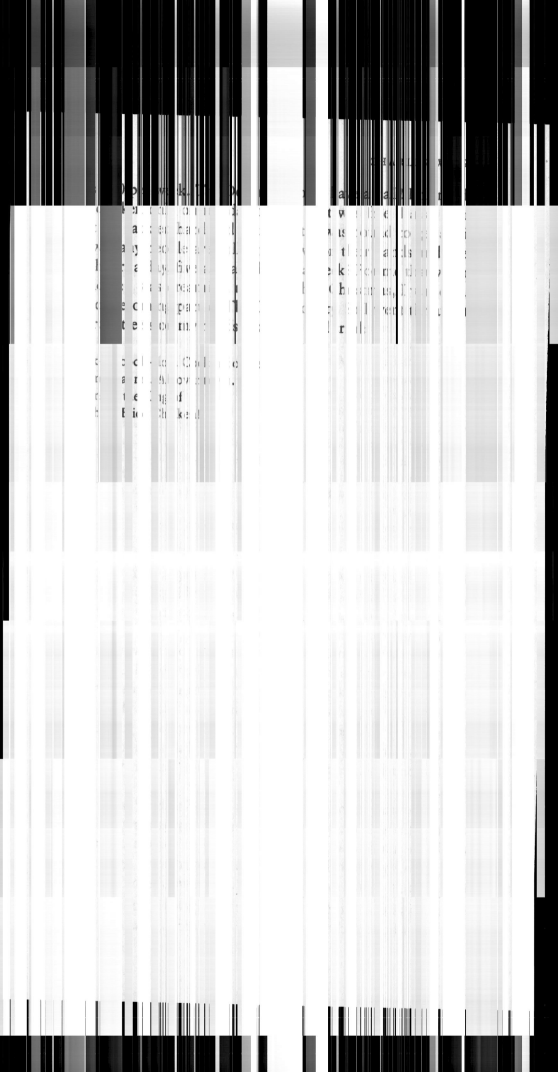

# FIFTEEN

I DID NOT LET the first day get me down, although when I got home that night I could still hear the voices of pedestrians ringing in my ears.

"I bet he's tough."

"No, honey. He's a spring chicken if I ever saw one."

"Here chickie-chick!"

"Mama, can we take him home and put him on the roof so the dogs won't get to him?"

"He's white but I bet if you plucked those feathers off of him you'd find out he's black as coal."

"I bet he's the numbers man."

"No, baby. Probably pushing pot."

"You can't fool me. It's the police. I knew they'd crack down on all of these carryings-on. Just think. In broad daylight. On Times Square."

"Bill, he's just what we need for our next party."

"Wish I'd thought of that gimmick."

"I bet a quarter he's deaf and dumb. That ain't him talking. It's a machine inside of him."

"Think he can get us tickets for the ice-hockey game at the Garden?"

"I w[illegible] b[illegible] r[illegible] Pol[illegible] [illegible]

[illegible]

"Sl[illegible]," [illegible] for the [illegible]

"I w[illegible] b[illegible] th[illegible]

"[illegible] or TV [illegible]

that [illegible] You'll se[illegible]

[illegible]

"[illegible] do for [illegible]

A [illegible] er inter[illegible]

[illegible]

[illegible]

I [illegible]

[illegible]

That's [illegible]

I [illegible] r [illegible] and, and [illegible] r.

I'd planned to touch up my hair with Silky Smooth because the hood of the chicken costume had pressed my curls against my skull. But for the moment Silky Smooth had lost its groove.

As I was going up the stairs, stunned and unhappy, I met the perky party girl, Miss Sandra Hanover. A male-femme in sundown antelope costume and matching boots.

"Les," she cried. "I thought I'd have to leave without saying good-bye."

"Leaving?"

"Yes, love. Your mother is going to Europe with the call girl. She just married this millionaire. Just like in the movies, and I'm here to tell you! I'm going along as her personal maid. I'll ride the high seas in full regalia. Talk about impersonation!"

"That's great," I managed to say.

Miss Sandra Hanover gestured, like the great soignée Baker from St. Louis, Mo. "Ain't it? I may even go into show biz in Europe. The truly smart-smart flicks always sport a dark face these days."

Ordinarily, the word "impersonation" would have interested me, would set me to thinking. But the only thought it brought me now was that my own impersonation had caused the death of a bright dream.

Finally, I managed to say, "That's great, doll. When you leaving?"

"Wednesday. At the stroke of midnight."

"Well, I'll see you later. I've gotta go to Madam X's."

"Madam X!" Miss Sandra Hanover exclaimed. "You must be off your rocker!"

"No," I said. "I'm not off my rocker. I wanna survive."

Madam X's is located in Harlem's high-rent district, in a real town house fronting the barrier of Morningside Heights and St. Nicholas Avenue. It looked faintly sinister to my eyes, so I stopped and hesitated. Quiet as a bird-watcher, I read the neat hand-painted black-and-gold sign:

WANT TO KICK THE LOVE HABIT?
Madam X guarantees that you will never fall in love again.
Low down payment. Easy terms can be arranged.
Open as long as there is love in this world.

She paused and said, "Do you feel it, son?"

I gulped tea and belched.

"Do you feel it, son?"

"It's a mother-grabber."

"You're much too kind."

"I wouldn't lie."

"I always try to brew the finest."

"What's the brand?" I asked.

"Brazilian marijuana," Madam X said grandly.

"It's too much, baby."

Laughing softly, Madam X said, "A lad after my own heart. But I've made a recent discovery. The state of Virginia, famed as it is for its tobacco, also grows the most wonderful marijuana. But please don't breathe it to a soul."

"On my word of honor."

"I understand Mr. Fishback is sponsoring you."

"Yes, and he's something else, too. He's in Europe now. Spain."

"Mr. Fishback is a very important man. But I don't quite cotton to his taste for deceased females. I might add, however, that we all have our own taste."

"That's true. I once collected stamps."

Madam X laughed merrily. "The things we think we want to be! I wanted to be the mad bomber, and then a city planner and an architect, so I could redesign Manhattan and make it beautiful and efficient. But that was before I became a saint."

"Manhattan is going to the dogs," I said. "I'm gonna move to Jersey."

Ignoring this statement, Madam X said, "Would you like another cup of tea, Lester?"

"In a moment, thank you."

"Yes," Madam X said. "The only way to appreciate marijuana is to brew it. Serve it hot and inhale the fumes, a custom in my family for many years." Pausing and smiling a stoned smile, she said, "Your bill has been taken care of. Mr. Fishback. You're very fortunate."

Fortunate? Suddenly I remembered The Deb. Forgetting myself, I shouted, "Fortunate, my ass! I'm in love and it's driving me crazy."

"Your troubles are over," Madam X said, proper and poised

[illegible] ing bound [illegible]

[illegible]

"You are the road to self-destruction," she chanted. "All is not lost, though. You may find the way, *despite* The Wig!"

I was really angry now. It was taking all my family training and self-control to remain calm.

"Don't try to put the bad mouth on me, old woman!"

"Never," Madam X intoned. She stood straight and tall. Then, with a great birdlike swoop, she sank to the floor.

Her head was bowed as if in prayer. The hood of her cape slid off, and her perfectly shaped bald head revealed one magnificent twelve-inch-long whorl of *golden* hair. It made me shiver.

"I'll see you later, Madam," I said.

"No, you won't see me," Madam X warned, without looking up. "You'll see the *portrait* of Lester Jefferson, and he'll be *without* The Wig."

# 3

. . . . . . . . . . . . . . . . . . . . . . . . . . . . . . .

*". . . and one fine morning."*

—SCOTT FITZGERALD

# SIXTEEN

It was now morning all over America. It was also morning in Harlem. The first of April in the year of my National Life Derby, there was a doubtful sky, laced with soft white clouds. And although it was not the day of reckoning, my Dutch-almond eyes were open at 7:30 A.M., E.S.T.

My, how the chicken days were flying! Three weeks of crawling around town on my hands and knees had made me a minor celebrity. Still, I didn't like some of the things the people said about me. My true i-dent was a guarded secret. I refused to appear on television (I was afraid The Deb might be watching). I was hopeful of a reconciliation, although, according to the gossip columns, she had become Café Society's darling. When she had gone out to get her "head tore up," she had evidently done it in the best places, I reflected sourly.

Harlem's new beauty is the girl with the short natural hair. She has fabulous style; she has never needed beads and bangles like some Cleopatra types, and she never will—Dorothy Kilgallen

Short-haired smasher making Broadway scene is The Deb. A swinging African princess incognito.—Walter Winchell

Everyone wants The Chicken cackling about town but he belongs to The

cried helplessly, gripping the edge of the washbasin with all my strength. No good. I made a mad leap over to the john just in time.

As the tensions left my naked body, exhaustion set in. I was in no condition to deal with the possible problems of my Wig. I listlessly heard the sweet cries of children in the hall, pleading not to be sent to school (an imposing red-brick structure that had split in half for some strange reason the week before, killing twenty children, all under the age of twelve). Nonnie Swift had cackled happily about it ever since. Her son, she said, would be tutored at home.

A New York mockingbird chirped in the mandarin tree.

I went back to my room but I couldn't stay there. I had to get out. Out and walk, walk and try not to think. I wanted to scream to anyone, to the sky: "But I didn't mean anything! All I wanted was to be happy. I didn't know to want to be happy was a crime, a *sin*. I thought sin was something you bought for ten dollars a major ounce and five dollars a minor ounce, both qualities highly recommended, and each wrapped in plain brown paper. I never bought any—not because I couldn't afford it. I just took pot for a dollar a stick . . ."

But why go on? Why try to explain? Was there anyone to hear me?

I dressed hurriedly and, magnificently Bewigged, went out, locked the door, and walked slowly down the steps, thankful that Nonnie Swift was not about.

Half of a neatly folded telegram stuck out of my mailbox. Filled with apprehension, I ripped the telegram open. It read:

I bet you can't guess where I am at. I wasn't doing nothing. These colored clubwomen wanted me for a benefit but the white clubwomen said I wasn't college. At least not Ivy and queer. The colored clubwomen agreed. I wished you could have heard the names they called me after the white clubwomen had left. I wasn't doing nothing but walking through the streets looking for my lavender Cadillac number three and the bluecoats arrested me for nothing at all. I only had a quart of Summertime wine and was just drinking. I paid for it, didn't I? So why can't I drink it on the street? So I'm back here. The white devils. I was getting ready to do a profile on TV, too, with Mr. Sunflower Ashley-Smithe. Don't worry none, though. They got a cell ready for you. Next to mine. How long you think the white devils gonna let you go through the streets with your hair looking like that? Why didn't you phone me? I left my number.

Little Mr. Jimmie Wishbone

[illegible] morning [illegible]

[illegible] Kings [illegible]

[illegible] telegram [illegible] blue [illegible] that sky [illegible] e. "Les [illegible] birth [illegible] ing. Th [illegible] tle to [illegible] what he [illegible] had ask [illegible] canvas [illegible] vare tha [illegible] is a pri [illegible] of [illegible] was in [illegible]

[illegible] o I [illegible] slins [illegible] flats [illegible] awk [illegible] ntel [illegible] on of [illegible]

[illegible] ing back [illegible] e stre [illegible] horr [illegible] vid [illegible] whe [illegible] y t [illegible] masses," [illegible] rench [illegible] ten Isl [illegible] h poodle [illegible] You ca [illegible] ly thr [illegible]

[illegible] conferen [illegible] te Haren [illegible] had sa [illegible] time of [illegible] payment [illegible] now you [illegible]

[illegible] round, [illegible] magic [illegible] to happen [illegible] hops I d [illegible]

[illegible] joi [illegible] Geo [illegible] twenty [illegible]

[illegible] claims [illegible] Sam [illegible]

"I knowed [illegible] ja [illegible] like [illegible] ly cultur [illegible] easy an [illegible] school [illegible] genu [illegible] the com [illegible]

plus neighborhood, city, county, state, and federal sales tax."

But I needed no poodle curls; I was my own Samson, a Samson with Silky Smooth hair. My true glory had flowered, I thought bitterly, remembering Nonnie Swift's words.

"Poodles, poodles," the sneaker-shod young man called after me, but I crossed the street and went on my way.

"Look at him," a small boy cried, pointing his bony hand at me. "I bet *he* ain't going to school!"

Smiling, I said, "No, Sonny. Not today."

"But *he's* going to school," the boy's mother said to me, doubling a suède-gloved fist and slamming it against the boy's mouth.

"Jesus, he must be a very bad boy," I said.

"He is," the mother said vigorously.

I stared hard at the crying boy. "What did he do?"

"He doesn't want to go to a segregated school. I broke my broom handle on him a few minutes ago. That's what the NAACP and the Mayor and the Holy Peace-Making Brotherhood advised. You wouldn't have a pistol on you, would you?"

"No," I shuddered. A sudden pain hit me so hard that I felt faint.

My throat was dry. "Isn't there some other way you can make the boy understand?"

"No," the mother replied.

"Maaa," the boy moaned. "Please take me to the hospital. I ache all over. I think I'm gonna die, Mama."

"Shut your trap."

Just than a soothsayer wearing a dark policeman's uniform walked up twirling his nightstick.

"What's wrong, lady? Having trouble with your boys?"

"Only the little one," the mother laughed. "He doesn't want to go to a segregated school. I've got to beat some sense into the boy's head if it's the last thing I do."

"Wanna use my nightstick? I'm sorry I don't have my electric cow prod with me because that does the trick every time. That always makes them fall in line."

"Oh, officer," the mother said, "you're so kind and understanding."

"Think nothing of it. Just doing my duty. I've got kids of my

"That's right," the ferocious shiner said. "We ain't done nothing. We just invented this dust machine to help our business downtown. The dust shoeshine boy stands on the corner with the machine in a shopping bag from Macy's, rolling his white eyeballs and sucking a slice of candied watermelon. You know. Like he's waiting on his mama. Every time a likely customer walks by, the dust shiner pulls the magic string. By the time the customer reaches the middle of the block he sure need a shine. He our gravy. And now this mother-grabber is gonna call Lily Law. He wants to suck white ass. He ain't thinking 'bout us little black boys."

The gleaming tall man broke away and ran inside a diner. "I'll fix you little devils."

"I'll go inside and see what I can do," I told the shoeshine boys. "Now you boys run like crazy."

I wasn't a hero and I've never aspired to be one (except in a private, loverly sense—ah, The Deb), but I've always, always, tried to help people. It's a kind of perverse hobby with me. Opening the diner door, I offered a diplomatic grin. The gleaming man was on the telephone.

"Mr. Police. This is Jackson Sam Nothingham. Yes, sir. The Black Disaster Diner. What do you mean . . . It's me, Mr. Police. Your sunny-side-up boy. That's right."

The diner owner hadn't noticed me. I eased over and deftly pulled the phone cord from the wall.

"What? I can't hear you. Say something, Mr. Police. I pays my dues . . . And what's more, I takes care of the Captain when he comes around . . ."

"Maybe they hung up on you, Mac," I said.

The bewildered owner swung around. "What you mean, boy? They hung up on me? Wait until the Captain gets a load of this. He knows I sell a little gin and whiskey in coffee cups after hours. All the Mister Polices on this beat says they don't know what they'd do without good old Jackson Sam Nothingham. My good down-home Southern cooking and a nip on a cold rainy day. I'm keeping up the morale of the police force and you try to say they hung up on me?"

"That's the way the cookie crumbles," I philosophized. "It doesn't have to be a Chinese fortune cookie either."

The angry tall man looked hard at The Wig. "You curly-

I was rehearsing the imaginary dialogue when I smiled at a middle-aged woman with a face that looked as if it had stared too long at the walls of too many furnished rooms. The middle-aged woman's tiny pink eyes went from my smiling face to The Wig. She leaned back on the bench, opened her mouth, and shut her eyes tight.

Well, I thought moving on, she is not accustomed to beauty.

An elderly couple were eying me. I heard the man mutter to his wife: "It's all right, Wilma. Times are changing. Remember the first automobile? World War One? We can't escape what we've never dreamed because we've always believed it was impossible. Wilma? Please don't cry. We'll be dying soon. *And then we won't have to look at such sights.*"

He meant me.

The sight went calmly on, smiling at a fat Negro who carried a shopping bag with Silky Smooth printed on the side. The fat Negro woman spat tobacco juice at my shoes, and a blond Alice-in-Wonderland type urinated in a plastic sand bucket and tried to splash me. Her mother applauded.

I was beginning to get a little sore. I felt like saying, "Nothing, nothing—do you hear me—nothing can stop me." Who the hell did they take me for? Was I the young man who had ground three hundred pounds of chopped meat out of the bodies of seventy blind people? Or the young man who had rescued a pregnant mother and her five children from their burning home, and then single-handed built them a ranch house overnight? Was I the champion rod who had respectively screwed wife, husband, mother-in-law, part-time maid, twelve-year-old daughter, fourteen-year-old son, white parrot, and family collie pup?

No! I was the celebrated chicken man, and none of them knew it. Ten hours a day, five and a half days a week, crawling on my hands and knees all over Manhattan. And I'd been a target for such a long time. Five-feet-ten, naked without shoes, normal weight one hundred and forty pounds. Boyish, with a rolling non-nautical gait, my face typically mixed: chamber-pot-simmered American, the result of at least five different pure races copulating in two's and three's like a game of musical chairs.

Following my own shadow, it seemed that I was taking a step in *some* direction and that The Wig was my guide. Progress is our

"Yeah," I replied, beginning to relax. Man, The Wig was really working! "I know what you mean."

"Most people are not very nice, are they?"

"No. Most people are not very nice."

Then we were silent. We danced arm in arm across Central Park West and up the five steps of a very respectable brownstone, just as the siren, like a proclamation, announced twelve o'clock.

The girl's two-rooms-and-kitchenette was very clean. There were no cockroaches, rats, mice, no leeches, no tigers.

Softly feminine, the girl said, "Relax, baby."

Then she came over and tried to rip the button-down shirt from my body.

"Take it easy, baby," I said, biting her neck. "We have all the time in the world."

"I know, I know," she said contritely, "but I must have this release."

She elbowed me so hard that I fell backward onto a big brass bed, where she proceeded to remove my loafers, socks, and blue jeans. I wore no shorts because the chicken costume was very warm.

The girl kissed the soles of my feet.

"Come on up here," I said, feeling my kingly juices.

"You have beautiful strong legs."

I kicked her lightly on the chin, she fell back on the floor. I jumped off the bed. Ready, at attention. She whimpered. I mounted her right on the floor. She sighed and patted my forehead. I sighed. Irritable, I also frowned. "Let's cut the James Bond bit. Let's get this show on the road."

The girl sank her teeth into my right shoulder. I slapped her hard and carried her to the bed. She whimpered again. I fell on top of her. Her tongue was busy in my left ear. I whimpered. Her right hand, like a measuring tape, grabbed my penis.

With my right hand I cupped her chin and thrust my tongue into her throat.

The girl squirmed and tickled my ribs.

Lowering her head, I kissed her chin and the oyster opening of her neck where her bone structure *v*'d, until my face slid farther down, and came to rest in the soft luxury of her breast. More delicious than fruit, I thought, teasing the wishbone below her breasts.

good. The frustrations of the day had been spent. The Wig, The Deb, and all those people I had encountered . . .

"Love," the girl called, breaking into my thoughts.

She sat down on the side of the bed and took me in her arms and held the glass of iced Coke as she would for an ill child. With her free hand, she gently stroked my brow.

"I want you to become my lover," she said quietly.

"We've just met," I protested. "We don't even know each other."

"You'll learn to love me. I'm a good woman. I've got money."

I bolted up from the bed. "Where's my jeans? I gotta run, cupcake. Perhaps I'll see you later."

"Please," the girl cried.

"Later," I said softly. I got into my clothes and made it to the door. Just as I shut it behind me, I thought I heard her cry, "I'm going to tell Mr. Fishback on you!"

Midnight found me on the Eighth Avenue A train for Harlem, wearing a pretty flower-printed plastic rainhood I'd luckily snatched up along with my clothes. It was raining out, and otherwise I'd have got The Wig wet. None of the passengers paid me the slightest attention. They had witnessed too many extraordinary happenings on subway trains: such as an old man getting stomped to death by a group of young punks because he didn't have life insurance; or someone getting sick and choking to death. Even statutory rapes had lost their appeal, they'd seen too many of them—so no one was likely to be impressed by a sad-faced, red-eyed young man wearing a plastic rainhood, shivering, biting his fingernails, staring at his reflection in the dirty window of the car.

I began to doze, thinking: when love waxes cold, said Paul in "The Third Coming . . ." then jerked up suddenly as the A train pulled into 125th Street.

I was the only passenger to get off. The platform was deserted. Workmen were spraying the platform with glue. Dazed and a little frightened, I ran up the sticky steps and out into the deserted street and hailed a taxi.

The driver, wearing a gas mask, stuck his head out the window.

"Oh, it's you," said Mr. Fishback, the funeral director. He

[illegible] is not [illegible]
[illegible] It comp[illegible]
[illegible] be anyt[illegible]
[illegible]
[illegible]
[illegible]
[illegible] offer som[illegible]
[illegible] big at [illegible]
[illegible] have [illegible] ible to [illegible]
[illegible] it. And [illegible]
[illegible]
[illegible] seen [illegible]
[illegible]
[illegible] Mr. Fish [illegible]
[illegible]
[illegible] experim[illegible]
[illegible] She [illegible]
[illegible]
[illegible] Mr. Fish [illegible]
[illegible] nod. [illegible]
[illegible]
[illegible] everythi[illegible]
[illegible] been [illegible]
[illegible] it never [illegible]
[illegible]
[illegible]
[illegible]
[illegible] ge. The [illegible]
[illegible] still [illegible]
[illegible] happens [illegible] and [illegible]
[illegible]
[illegible]
[illegible] kindly. [illegible]
[illegible]
[illegible] n, thank [illegible]
[illegible]
[illegible] all alon[illegible]
[illegible]

"Do you need my gas mask?"

"No."

"It's dangerous."

"I don't care," I said.

Mr. Fishback's mortuary was under the Triboro Bridge, at the edge of the polluted, muddy river. It was a one-story building of solid plate glass, with the roof also of glass, rising up dramatically like the wings of a butterfly. Mr. Fishback parked the taxi (which belonged to his brother-in-law, who was dying, he said) near the bridge and then walked down a lonely garbage-littered slope with me.

Side by side, we walked under a deep gray sky that was just beginning to break with the first light of day. The cool air was refreshing against my feverish face.

Once, for a brief moment, I panicked. "I can't go on."

"Now, son," Mr. Fishback said gently.

"What can I do now?"

"You know what you have to do."

"Yes," I nodded, clutching Mr. Fishback's arm for support.

We entered the glass building and walked like mourners to the direct center of the floor. Marble tiles slid back. Mr. Fishback removed his mask. He had a kind, dark, wrinkled face, the face of a genius, though being modest, he had always considered himself just God.

He escorted me down steps into a room the size of a standard bathroom. The room was mirrored and brightly lit, odorless. There was only a red bat-wing chair.

"I'm glad to get rid of these things," Mr. Fishback said, jerking out his false teeth and spitting blood on the floor. "Everything is so unsanitary!"

I flopped into the bat-wing chair: "The poor Deb!"

"Hush, now. You'll feel better after I cut off The Wig. Then one more act and you'll be happy for the rest of your life. While I was abroad, I kept in touch with Madam X. Remarkable woman."

Mr. Fishback pressed an invisible button in the mirrored wall and out popped a brand-new pair of sheep shears.

I closed my eyes. I felt no emotion. It was over. Everything. Love waxed cold. The Deb—dead.

"Watch out for my ears," I warned. "And hurry up. I'm hungry."

# ABSOLUTELY NOTHING TO GET ALARMED ABOUT

....................................

*In memory of Langston Hughes,*
*Conrad Knickerbocker,*
*and Alfred Chester*

IN THE HALF-WORLD of sleep where dreams and consciousness collide, I turned on the narrow, sticky plastic mattress. The brilliant ceiling light seemed to veer toward me. But with less than four hours' sleep, fourteen shots of vodka, six twelve-ounce bottles of beer, two speed pills, one marijuana cigarette—I chuckled in my pale, lemon-colored cubicle. The stone floor had a fresh coat of battleship-gray paint. After less than a week, the old terra-cotta paint was surfacing. The armless bentwood chair functioned as a night table. Narrower than a standard clothes hanger, the wardrobe was doorless. The new opaque window was jammed. Unlike other residents, I never came upon rats or snakes. What unnerved me were the goddamn arrogant cockroaches. Who cared? The cubicle was at least a roof, reasonably clean, reasonably safe and inexpensive, thanks to the charitable foresight of the Salvation Army's Bowery Memorial Hotel.

Now, the 6 A.M. voices of Sallie's men blended; became a litany of fear, frustration. Voices calling for ma, mama, and mother. Pleading: Stop and help—occasionally stamped with the moan of a dying male tiger. These nightmare voices were the twin of the daytime voices. These were weak men who no longer cared. Cheap wine chemicals had damaged their brains. As I listened, fear touched me. Would I become a soldier in their army? *Fool! Get yourself together. You've got to get out of here.*

[illegible] spiring; [illegible]

[illegible] ted. [illegible]

[illegible] ly. [illegible]

although they crowded their windows, talked, and looked down into the almost deserted arena of the street. No P.R. men were lounging against cars tonight. A few of them sat on stoops or braced themselves against Victorian carved doors.

I had to buy a six-pack in a bar and returned to the flat, popped a few, talked with Tony. TV gave out *Take Her, She's Mine,* while the sound of shots, Molotov cocktails, angry voices drifted across the vacant back lot (filled with about twenty-five inches of rubbish and where at this very moment a slender middle-aged Negro man was studying the lot as if it were a mound of old gravestones) and into the flat's windows.

There was absolutely nothing to get alarmed about. Just another domestic scene in current American life. But they will use more sophisticated methods next summer. The kids will have matured by next summer.

Earlier a group of them had stopped me.

"Have you seen Joe?"

"No, man," I said. "I ain't seen Joe."

A mistaken identity. But I was with them—someone has to be on their side and I cursed their goddamn parents and this goddamn mother-sinking country that has forced them into the act of rioting. In the act of reaching the portals of the seemingly prosperous poor, their parents had lost them just as this country had forgotten the parents.

Certainly I felt these black kids had a legitimate right to break store windows and throw rocks and bottles. Recently, I had worked at a resort where bored, wealthy kids kept the security guard on the go as they ripped lobby sofas and broke into the underground lobby shops between midnight and dawn.

Meanwhile, the black children will continue to riot and die.

M. D. said, "There is a man that I want you to meet." We taxied over to Intermediate School, No. 201, 2005 Madison Avenue, and I met the man. I also saw, for the first time in my life, former Senator Paul H. Douglas of Illinois, chairman of the L.B.J. Commission on Urban Problems, and Senator Robert F. Kennedy and two of his handsome children.

We arrived late, and I could not hear what Senator Kennedy was saying. It did not matter. He seemed likable. And despite the rumor of the ruthless reputation, the cold blue eyes, I could pic-

Clasping her hands, Anne said, "I was born in Jersey."

"Shut your trap," Bruce said. "You don't know what you are talking about. You were born in New York. At Beth Israel."

"Charles," Mick said, "Ron and me was born in New Jersey, and the rest of them were born in Beth Israel. We moved after the apartment building caught on fire. There was a deaf-and-dumb boy who was always doing things. One day he set the building on fire and we moved."

"Doing his thing." Bruce laughed, twisting on the bar stool.

"Bruce," Ron warned. "Cool it. He couldn't help it. No one loved him."

"God loved him," Anne said.

"Yes," Ron agreed. "God loves everyone. I've got a picture of him. Do you wanna see it?"

"It's Jesus, stupid," Mick said when Ron returned with a color reproduction and another can of beer.

"Mama's dancing," Ron said.

Then I heard heavy footsteps and lusty masculine voices in the hall, and we all looked at each other.

"I hope she doesn't get drunk," Ron said.

"Man! She's already stoned," Mick told him.

I wanted to hear Bob Dorough sing "Baltimore Oriole" and went into the living room. I heard Bruce whisper, "I'm going over and see what's happening. I'm gonna get some loot."

"Git some for me," Mick told him.

I could see their mother sitting at the chromed table, wearing the perennial purple-splashed muumuu gown. A pleasant, plump woman with a wardrobe of hair pieces, Nellie's teeth look like ancient Spanish gold. A dark-haired young man was behind her chair, tonguing her left ear, his long slender hands racing up and down her bosoms as if trying to determine their length and quality. Between "No, oh no!" Nellie moaned.

Mick eased over and peeped through the crack in the door. Anne was looking, too. Beatle-maned Ron did not get up. Pierced with cut-crystal sensitivity, he sat at the table writing his name over and over again.

"It's time for you to go to bed!" Mick exclaimed, slapping Anne violently. She screamed, her little arms outstretched as if to curtsy.

"Mick," I said. "Watch it."

of the night, regardless of what had happened or would happen.

I lit another filter and announced, "All right. Let's see if you remember how to type your name. Everyone will type except Mick and Ron. They're drinking beer, and I don't want them to spill it on the typewriter."

"Oh man." Mick frowned. Ron took a long sip of beer, ran over, and put it down on the cabinet.

Nellie called me. I went to the door and walked across the hall. The lights were still off. Nellie was naked.

"Here's a present," she said, offering a newspaper-wrapped package, half the size of a bank book. "The kids no trouble?"

"No," I said. "And thanks."

"Mama's naked." Anne giggled.

"Shut up," Bruce screamed, and then all of the brothers ganged up on their sister on the blue-tiled floor.

I pulled them apart and plotted the typing lesson. "All right. Knock it off. Anne is first. Everyone will have a chance to type. The twins will type too."

"Ah man," Mick said. "They're babies. They don't know nothing."

"Charles Wright," the young woman said, smiling. The young woman was a black reporter for a magazine. She was interviewing the writer for the magazine's forthcoming lead story, "The Real Black Experience."

I had had a couple of pills and enough drinks to make me feel warm toward almost anyone I might run into between 5 P.M. and dawn. Certainly I felt very warm toward the lady reporter. We both had, in a limited sense, climbed the black progressive ladder in white America. It was a difficult time for blacks to be truly black in a black reality. It was very easy to get bedecked in an ethnic showcase. But I had been black for a very long time. Before black was beautiful. Marcelled blacks gave me the cold eye ten years ago. I had an uncoiffeured, bushy Afro. I loved blues, collard greens ("pot liquor," as the collard juice was called), ham hocks before they became fashionable. And now I faced the young black reporter with lukewarm charm. I knew the magazine's editor had supplied the questions. I was going to be a gentleman about the whole damned thing.

AT 10 P.M. ON AUGUST 7, the moon was full and the air had turned cool. Vincent Jew and Wing Ha Sze were returning from the movies, walking down Bayard Street, next to the Chinese Garden—a semi-official, peeling, red and white plaque says in English and Chinese, "Manhattan Bridge Park." José Ortez, his girlfriend, and another young couple were on the same side of the street. They had been to a social club and were going toward the subway, they said later.

Returning from the liquor store with a chilled bottle of vino, I could not see them from where I was on the opposite side of the Garden, walking down Forsyth Street, about fifteen or twenty feet from the corner of Division. On the opposite corner, I saw a stocky young man standing next to the parking lot. He had shoulder-length dark hair, wore a light-colored shirt of the T-shirt style, dark trousers. A leather type of shoulder bag was strapped against his barrel chest. He fumbled with the bag and looked around as if uncertain which way to go. Then suddenly turned under the bridge, and out of my vision.

Normally, I'm spaced out, move with the speed of a panther. But that night I was relaxed, my stride slow. Emerging from under the bridge, I started up Bayard and heard the first popping sound. Leftover firecrackers, I told myself.

The street curves here and is not very bright. Remember: the

moon [illegible] light [illegible]
fast [illegible]
saw [illegible]
started [illegible]
ing [illegible] dark figure [illegible]

The first [illegible]
of the [illegible]
someone [illegible]
looking [illegible] difficult [illegible]
shoulder [illegible] for a [illegible]
know [illegible]
of the [illegible] did [illegible]
headed [illegible] which [illegible]
ran [illegible]
where he [illegible] fifteen [illegible]
and [illegible]
dark, [illegible] street.

[illegible]
Garden. [illegible]
appeared [illegible]
streamed [illegible] stend [illegible]
Dazed [illegible]
feet [illegible]
shoe [illegible] down [illegible]
wounded [illegible]

Baldwin [illegible]
advised [illegible] ice [illegible]
street."

But [illegible] his [illegible]
with said, [illegible] dead [illegible]

At the [illegible]
He asked [illegible] the [illegible]
Baldwin and [illegible]
policeman [illegible]
protested. The [illegible] same [illegible]
people [illegible]
unguarded [illegible]
you could [illegible] people [illegible]

The first [illegible]

and sat on his copy of Sunday's *Daily News*. Other squad cars arrived. People began appearing as if God had snapped his fingers and created them by the Garden wall. All of them were peering in the car at me. I had that uncomfortable feeling which afflicts celebrated people: I was afraid the crowd would kill me. But I kept my cool, lit a cigarette, and looked out at them and saw José Ortez for the first time. Frequently the police park at Bayard and Chrystie Streets. They were there when they heard the shots. They saw Ortez running, they said, and added that although they fired six warning shots, Ortez did not stop. He was finally apprehended on Division Street.

A café-au-lait-colored man, his dark hair was kept in place with a thin, old striped tie, and he wore a fancy knit shirt, the type which is popular with blacks, Puerto Ricans, and Italians. His trousers appeared to be less costly than the shirt. He was handcuffed and had a serene, saintly expression.

Presently, Ortez, his girlfriend, and her friends, Baldwin, and I were driven to the Elizabeth Street Station of the Fifth Precinct—a slum of a station. A disgrace to the city and the men who work there. All of us except Ortez were ushered into a large room. *Willard* graffiti were printed all over the room. *Willard* the rat horror movie.

Baldwin and I had a good rapport. Neither of us knew the other people. José's petite girlfriend had an earthy sexuality, and she cried and cried and cried. The other young woman had the open face of a child. I might as well tell you: Charles Wright is a distrustful son of a bitch. But the girlfriend, the young couple gave off the aura of good blue-collar people out on a Saturday night. If they were acting, their air of innocence was the world's greatest triangle act.

We were asked our names and addresses. Then they brought in Ortez and took him into a back room. The girlfriend started crying again. Around 11 P.M. we went up to the fourth floor. "Willars hole," the wall read. That was the way it was spelled.

The five of us waited in the fingerprinting room for about twenty minutes before being escorted into another room—the large, depressing room of the detective squad. Bored, I began drinking vino. The detectives did not seem interested in my stocky young man or that he was white (later I would be asked if he were

* * *

By the time you read this, the celebrating will have cooled. The friendly neighborhood grocer will be paid, the common-law husband will have met his pusher, and the children will be stuffed with sweets. Perhaps there will be a visit to Busch's, the famed credit jewelers, or a sharp new leather coat. The old-age pensioners and the "mentally disturbed and misfits" will pay their bar tabs and get jackrolled. However, all welfare stories are not grim. There are the old, the lame, and the helpless poor. This is their only way of life. But for others it is a new lease on living, almost as easy as breathing. Now all that remains are the twelve days of survival, the next check. I want to tell you about some of these men and women.

Mary X. is "off." Temporarily off. Brave, long-haired girl in midi-dress, the smart suède shoulder bag, living here and there. Starving. Almost tempted to take a job in a boutique. And why should Mary X. suffer in the richest country in the world? She had to miss Dionne Warwick at the Apollo and Soul Sister Franklin at Lincoln Center. She had been receiving her check at a friend's pad. But the caseworker paid a routine visit. "Where's Mary?" The friend's old lady said, "She ain't been here in over a month."

"And I'm off," Mary, who is twenty-nine, lamented. "Lying bitch. She's mad because I won't ball with them anymore."

A few days later, Mary saw her social worker. Life is getting brighter. "Even if I have to go over there and throw a fit. Look, I haven't worked in four years. I could if I wanted to. But I think I need glasses, and I have to get my teeth fixed. And you know I have to take pills. I'm a nervous wreck." Speaking of a semi-drag queen who is almost at the top of the welfare-dollar ladder, Mary said, "That bitch. She gets $99.50 twice a month. And she's living in the street. I saw her trying to hustle over on the Apeside."

The Apeside is the East Village beyond Tompkins Square Park. In TSP I met Jojo. He was very uptight, his paranoia gave off sparks. "Man. They sent my check back. Got a cigarette?" Jojo, ex-garage mechanic. Blond, extremely bright, but frightened of touching his brain. He's spent three years in jail (robbery), dabbled in dope, and is now deep into a wine scene. He breathes like a man in deep pain. We stop off for a pint of Orange Rock. "Gotta steady my [illegible] ports [illegible] es. We [illegible] ght, we [illegible] to the [illegible] re have [illegible] st Thirteenth Street, where the [illegible] sphere [illegible] dy, hop [illegible] e a [illegible] the chorus gyps [illegible] a little [illegible] I was su [illegible] at [illegible] well-dressed welfare recipients. R[illegible] ties, every [illegible] ws [illegible] the [illegible] ement. [illegible] the [illegible] ch [illegible] ally [illegible] cks and who [illegible] s off [illegible] try [illegible] get back [illegible] ere were [illegible] old people. [illegible] presch [illegible] l school-age children [illegible] each other between plastic [illegible] ess chairs. [illegible] bu [illegible] y mothers everywhere [illegible] paid [illegible] attention to the children. [illegible] plenty of time to go[illegible] sip. [illegible] take over. [illegible] the welfare [illegible] welfare [illegible] as a [illegible] sat [illegible] to [illegible] tell [illegible] only [illegible] thought [illegible] the stock exchange. There [illegible] be some [illegible] king [illegible] up [illegible] cross-examination. Jojo [illegible] But we [illegible] up at last [illegible] conversation [illegible] with a [illegible] ence.

Al[illegible] Jojo received [illegible] for exactly [illegible] 33. He [illegible] more. He [illegible] A serious Jojo [illegible] the [illegible] ker. [illegible] a kitchenette [illegible] Jojo [illegible] Jojo [illegible] $[illegible] loa[illegible] bers, hard-boiled eggs. [illegible] s[illegible] ine and [illegible] pool. Life [illegible] good [illegible] vors.

Ne[illegible] words [illegible] will [illegible] want [illegible] say [illegible] told me [illegible] an [illegible] there [illegible] $7 fare money home and [illegible] friends, sitting around the [illegible] waiting [illegible] lay. N[illegible] seven [illegible] children [illegible] they [illegible] mothers [illegible] style [illegible] in their [illegible] made [illegible] ive [illegible] ever [illegible] are always [illegible] defensive [illegible] they [illegible] lay [illegible] that [illegible] d, [illegible] them [illegible] and [illegible] with them, and [illegible] they [illegible].

[illegible] they [illegible] alcoholic becomes a

dagger. They are disappointed: I will not marry their mother and become their father. It is only because of the children that I have never bedded the mother. Although my childhood was quietly religious and happy, I, too, was briefly a child of welfare. After my grandfather died, and before my father's World War II allotment, there was nothing my grandmother could do but apply for public assistance for me. It was a pittance in every sense of the word. Sometimes she did daywork for white families (in the village of New Franklin, Missouri, not too many white families could afford part-time help, much less full-time servants).

I remember that in winter we became the local F.B.I. of the railroad tracks, looking for coal that had fallen from the open-bellied freight cars. Even today I can taste the delight of a Sunday supper: day-old bread in a bowl of milk sprinkled with cinnamon and sugar. I remember the Christmas we were too poor to buy a tree. But luck was with us, one cold, sunny afternoon a few days before Christmas. We found clumps of pine branches along the railroad tracks. My imaginative grandmother decided that we would make a tree. We found a small leafless young tree and tied the branches to it. It was a beautiful Christmas tree, the delight of the neighbors. And we did not even have multicolored lights for the tree. I frame this memory briefly to let you know that I understand the plight of welfare. I hold no bitterness against those days. It was a happening of that particular time.

Yet there is dark music in the towns, cities, about the welfare recipients. We have to pay taxes to take care of these lazy, good-for-nothing bums. Still, there are the happy Lawrence Welk voices who sing, and this works to our advantage in the end. This is where we want to keep them. We will give them enough so they'll be content and will cause us no trouble. Welfare is their addiction.

Anyway, for those of you who are interested in trying yet another new life-style, here are a few surefire suggestions I have compiled with the help of Green Eyes, who never had to use them:

1) Become an addict.
2) Become an alcoholic or fake it.
3) Get busted, a minor bust, though you could have a fairly cool winter in the Tombs.

Gather this:

Have a...
Kings...
...extend...
...

. . . . . . . . . . . . . . . . . . . . . . . . . . . . . . . . . . . . . . . . . . . . . . . . . . . . . . . . . . . . . . . . . . .

THE AFTERNOONS OFFER more than a sharecropper's bag of humidity and rain. But the lunar boys are exceptionally cool, as if the age of Aquarius had instilled in them a terrifying knowledge of silence. In groups of twos, threes, and fours, wearing brilliant-colored nylon T-shirts, jeans, John's Bargain Store khaki walking shorts, tennis shoes, and athletic socks with deep cuffs, they are not long-haired. Immaculate, one of them wants to become a trumpet player. Another, at the age of fourteen, has had faggot grooming. Five of them are school dropouts. The boy with the "hot" $35 knitted shirts is one of six illegitimate children, all of them under the age of sixteen and on welfare.

These budding lunar professionals will, say between two and three of an afternoon, stroll into the Old Dover Tavern (the very "in" Bowery bar). In the beginning, at the end of the school term, they stood outside, while the leader entered. Later, as confidence ripened, they entered and huddled near the door, near the cigarette and candy machines. Now they prowl up and down the bar like altar boys, seeking some rare chalice.

The leader of one gang will ask the bartender for change or order his usual grilled-cheese sandwich. They never buy cigarettes, and it was only last Saturday night that we discovered that they have been trying to jam the candy machine.

Then silent, their young eyes revolving, they walk out into the

[illegible] ow [illegible] ain [illegible] f the Bo[illegible] a[illegible] tis[illegible] st[illegible]
[illegible] roll[illegible] rate[illegible], Germ[illegible] ce[illegible] Do[illegible] [illegible] oir sch[illegible]
[illegible] ime[illegible] the [illegible] ddings of [illegible] sai[illegible] wil[illegible] [illegible] d rap[illegible]
[illegible] drin[illegible] ing [illegible] ter room [illegible]. [illegible] re hea[illegible]
[illegible] say [illegible] ing trips for [illegible] bro[illegible] [illegible] oo br[illegible]
[illegible] ys [illegible] t quiet [illegible] he [illegible] ss.
[illegible] s [illegible] la [illegible] y, [illegible] they [illegible] le [illegible] side st[illegible]
[illegible] tens[illegible] and the [illegible] their [illegible]
[illegible] s if [illegible] ve [illegible] the fir[illegible] of [illegible] er tha[illegible]
[illegible] g o[illegible] re [illegible] ly and [illegible] un [illegible] the [illegible] oned k[illegible]
[illegible] bor[illegible] ba[illegible] at Sp[illegible] c [illegible] ark t[illegible]
[illegible] ous [illegible] rti[illegible] comple[illegible]. T[illegible] is [illegible] lated [illegible]
[illegible] shoc[illegible] s in [illegible] m We[illegible] [illegible]
[illegible] these [illegible] ea[illegible] ur boy[illegible] [illegible] acro[illegible]
[illegible] ing; [illegible] s of the [illegible] or not [illegible]
[illegible] are leg[illegible] ds of t[illegible] [illegible] e old [illegible]
[illegible] tch, [illegible] eeds, a [illegible] weet, [illegible]
[illegible] bills [illegible] hese bo[illegible] [illegible] ro[illegible]
[illegible] ave [illegible] ed the [illegible] ve the [illegible]
[illegible] t's [illegible] so co[illegible] sport. [illegible]
[illegible] wit[illegible] told me "[illegible] Pop[illegible] y juic[illegible]
[illegible] ys [illegible] I was j[illegible] ound. [illegible]
[illegible] and [illegible] take [illegible] te wit[illegible]
[illegible] d. [illegible] through [illegible] all that [illegible]
[illegible] 834 [illegible] selling [illegible]
[illegible] vis[illegible] part of the [illegible] re sel[illegible]
[illegible] th[illegible] heads. [illegible] ou do [illegible]
[illegible] Occ[illegible] ly, a v[illegible] the tee[illegible]
[illegible] igh[illegible] or call[illegible] ne. O[illegible]
[illegible] od. O[illegible]
[illegible] us[illegible] re. [illegible]
[illegible] Affl[illegible]
[illegible] ds.
[illegible] are [illegible] us ag[illegible]
[illegible] not ma[illegible] he B[illegible] fifte[illegible]
[illegible] the [illegible]. This [illegible] act[illegible]
[illegible] ers [illegible] mainl[illegible]
[illegible] p-and-[illegible] ican [illegible]
[illegible] Da[illegible] brains [illegible] mall-t[illegible]
[illegible] ves [illegible] or the l[illegible]

On August I, at seven in the evening, five blacks ganged up on one old white man at the corner of Prince and the Bowery.

Traffic jammed to a halt. The Bowery bar philosophers watched the happening. The white majority (Irish and Polish) were incensed by the bold black act. But they made no effort to do anything about it, except to spray two black regulars, two queens, with a water pistol of words. "Have I ever tried to rob you?" a hard-drinking black queen asked. "Shit. I could buy and sell all of you. Don't talk about my people."

Sitting four stools away, I suddenly laughed at the perverse reality of *this* sporting Bowery game.

The jackrolling blacks took from the old whites in the light of the day. At night the young whites drank freely of the old black queens and often stole from them, providing the queen bedded them.

Governor Rockefeller, campaigning for reelection, said yesterday that the addiction problem in the state had grown much bigger than he had expected four years ago.
*The New York Times,* August 4

"Young people today are being subjected to the most profound temptations and stresses—"
Robert Sargent Shriver,
*The New York Times,* August 6

"We didn't actually break in. The door was open so we just made ourselves at home."

"Hell. Charlie don't give a shit."

Sitting in the living room of a building marked for demolition, I wondered if I did care. After all, squatting out has become most fashionable. Earlier, I had been sitting in a bar, when an acquaintance had invited me to a party. In the past, I had offered Duk Up Soon a place to flop for the night, an occasional quarter, advice. This invitation was a thank-you gesture. And now we were in this living room, sitting on milk crates, a car seat, and the floor. Street lamps spotlighted the room. Votive candles created a ritualistic mood. The buffet: wine, pot, beer, and pills, plus the works. The kids were very polite, and I decided to sit in and see what would happen. Then Pepe came in. We were a little surprised to see each other; our smiles bordered on warmth. I had written about Pepe

...summer jacking debut that Pepe's thing was pot, wine, and girls. He was fourteen then... Navy, almost seventeen, with a delicate dark mustache, looking as always Italian... shirts. The sneakers have replaced the Oxfords, his boots are... running. His well... others... own head and... pinned the weekend lover. The other five children are in school and doing well. Pepe looks like a prep vocational student as he takes the bags from the deep pockets of his socks... his... chill until an hour ago were in the Frigidaire on Seventh Avenue, who weighs about 120 pounds, and a Coke can and... her frightened as she takes off his belt and turns to Duke Up... and... lover, would been... like pin high jockeys, silently, with... only seems to touch... face like a... But they... their arms at the needle and the strapping, they... tall and... intensely cool. He shoots the up jamming into his middle... upon the needle still in his arm. "Man, look. Look at that. You... fucking bullseye. That is everyone."

...Pepe began to nod. Leo... with the cut dab... key... stacked to Duke up. Soon it trembles. There were eleven keys on than. Only one fit Duke's trigger door. Bea cupping... held over his nose and snoring in... his clean campaign... No. This pad looks like a prison. If I got... a clean pad... but see my sister's pad... turning equip... watching him, Leo listening to Frankie Crocker on WMCA. A certain number... teenage boys and a very... girl walk... peer... in the... dark room a little... they brought block... war... and bread.

One of them said. "You should you had a bad... man you... bring a pan...

...the pretty girl said to the... particular... fine been... a... bid like a Bingo Bri... white Burl's voice grew... and she began to put down her words. ... Tommie. You deep," they... girls said before she... could...

"...friend had turned on and wanted to leave, bitch. I'm going with all of you," Tommie said. "Git your lazy ass get..."

But the pretty girl was high now... through the numb... cool... as she sat down on a milk crate, crossed her long legs, opened her fringed suède handbag, and began making up her face. It took her almost twenty minutes to paint her lips. "Dumb bitch," the boyfriend taunted. The girl tried to put on false eyelashes with one hand and hold the mirror with the other.

"You ain't got no brains at all," the boyfriend said, snatching the mirror from the girl's hand. The girl was very quiet now as if she were alone. Our voices with the rock music were the sounds of people who were in hell and would never get out.

"Well," I said finally, "I've got to make it."

They were damn nice kids, despite the junk. The rapping had mainly been for my benefit. It was their way of showing that they were with it. Why didn't I call the cops or the narc people? Well, I had talked to these kids and kids like them for a very long time. I knew they had to do their own thing. That is unless they were busted.

Just the other night, I had an encounter with the cops. "Why don't you do something about the junkies and pushers?" I said.

"You should go back to Spanish Harlem," the cop told me.

"Sorry. I'm not Puerto Rican."

"Then go back up to Eighth Avenue and 125th Street."

I laughed.

Junkies like scavengers overturn litter baskets, looking for the heroin that has been stashed there, or they circle the full green-leafed trees looking for the bags, and no one cares as a slim junkie (using a master key) opens a car trunk, directly in front of Daytop Village on Chrystie Street, and makes off with a flashlight, a battery recharger in the Chinese Garden (officially named Manhattan Bridge Park in English and Chinese). The young Chinese boys play a new sport: baseball. The sun is high in the watery blue sky, and it is a quarter of two in the afternoon. Three junkies shoot up, while on the bridge a hard-hat construction worker looks on in amazement: Yes S. X. was gagging to death, and the others were high and giggled, but Beaver comes in, drags S. X. to the bathroom for a cold shower and ice cubes on his testicles. Dial 911 and watch two teenage boys steal a tire off a car at high noon. Later, I take a junkies count: two hours netted eighty-seven in a limited area, and I wasn't trying very hard. On Bleecker, a bearded hippie stops me with "Hey, baby. I need seven bags." Sorry, I say, and another cat comes up and asks what does that honky want, and I

real. One dares not mention that this was the only way for him to get published and that he had to eat and buy shoes. And none of it was easy. And it seems to me, Langston, that you knew what your literary black sons haven't learned: it's a closed game played on a one-way street.

Ah! The bitterness, some jiveass mothergrabber will say.

But we know better, don't we? The smile on your face in the white quilted coffin says so. The undertaker had a touch of genius, for the smile is nothing like your smile but the smile that was always underneath the surface smile. The smile that was in your voice and your laughter.

The serene mad smile of one who is trapped!

At the funeral home I heard a woman say, "Don't look like he suffered one bit."

No, no, no!

If you had lived, you would have been in Morocco now with the photographs and introductions I had given you. Florence, whom you met here, and Cadeau, the white Peke, were waiting for you. You spent four days in Tangier last year and liked it well enough to return and spend the summer there. That is, if you solved the money problem. And most of all you wanted to go to the folk festival in Marrakesh.

And it was strange that Tuesday morning, Langston. I hit the streets, slightly stoned, talk-singing that old Billie Holiday tune, "Good Morning, Heartaches . . . Here we go again . . ."

And there you were on the front page of *The New York Times*, dead.

I hated to leave you up on St. Nicholas Avenue . . . just when I had gotten to know you.

I hate to close this note, but I must put you out of my mind for the time being. And it is not your death that I'm mourning. It's the horror of it all. "Ah, Man!" you would chuckle sadly.

Poor black poet who died proper and smiling.

Langston Hughes was always concerned about my eating habits. Frequently, he invited me to dinner, restaurants or to his Harlem brownstone. I was always a smiling liar: "I have eaten, old sport. All I want is a double vodka on the rocks." But a few nights after his funeral, I returned to Harlem, buoyed with the memory of my

third of Chambray vermouth, chain-smoked, and tried not to think.

Around midnight, I hit the streets. No heralding trumpets greeted me. No royal streets led to the House of Orange. However, Hershey's Bowery bar became an orangerie, a smoky crimson stage where approximately thirty-five intoxicated men tried to upstage each other. Like ash-can whores, they tried to con each other and the bartender. A mangy, crippled dog sauntered in and bequeathed fleas. I ordered another wine, looked up at the mute television, which seemed to gradually rise toward the ceiling. Unlike the drinking men, the television apparently wanted to get closer to God.

That's when I turned, looked out the door, and saw the girl. I ran to the door and watched a black teenage girl walk down the Bowery. Walking as if it were day and the street, a pleasant, tree-lined country lane.

I caught up with the girl and remembered where I had first seen her, playing softball in Chrystie Street Park about a week before. She played very well and commanded every male's attention. What I'm sure most of us were admiring was not her pitcher's left arm but her ice-cream-cone tits, the wide womanly buttocks, although she appeared to be no older than sixteen.

"Hello," I said. "Where are you going?"

"Home," the girl replied, averting her eyes.

"You shouldn't be out this late alone."

"I was over at my girlfriend's on Houston. We were listening to Smokey Robinson and the Miracles, and I forgot what time it was."

"Where do you live?"

"Ludlow," the girl said, sounding like an eight-year-old.

"Do you want me to walk you home?"

"If you want to."

In the beginning, I had told myself that I wanted to protect her like a brother, like a father. But when we reached Delancey Street I had my arm around her. She rested very easily in my embrace. Innocent and sweet fantasies waltzed through my mind. But the Midwestern, Methodist country boy did not applaud the waltz.

"I don't have to go home yet," the girl told me, looking straight ahead.

We crossed Delancey and walked through the park, deserted

NOW I WAS MANAGING to write for *The Village Voice* every other week, supplementing that income with an occasional slop-jar job; washing dishes in penal delis, carrying one-hundred-pound bags of rice on my 129-pound shoulders. But I had my big toe in the door of my world again. The dusty black telephone which sat on the floor like a discarded toy and never rang except when management called bitching about the rent began ringing. There were letters, invitations to parties. I began seeing old friends again. One of the best was beautiful black Hilary, an artist-model.

After a pushcart hot-dog lunch, we decided to go into the Cedar Tavern and have a few drinks.

On the fourth Scotch and water, Hilary said, "You must be more social, Charles. Parties are where things happen."

"And don't happen. I'm tired of assholes and freaks and phonies."

"Now, baby," Hilary pleaded.

"Shit, Hilary," I exclaimed. "I wasted a whole weekend with those black middle-class cocksuckers on Long Island. Why? Because I was promised a job. And all they wanted to talk about was my experiences in Tangier and Mexico. Plus the hostess had 'always wanted to write.' Shit. Let's have another drink."

Hilary giggled. "At this rate, I'll be stoned before I get to the Art Students League."

black breed that was conceived in the idealistic Kennedy years, passed their youth in Johnson's Great Society, grew to maturity, prospered in the subtle South Africa of the United States of 1971. The majority of these young black men and women are clever, extremely intelligent. The majority of these young black men and women are only superficially militant. Of course, they give money to black causes and buy the Black Panther newspaper (how can they refuse with their manner and dress on a blue-sky Saturday afternoon?). All of them agree that New York's finest pigs are "terrible. Just terrible." And like skimming fat from milk, they are as bourgeois as a Republican Vice President. Y'all hear me? Riot all over the goddamn city, but don't bomb Macy's, Gimbels, or Bloomingdale's. Do not open a drug-addict center within five hundred miles of Tanglewood.

Some of these young black men and women are my acquaintances. I knew and liked T. C. Moses III. I was finger-popping as I rang his doorbell.

T. C., who went to Howard University, received his law degree from Columbia University, sported a conservative Afro. Dark-skinned, he wore an English suit, white shirt, and dark tie. Smiling warmly, he shifted one of his sixteen pipes from his right to his left hand.

"Charlie. My main man. We've been expecting you."

"Sorry I'm late." I smiled, hoping it was real.

Just then, Julie, the fat blonde in something long, flowing, and purple, squealed. "Angel, baby," she cried and gave me a solid hug, about a dozen wet, little kisses. She smelled of gin and perfume.

We went into the white-walled living room with its highly polished floor, garden of green plants, paintings, and drawings by black artists. As far as the eye could see, fake imported African artifacts took possession of walls, floor, tables. The most imposing had their own lucite pedestals (T. C. went to Africa last year and forced a protesting Julie to remain in Paris).

The lights were low, people milled about like museumgoers. Aretha Franklin was on the stereo, and I knew it was party time. Time for most of them to let their hair down about an inch. Earlier the music would have been a little Bach or a Mozart fanfare, and the talk would have been heavy: the fate of mankind, crime in the

Before we could reach the bar, a black voice commanded, "Charles Wright!"

"Oh, Charles," Hilary said. "It's A. X. and his gentleman friend, the poet." A. X.'s court consisted of two white men and one serious, plain young woman who looked as if she was a graduate of an expensive avant-garde girl's college and might at one time have considered joining the Peace Corps. A. X.'s poet was Afroed, bearded, serious, wore a rumpled suit and tie. He was searching. "Trying to get the feel, baby"—for a proper African name. Africa was where it was at. Poetry was where he was at.

"But is it art?" I wanted to know. "And why do the majority of black poets sound alike. I'm not talking about the kids from the street."

"But there's a war going on. We're at it with whitey," the poet said dramatically.

I looked at A. X. He nodded gravely. Was he thinking of his Irish doorman, who said, "Good evening, Mr. Coombs"?

"I wanna dance." Hilary pouted. "I wanna dance with my dress up over my head."

"Hilary," A. X. said, "there are ladies present. You are not in the Village."

"And, my dear, you are not in the subway john on your knees."

"Hilary," I exclaimed, pulling her away.

"Let's have a drink and drown all the schmuck faces. Am I really naughty?"

"Never," I said, bestowing a prize kiss on her unlined forehead.

A week later, a Monday, following the Newark riot, I was delivering circulars door to door in the Bronx. Now a good circular man is aware of dogs. Therefore, I stuck the supermarket throwaway in the iron gate, which was open. A healthy young dog came running from the side garden with his teeth bared. I managed to grab the gate; the dog, hunched like a quarterback, tried to chew my left foot through the fence.

"Don't kick him," a woman screamed. "This ain't Newark."

In the voice of a serene, opium-smoking saint, I replied, "I was not trying to kick your dog, madam. I was merely trying to close the gate. I didn't want him to bite my foot."

She has been with me for a very long time, even before I could read and write. The guys at Smitty's gas station in Boonville, Missouri, called me dago. Aged five, I knew dago was not nigger. But they have remained stepbrothers to this day, forming an uncomfortable army with kike, Polack, poor white trash. But I had nigger, Negro, coon, black, colored, monkey, shit-colored bastard, yellow bastard. Perfect background music for nightmares. The uric sperm of those years has flooded my mind. Was I ever Charles Stevenson Wright? In private moments, I say aloud, my face igniting a sulphuric grin, "Your name is Charles Stevenson Wright." Occasionally, I applaud this honest sea dog facing me. Charles Stevenson Wright, the man. Face myself or else suffer the living horrors, the grind of a real fuck, guaranteed to keep you moaning until death.

Inherited bitterness, barriers, color nightmares. A rainbow then. Not Finian's "I've an elegant legacy waiting for ye," but a remembrance of you trying to rim the daylights out of me in the hope of producing another petrified black boy. My grandfather, Charles Hughes, was a boy at the age of seventy. It is remembering my grandfather and all the other boys who have been buggered through the years by that name.

Like a quarterly, ghostly visitor, one nightmare always returns. I am facing a Kafka judge (perhaps a god) and his court. Their skin and hair are as clear as rainwater. The quiet is frightening.

"But I always thought I was simply Charles Stevenson Wright," I protest desperately, then roar with mad laughter, knowing that whitey, too, has great problems, nightmares. At this stage of gamy, Racial American Events, it is impossible for whitey to produce good niggers. But he still is capable of producing Uncle Toms. But always remember: hoarded prejudices beget slaves who impale their masters on the arrow of time.

monument to another age of splendor. But the bentwood hatrack and chair, the vile painted furnishings dominate—a seedy stage for Tennessee Williams or Graham Greene (the stage is not waiting for me; I live here). But the mattress is clean, firm, and makes me feel good. Already I am debating whether I should christen it with the pretty black junkie girl. A daily visitor, Betty is always trying to "straighten up your pad, man," asking me to kiss her, or doing one of those brief junkie naps. I "respect" her; we get along damn well. But pride and the cold technician have always kept my emotion in check. At the end of each visit, Betty looks me straight in the eye and announces, "I will be back."

And Betty always leaves something. Things that females can't bear to part with in this age of liberation.

Bopping through a pauper period, I have nothing of value for Betty to steal. "Would you take money from me?" she asked.

"Nope," I replied.

"What about a little gift?"

Betty could steal a "boss" pair of sunglasses or an umbrella (it was raining that afternoon).

"Oh, Charles." Betty pouted, then laughed madly, displaying a solid gold wristwatch she had taken from a man in a West Side motel.

Depression knights my forehead. I cannot move.

Finished the wine. The lukewarm beer, a bummer. I go to the window. The gray street looks fresh and clean after the rain. Directly across the street, the city branch of Swiss Farm nurseries displays young green trees, plants, and flowers in red clay pots. I am seized with hunger for the country, the sea. Surrounded by the Hudson and East Rivers, the Atlantic Ocean, I second Eugene O'Neill's cry: "I would have been much happier as a fish." Yet like an addicted entomologist, I am drawn to people. Let them flutter, bask, rest, feed on my tree. Then fly, fly. Fly away. Goddamnit. Fly mother-fuckers.

In the afternoon, bless the solitude, salute it with vodka. Finished reading Henry Green's *Loving* and Muriel Spark's *Memento Mori*. Talk about a good high. Read a paragraph from an Imamu Amiri Baraka essay (no matter, no matter. I remember LeRoi Jones when

He had given one of the two occupants a perverse young female dog. The boy fed Blackie and unlocked the entrance door. But he exited by the fire escape, lugging a brand new tape recorder.

A cardiac man (a constant people watcher) saw the boy and called his wife. The couple lived directly across the street and watched our Tom try to hawk a "heavy, black case." Watched until the boy disappeared out of their view. Shortly after this, the boy returned, minus the tape recorder. The cardiac man did not have a phone, but vowed to tell the people in the fifth-floor apartment about the "heavy, black case." The Welfare Bonanza was nine days off, and it was a gritty time for the poor, especially for people who lived beyond the monetary welfare standard, for party people. But the couple across the street saw chubby Tom's mother dash out and return with "heavy goods" from the Pioneer supermarket.

Now it was almost 11 A.M. Eugene, one of the occupants of the apartment, returned and found the apartment in a shambles. He called his cousin Dash, who arrived an hour later. By this time, the police had arrived and departed. Dash waited for the detectives. Then it was time for Gene to go to work. Dash called me. I arrived at 3 P.M. and performed amateur spade-work. The locked American armoire was almost unhinged. The two doors were like two flags at half mast.

"Well," I said, "I doubt if it was a junkie. They didn't take clothes or record albums. And the phones are still plugged in. They could have taken Gene's stereo. It isn't that heavy."

Laughing sadly, Dash, an IBM man said, "But they took the tropical fish and the bird."

Blackie, the perverse little bitch, had eaten the other bird. "I have a funny feeling," Dash said. "I bet it was the little boy downstairs."

Tom's boyish charm seemed too smooth, like rich country butter, and I had been watching him for a long time.

"I've been thinking the same thing."

It was now around five, and the sky was an explosion of red, and we eased the pain with Gordon's gin and waited for the detectives.

"Call the detectives again," I said.

"Hell. I've called them three times. They said they'd be over."

[illegible] you got [illegible]
[illegible] n Precin [illegible]
[illegible] nything [illegible]
[illegible] s tick [illegible]
[illegible] deter [illegible]
[illegible] d be [illegible]

[illegible] proof [illegible]
[illegible] his wit [illegible]
[illegible] igh and [illegible]
[illegible] lefecate [illegible]

[illegible], and [illegible]
[illegible] ent to [illegible]
[illegible] nst my [illegible]
[illegible] gels [illegible]
[illegible] and de [illegible]
[illegible] r hands [illegible]
[illegible] the Ca [illegible]

[illegible] chants [illegible]
[illegible] dogs in [illegible]
[illegible] netimes [illegible]
[illegible] e and [illegible]
[illegible] Will yo [illegible]
[illegible] n, and h [illegible]
[illegible] and tak [illegible]
[illegible] dy, he [illegible]
[illegible] great d [illegible]
[illegible] dren, [illegible]
[illegible] et, that [illegible]
[illegible] r apart [illegible]
[illegible] and th [illegible]
[illegible] hbors. [illegible]
[illegible] s, but [illegible]
[illegible] to Tou [illegible]

[illegible] Fifth P [illegible]
[illegible] e four [illegible]
[illegible] n One [illegible]

was silent. He was chubby and might have been Tom's father. The other policeman was young, slender. A philosopher. He said, rather sadly, "There isn't much proof to go on."

"If you don't catch the boy with the goods, what other proof could you possibly have? Except a man and woman who saw the boy—and our willingness to testify."

Up to this point, the slender policeman had ignored me. Now he gave me his attention. We talked about crime in the street, kids. I wanted to go to the bathroom. Finally, we said good-bye, and the two men in tired blue departed. Once again Dash and I got high and waited for the detectives.

Sunday was sunny and pleasant after the rain. It was also a busy day for our Tom. Apparently he sensed that something was up, for he was in and out of the building about ten times. But we never saw him.

Later that morning, the detective who had been assigned to the case called. He warned us not to talk to the boy or harm him. And please, please, do not stage a personal raid on his mother's apartment. The detective would be over later in the day with a search warrant. He was an overworked, sympathetic man, who arrived on East Eleventh Street at exactly 6 P.M. that Sunday evening, almost three days after the robbery had taken place.

It was party time in Tom's mother's rear apartment. A toast to the delight of Miller High Life. Music, laughter created a stereophonic noise in the crowded, dimly lit four rooms. The detective had trouble getting in; people pushed and ran from room to room, at times creating the effect of a crazy, jet-paced counterdrill. There was almost no furniture in the apartment. All the detective could do was issue a summons to Tom's mother. They were requested to appear in Juvenile Court.

Dash and Gene arrived at Juvenile Court. It was 9 A.M. Their case came up at 2 P.M. Tom's mother would not accept legal aid. She would get her own lawyer. The judge warned her not to return without a lawyer. A new date was set for the trial.

But the sullen woman returned without a lawyer. She was alone and occasionally smiled at the judge.

Where was our Tom?

In a clear, today-the-sun-is-shining voice, Tom's mother told the judge, "He didn't feel like coming."

The brief silence in the courtroom was deadly. The judge was

...raged and issued a sum... ...or Tom... ...placed in j... ...the jail until h... ...came to g... ...made a qu... ...it from the... ...room. The... ...sa...d, "I'll... ...know whe... ...ck up the k... y...

That wa... ...lost five w... ...o. Sitting... ...afternoon... ...asked Da... ...the ca...e B... ...the ...ject and... ...about ge... ...d. We ha... ...tered to... ...h...t Harris...g...t Wel...

Then I... ...bered a U... ...t: "Hove... ...Counc...l ha...d to build... ...more pu...lish...d... ...llowing...ental use... ...fenced... ...with du...e... g...ose."

Ca...edian s...d. Dogs. Do...

ANOTHER CASE VIA AIRMAIL, another perfumed note from Paris, France.

Dear Charles:

Anne T. returned from Portugal with a terrific suntan and bruises. Bruises, hon. The poor thing is black and blue, thanks to a fat, Princeton type of young man (he said he was working for the C.I.A. "Top-level stuff"). This young man stole a twenty-dollar bill off Anne's dressing table. She left it there deliberately. And now she's back, all bruised up, and wants to go to the south of France. But I haven't got a bathing suit. I haven't bought a thing all year except hose and a panty girdle. I'm so poor. George's alimony is a pittance, and I was such a fool. I should have taken that bastard to the cleaners. But I was thinking of the kids. *His* kids. I never could conceive, and I'm too old now, anyway. All I can do is play solitaire, work crossword puzzles, and read detective stories. Paris is terrible, terrible. The City of Lights doesn't mean a damn thing to me anymore. I'm seriously considering returning to the States. Ask Miss Feldman or Mr. Miller at the Albert or those nice people at the Hotel Van Rensselaer. I must live in the Village. Gone are the Barclay days! Have you seen Charles Robb or that bitch Hilary? I hope you are writing and everything is going well. I'm baking bread and drinking black-market Scotch. That's Paris for you. Bebe sends his love. He still thinks he can talk. Silly dog.

Love,
Maggie

## CHAPTER EIGHT

"No kidding, Charlie. You're together, and I had to see you."

"Here's to the vineyards and the people who toil in them," I said, thinking: At least he doesn't want to borrow money, doesn't need a place to flop for the night.

Clancy shook his head again. "I don't know, sport. I had this gig and was starting to get myself together. I bought some clothes. A TV. Then I start messing round with Martha. Shit. I'm gonna get me some dope."

"Well," I said, sitting down on the unmade bed, "you've had it before. And you're all screwed up. Why not a little dope? Maybe you'll get lucky and get hooked this time."

"Charles," Clancy pleaded. "Don't put the bad mouth on me."

"Did you call your brother?"

"No, but I will." Clancy sighed and filled the tumblers. "You know he's got a cabin up in the mountains, and this fall we could go up there and hunt. Do you good to get out of the city. Maybe you'd like it up there and could write."

Clancy and I did not hunt last fall, nor fish in the spring, but I said, "Yeah. I'd like that. I like the country. Anything to get out of this fucking city."

We had more wine, and Clancy began singing in a Rex Harrison voice, "California Dreaming," then bolted up and smashed his fist against the wall.

"That bitch. My fucking mother is in California. After Daddy died in prison, she left all of us kids and went to California with a shoe salesman. What kind of mother is that? Don't wanna bring you down, Charlie. Let's have some more wine."

"God said, Let there be light, and there was light," I said.

"You should have been a preacher or a teacher. You're good with kids."

"Yes, my son. Pass the jug."

"You can't destroy yourself, man. You just can't."

"Clancy, I think you've got a point."

"Goddamnit!" Clancy exclaimed, banging his hand on the table, spilling wine. "You can't destroy yourself."

I watched Clancy stagger to the bathroom, staggering like a man trying to avoid a great fire.

The afternoon wine flowed. Cigarette butts filled ashtrays,

[illegible] smok[illegible] [illegible] goos[illegible] [illegible] "Th[illegible]

"[illegible] sleep[illegible]

"No[illegible]," [illegible] said, frown[illegible] [illegible] dream[illegible] [illegible] and [illegible] with b[illegible] [illegible] have [illegible] on."

[illegible] glanc[illegible] [illegible] his f[illegible] [illegible] Every[illegible] again[illegible] [illegible] scre[illegible] up [illegible]

"Oh [illegible]

"Yo[illegible] [illegible] You thi[illegible] [illegible] [illegible]ucki[illegible] [illegible] God[illegible] [illegible]d."

"Wh[illegible] [illegible] laughed[illegible] [illegible] anoth[illegible] [illegible] game [illegible] out [illegible] Wh[illegible] [illegible] perhaps [illegible] friend[illegible] [illegible] know[illegible] edge[illegible] [illegible] wh[illegible] [illegible] trick [illegible] might [illegible] with my [illegible] [illegible] ed eg[illegible] [illegible] I know [illegible] they w[illegible] take a [illegible] of my [illegible] [illegible] [illegible] the mom[illegible] [illegible] [illegible] whe[illegible] [illegible] pow[illegible] [illegible]

I [illegible] head[illegible] [illegible] up [illegible] St. [illegible] see what was happen[illegible] [illegible] of th[illegible] [illegible] imag[illegible] [illegible] The [illegible] love[illegible] [illegible] mod[illegible] [illegible] J. W[illegible] [illegible] wor[illegible] [illegible] own, [illegible] cent[illegible] [illegible] exit. [illegible] He ha[illegible] been [illegible] sa[illegible] [illegible] almo[illegible] [illegible] spe[illegible] [illegible] a young [illegible] on u[illegible] [illegible] shirt, [illegible] jeans. [illegible] sai[illegible] "B[illegible]y, [illegible] spa[illegible] [illegible] change[illegible]

Larl turned swiftly, enraged. "Can't you see my face is black, boy! How the hell can I spare anything?"

The healthy boyish charm faded. The young man went away as if he had been punished.

Another small St. Marks encounter. The beggar is a wiry black man who bolted down from a stoop and began rapping with a young man whose face was a map of suburbia. The black man really rapped. Suburbian, Jr., would not release any coins. The black man put his arms around Junior and gave him a peace-movement kiss on the cheek. A few more words and Suburbian, Jr., reached in his pocket and gave the black man a quarter and a dime. The black man told me, "I wish America had another hundred thousand hippies. Then I could make a steady living."

But the fat black hairless queen does not have to worry about a steady living. He is a male nurse, has a sideline hustle. Waddling like a grand female duck, large brilliant eyes, going from left to right, he comes on like a Southern mammy. The queen specializes in young white beggars. "Oh Lord! So many homeless chickens. All they want is a little change or some pot and pills. So they put the make on mother. But I been round since the year one. I take'm to my penthouse on Avenue A. I got plenty of pills, pot, and poppers, and I turns them over faster than you can say eggs and grits. Sometimes they comes back and brings their little long-haired girl-friends. And they just all love mother. Oh, my word. Look at that boy crossing that street. What a basket. Well, I must rush off and tend to my chickens." The black queen's dimes, quarters, dollars are a good investment. If a black gives money to whitey, he will be the winner, regardless of what game is being played.

Like Shuffling Joe, who is determined, threatening. Union Square is his base. Union Square is filled with rats; Shuffling Joe has to find "fresh ground." One reason why Shuffling Joe is determined is that he will not drink La Boheme wine, which costs fifty-five cents a pint. "Gallo, man," he says. Gallo is seventy cents a pint. I watch Shuffling Joe hustle a bearded photographer and his lady friend. They are about twenty paces in front of him. The photographer shakes his head, gestures with his hand. His lady friend turns, looks serious; Shuffling Joe watches them move on, still rapping. He grabs the photographer's arm. Photographer grabs camera. Now Shuffling Joe is really rapping, gesturing dramatically. The lady friend has been watching gravely. Suddenly she opens her

Especially if they're clean and bright as daisies. But what I want to tell you about is a black and white team, a classic encounter. Larl was at Astor Place and Fourth Avenue. Two teenage girls, one black, the other white, skinny as jay birds in their hip department-store finery. The girls asked Larl for some spare change, Larl ignored them. In unison, the girls shouted, "Cheap cocksucker!"

Larl swung around, marched toward the girls. Then silently raised his hand and, with one powerful stroke, slapped both girls. A crowd gathered. Larl, very aloof, walked away and did not look back. He had to pay $40 to have his watch repaired. A costly street encounter. The games of affluent space-age children, I told a group of supposedly hip hustlers recently. They suggested that I'd make a great panhandler. But panhandling doesn't interest me, just as playing tennis or owning a string of polo ponies doesn't interest me.

except that there is a Lapp tribe in Karasjok. I have a crazy idea that Norway is like California's Orange County. In fact, the vodka just informed me that Norway is exactly like California's Orange County. So conservative that the barks of trees are covered with burlap bags. A country that produced Knut Hamsun, the novelist, and Henrik Ibsen, the playwright, has to be uptight.

The Norwegian sardines have a key opener, which means that I do not have to use my dime-store can opener. Except that I do have to use my opener. The key opener breaks under my muscle-man pressure. I even have difficulty using my own, the tin being soft, so soft that a child could bend it.

I try to make a long cut here and there. Finally, take the stem of my opener and pry the goddamn thing open. Mon Dieu! The tin is smaller than the average bar of soap. But what do you expect for twenty-five cents?

The smoked sardines are a perfect complement for the vodka. But I'm thinking about the cost of labor, the men or women who fished the sardines out of the sea, the people who packed them, the profits of the Norwegian businessman and the American importer and the Chinese owners of the store where I bought them, and how kind and smiling they are as if I were a new billionaire and had walked into their Knoedler's or Christie's or Parke-Bernet's and said, "Gimme twenty million dollars' worth of art."

Let me lay it on the line: I think progress is simply grand. The chilled vodka agrees. I believe in free enterprise, and hate indifference, cheap products, cheap people, careless people. Two nights ago at Numero Uno, the Pont Royale caterers, the steward, the pantry man forgot the parsley garnish for the prosciutto and melon. With the poise of third-rate comedians, the red-and-green-coated waiters wheeled the carts of prosciutto and melon into the main dining room, for the reception was breaking. Cursing like a nut-ward chorus, they returned to the kitchen with the carts. Dishwashers, bus boys, cooks frantically jerked plastic bags off the parsley, untied strings, snapped stems.

"The parsley hasn't been washed," I said, looking at my wet, dirty hands.

"The parsley hasn't been washed," I protested in a loud voice.

No one answered me. I became frightened and felt like a character in a Kafka novel. Dishwashers, bus boys, cooks, waiters, the

I looked back and ducked in time. A white port-wine bottle zipped through the air, landed at the base of a young tree, where pushers dropped their three-dollar bags of scrambled eggs.

Children are great. Our future. Children are great. Charming little buggers. Especially at midnight. Always midnight. Especially if they are prekindergarten age. Especially if their parents aren't around.

Charles Wright was born in New York City and not New Franklin, Missouri. Charles Wright grew up in the ghetto, joined a gang, which staked out a piece of the turf and took possession of it. A cold Walter Mitty dream? But what takes place in the following dream? No doubt street money and politics would have been involved. A sharp pimp, pusher, addict? There is no doubt in my mind that I would have served time. Perhaps I'd be writing my lawyer, family, friends, asking for books, candy, and cigarettes—instead of writing an entry into a journal.

MOTHERS: California ain't Mississippi. New York ain't Georgia. All offer the same old racial climate. You do not have to go to the heartland of America—say, the Middle West—to take the pollen count of pro-George Wallace sentiments. Simply open the door that fronts on your own back yard. The death of George Jackson, one of the Soledad Brothers, made me realize that the Auschwitz gates are not closed. They are not awaiting instructions from their superiors. They are waiting to act on their own. Who will be next? Angela Davis? You, me? In Manhattan each day, blacks and Puerto Ricans are roughed up daily before they see a judge or jury. It happens every day to the little people from the urban jungle. Seldom do we hear or read about it.

Sometimes these happenings have the deceptive innocence of childhood, have absolutely nothing to do with drugs, mugging, or even disturbing the peace. It can be nothing more than a handwritten note: "Come for a drink around six. My aunt is coming down and there will be a few other people. Perhaps we'll have dinner. Anyway, please come. They want to meet you." Because I felt guilty for not calling friends, for accepting invitations and never showing, I went to the dinner party, wearing my best suit of depression. Before the hostess offered a drink, she invited me into the kitchen. "I'm so glad you could come. Randy's in the bed-

[illegible] couple [illegible] the be[illegible] [illegible] street, [illegible]

[illegible] has a [illegible] highest [illegible] before [illegible] spot [illegible]

[illegible] Randy [illegible]

[illegible] who [illegible]

"What's wrong with him?" a cop asked.

"Nothing," I said. "He's stoned."

"Who hit him?"

"I did. He took a swing at me, and I hit him with a can of beer."

"A full can of beer?"

"Half full."

The policeman searched me, but I was clean as a whistle. And if I never, never had seen hatred before, I saw it in their eyes. Need I tell you, Randy is white and I am black.

The policemen went over to Randy. "Are you all right?" one of them asked.

Randy mumbled. I laughed at the absurdity of it all and was led toward a building with a nightstick in my back. The cop questioned Randy. He continued to mumble.

"Can't you see he's stoned?" I asked. "There's nothing wrong with him but his head. His old lady left him, and his mother moved and told the neighbors not to give him her new address."

The nightstick-lover of a policeman said, "If you don't shut up, I'm gonna beat you."

Just then a squad car pulled up to the curb. One of the street policemen went to the squad car. The two smiling men in the car had arrested Randy the night before; he had tried to attack a bum with a broken wine bottle. Then they drove off. The cop asked Randy if he wanted to press charges against me. Randy shook his head. The nightstick-loving cop was really angry now. He swung the stick like a demented drum majorette.

The four of us stood on the street corner silently for more than twenty minutes. Apparently the two policemen did not like the end of the happening. Finally, one of them came over to me. Pointing his nightstick down Grand Street, he said, "See those two guys coming this way? One of them has on a red shirt. I want you to start walking in that direction, and don't look back. I don't want to see you in this neighborhood again. I'll lock your ass up."

I walked away, inhaling the absurd Saturday-night air. Later that night, I saw Randy.

"Charles," he said, "I'm sorry. I need help."

I nodded but did not say anything. Mentally I was saying, Come on, feet. Let's make it.

\* \* \*

SEVENTH AVENUE, NORTH of Forty-second Street. Traffic flowing downtown. The streets are uncrowded at this hour. But the old gray buildings and the old shops with their face-lifted fronts are a staunch reminder of the materialistic present—the present of New Yorkers, Ltd. Three Japanese tourists photographed a florist shop, but I looked away and walked toward the Hotel Passover.

The first person I saw in the hotel was Abe Singer, a widowed accountant. He had his fifth-floor door open. An airline bag and camera case were on the bed. Seventy-year-old Abe Singer was in his underwear, drinking a water glass of bourbon as I passed.

"Jamaica, this time," he said, then added, still beaming, "I'm sorry."

The South Carolina maid was a large woman. She looked like an enormous lamp shade in her jungle-print cotton dress. She wore felt houseshoes and always complained of being cold. Age forty, the maid walked beside me, sighing.

"The poor thing," she said. "Sally wouldn't hurt a flea. The police were here, son. Don't touch a thing."

Sally Reinaldo's room was immaculate. A headless Hollywood bed, covered in dark blue satin, was the hub of the room. The turquoise walls were as bare as the gleaming wood floor, except for three white fur rugs. Silver-framed photographs of family and friends formed a semicircle on a round table by the bed. But I did

Handy Writer's Colony in Marshall, Illinois. Sally made the Las Vegas–Hollywood *la ronde*. It was rumored that she was making $100 a day in Hollywood. No one knew why she returned to New York. No one would ever know. Sally Reinaldo committed suicide on the fifth floor of the Hotel Passover.

I walked all the way back downtown, oblivious to the teeming, early-afternoon streets. Grief, loneliness, self-pity never touched me during the long walk. I simply felt that I had lost something. I opened the door of my hotel room, turned on the radio, drank a beer, showered, and took a sleeping pill. But I couldn't sleep. So I whipped the memory of Sally Reinaldo, who danced a little, sang a little, modeled a little, whored a little, and who wanted to become a star or a housewife, into an olive-green towel and threw it across the room.

Stoned, walking through the early-morning streets, clutching a tumbler of despair. The bars closing. Gradually people appear in the early-morning streets, unsteady in their walk, uncertain of which way to go, what to do. The full white moon, stationary, like a manmade object flung into space, like a flag announcing, "We have arrived. We have set foot on the floor of your dead planet."

And it seemed to me that the street people were tourists on that dead planet. Against their will, they had detoured from the route of dreams. Frightening, oblique—loneliness became the fellow traveler. But there was nothing I could do about it. I felt that I had left part of my insides in Sally Reinaldo's fifth-floor room at the Hotel Passover. I considered myself extremely lucky. A practical man, I gave up Waterloo and concentrated on exile. New York. Hades-on-the-Hudson. It is time to take leave of it. But for the moment, I am comforted with nothing but the prospect of another sunrise, buried in my own mortality.

On the Bowery, bells do not toll. But cocks crow at the Shangwood Live Poultry Market, and sincere hymns blare from the two Bowery Salvation Army havens, pleading with the classless, transient army of men to come unto God. And it seems to me that they should try Him or seriously think about hitting the road. Urban renewal is upon them. A broom is all that is needed for these powerless, nonpolitical men. (Most of them believe they are part of the

[illegible] tical sp [illegible] ...ated [illegible] wine [illegible]
[illegible] never [illegible] g [illegible] of t [illegible] e [illegible]
[illegible] been [illegible] w [illegible] ye [illegible]
The Bo [illegible] ch [illegible] a very [illegible]
nothi [illegible] th [illegible] . Thr [illegible]
dents w [illegible] e [illegible] om- f [illegible]
e. The [illegible] calle [illegible] One [illegible]
Second [illegible] ve [illegible] th [illegible] go [illegible]
's [illegible] tr [illegible] from [illegible]
ce bar [illegible] wh [illegible] old-time [illegible]
early d [illegible] , [illegible] cott [illegible]
" and [illegible] d [illegible] , " [illegible] still [illegible]
e Mar [illegible] re [illegible] fo [illegible] laced [illegible]
, whic [illegible] The [illegible] going [illegible]
Clover, [illegible] D [illegible] Bu [illegible] red [illegible]
mmy's [illegible] v [illegible] es, a [illegible]
rs. It w [illegible] like [illegible] Horse [illegible]
n's an [illegible] a [illegible] C [illegible] y [illegible]
owliv [illegible] c [illegible] on [illegible] . The [illegible]
wa [illegible] orse [illegible] B [illegible] 's pl [illegible]
zing an [illegible] r [illegible] . [illegible] col [illegible]
nt chil [illegible] mus [illegible]
xpens [illegible] c [illegible] s, [illegible] co [illegible]
930s [illegible] o [illegible] gar [illegible]
They a [illegible] s [illegible] ca [illegible] the [illegible]
the bu [illegible] r [illegible] ce. [illegible] the [illegible]
ethen [illegible] A [illegible] b [illegible] is [illegible]
ou ab [illegible] t [illegible] ys [illegible] t an [illegible]
ll the [illegible] s [illegible] ea [illegible] and [illegible]
. The [illegible] it [illegible]
on Ea [illegible] "h [illegible] s, [illegible] ough [illegible]
is ca [illegible] "t [illegible] ." [illegible]
ne al [illegible] o [illegible] Th [illegible] wh [illegible]
y hot [illegible] h [illegible] ece [illegible]
xo [illegible] ne [illegible] -in, [illegible]
the an [illegible] M [illegible] mr [illegible] file [illegible]
gro [illegible] f [illegible] , ge [illegible] we [illegible]
. The [illegible] n [illegible] ever [illegible] ual [illegible]
the [illegible] are [illegible] a clo [illegible]

Especially with young blacks and Puerto Ricans. Indeed, Eugene O'Neill's Iceman would come down to the Bowery looking for a fix.

Like New York night life, business is off in the bars, although men are sitting at the tables before the official 8 A.M. opening. But they sit all day, trying to hustle drinks like pitiful old whores, like shameless clowns.

Sitting and waiting for the silent mushroom in the sky, watching the desperate jackrollers, who in turn are watching them. Money is tight. A daytime robbery is a common happening. Most of the older men try to make it back to the hotels before darkness sets in or go in pairs, groups.

There are no black bars on the Bowery. The blacks prefer to drink on street corners, which is cheaper. There are hotels that will not rent rooms to blacks, and there are hotels which have separate but equal floors for blacks and whites, although both use the same bathrooms. The wine climate of the Bowery has always been racial. This has not changed. The majority of these weak drinking men come from the primeval American South. Wine has not shrunk their racial war; it has enlarged it to the point of fanaticism. Ethnic to the last pint of La Boheme white port (the most popular brand), the mix is roughly Irish and blacks running neck and neck, followed by Poles. There are few Italians, Jews, Chinese. But keeping pace with the national cultural explosion, increasing numbers of young men are nestling in the ruins. Most of them are very hip, according to the old-timer's social register.

The story goes that the police are tougher on white winos than on blacks. Whites are superior and shouldn't sink to that dark level. But it is only the old black men who retain the hairs of *machismo*. Before sunrise, black and white men are in the streets, walking up and down like women on market day, like desperate junkies. At that hour they are waiting for the early-morning "doctors," peddling illegal wine. Illegal wine is now $1.25 a pint. Yet the men who sleep in their own urine on the sidewalk and wipe car windows with dirty rags manage to pay the "doctor," just as more affluent Americans manage to have charge accounts.

For these Bowery men are American, too, with that great American dream. Tomorrow we will seek a new design for living, new territories, which is why the Bowery has expanded into little

about thirty feet where the Bowery and Canal meet to channel traffic to Brooklyn and elsewhere. Motorists consider it an unexpected, delightful slice-of-life landscape. Soon it will become a mini-tourist attraction.

Recently, a group of young black, white, Puerto Rican, and Chinese artists set up shop between the hours of eleven and three, painting pop designs on all surfaces except dirt and grass. Against the weathered gray of concrete, black silhouettes. A prisoner hanging from his cell. Two Afro heads in a heavy chess game. And from the old world, stencil designs of Chinese dragons. Although I applaud their slow, sincere efforts, this is of no value to me. All I know is my garden has been invaded by people who represent the blowup of New York. People arrive, perform, depart. Countless variations on an urban theme. These people make police reports, signal, Bellevue, Kings County, pay the bread man of drugs. These people confront policemen, merge with the winos and the gold-bricking Department of Parks workers, the artistic elite from the neighboring lofts and the Chinese immigrants, who instantly, magically, accept the American middle-class outer garment. You see, I am the senior citizen of the garden. Six years, day and night, summer and winter—I have sat on that stone ledge, surrounded by thirty-nine trees, watching people arrive like ghosts in a real dream.

Except for the long stone ledges, there is nothing. The playground equipment has been removed. The toilets have been sealed for eternity in concrete. All that remains are the ledges, trees, and elegant lampposts. Most of the time, only a few lamps are lit. The other night, four teenage boys marched through the garden and surveyed the scene. Then three of the boys ran out of the garden. The fourth boy returned. He walked through the garden like a Midwestern basketball star before a county championship. But his turf was urban. Stone under those imitation French cycling shoes. His hand was steady as he shot out all the lights. And in the semi-darkness the boy looked over at me and smiled. I saluted him. Hadn't I reported him to the police (at their request) before? Once, surrounded by a gang, I cleverly signaled to a policeman. He knew that the boys were throwing bottles and rocks into the street, had hit a woman with a baby and had broken the window of a Ford station wagon.

Center rise above history, as if to embrace the sky. In Chatham Square, chained to a young tree, three metal chairs proclaim JESUS SAVES.

But there are eighteen broken parking meters in my garden, like the end of a rip-off happening of abstract sculpture. Drug addicts, functioning as human jack-hammers, carried them up from the streets between midnight and dawn. I arrived at 6 A.M. with coffee, the Sunday *New York Times,* and thought: Where are the police, the concerned citizens? Indifference might have a past. Am I right in assuming that it has a future?

Of late, small armies of policemen (usually Chinese, with a couple of novice Wasp detectives) march through my garden on a groping, fascist search. But there is no one except me, two young lovers, and the winos. Open, open! There is no place to hide. Frequently, New York's finest question me, their hands roughly moving from the top of my head to my feet. Then, apparently unsatisfied, they flash their brilliant flashlights in my face. This does nothing for them. So they turn the flashlights up into the thirty-nine trees. And as they walk toward the Bayard Street exit, I ask if I can help them. Their voices, like their eyes, are elsewhere. You see, New York's finest say they are simply on a routine patrol, which is a goddamn lie. I am the senior citizen of the Chinese Garden, the resident historian, the wild-grass accountant. I also do extra duty outside of the garden. Within a ten-block radius of the garden, I am familiar with crime and corruption. Therefore, I hope no one will be foolish enough to think the rise in crime has anything to do with the police's presence in my garden.

The sentry knows who patrols the desecrated island of concrete and trees. Just the other day, a daring group of British tourists marched into the garden. The excitement of discovery seemed to color their voices and eyes. A Byzantine ruin, or a secret Persian Garden? Here, marijuana, wine, baseball outrank young love and volleyball. Here, the sons of Chinese immigrants are becoming skilled American baseball players. Dressed in red, the Free Mason volleyball team plays an excellent game, lacking only American competitive drive. Their game is passive, as if volleyball were programmed and, chop—a programmed karate class, still working out at a quarter of nine in the evening.

her a question. Her young daughter was fine. But mothers and fathers were out this year, she said.

"The cat," she exclaimed, offering me a drink from a Hiram Walker pint. "You remember. Well, I've got good news for you. He came back to life, and I'm so happy."

Was there a time when a once dead, now live cat, or a child with a balloon, would have startled me in the Chinese Garden? Yes, there was a time. It was during the early stage of the Great Society.

rated with white flowers in her right hand. A perfect Fellini whore, she moved through the tall grass toward a large tree about fifteen feet from where I sat. The man, who had his hands in his pockets, followed at a fast pace.

Still clutching the white bag, gloves, umbrella, Miss Nell went through the ritual of going down on the man. She worked very hard. She worked with great feeling. She worked like a professional. Miss Nell worked for a very long time. Now and then, she'd look up at the man, and you could almost read her mind. Finally, she stood up, lifted her skirt, and offered her buttocks. This did not help the man, who was now working very hard. Miss Nell decided to try the door of life. Still clutching the bag, umbrella, gloves, she put her large arms around the man. She might have been a mother comforting a small child. But Miss Nell and the man moved with great passion. He was very relaxed and even smiled. He did not reach a climax.

Exhausted, Miss Nell led the man over to the ledge where I was sitting. The man smiled and joked. Miss Nell was angry. She looked down at me, opened the clear plastic umbrella with the pretty white flowers on it, and tried to block my view. It was like trying to cover the Empire State Building with a single bed sheet.

Once more the hard-working professional went down on her customer. And I thought they would make it this time. But Miss Nell jumped up and screamed, "My God! What's wrong with you? I ain't got all night. I've got to take care of business."

The man was still smiling and asked for a two dollar refund.

Miss Nell snapped open her white handbag and said, "With pleasure." Then she walked out of the garden swiftly, her head down like an unhappy queen. The man followed at a distance.

Then the young lovers, who are almost nightly visitors, rose and walked out of the Chinese Garden, the small auburn dog running ahead of them, his metal leash hitting the pavement dully, sounding as I imagined Miss Nell would sound with a very bad cold.

*A profound statement from a country-club divorcée, age forty-two. A former secretary, the divorcée had also worked in advertising and public relations. It was almost midnight, and the tranquilizers and Scotch had failed to extinguish the lady's anger: "Hell. People think alimony is easy. I worked sixteen years for that*

had his arms around two of his girls, and all of them were smiling, and they might have been rehearsing for a 1980 television commercial.

"Would you whore?" I asked a young actress who had worked briefly at a whore bar.

"No."

"Why?"

"No moral reason. I just wouldn't enjoy the work." But like most women, the actress found the whore-pimp scene fascinating. "I can understand how straight women fall for it. Especially emotionally insecure women. The rap is beautiful. Reassuring. If straight men used the rap of a pimp, male and female relations would improve."

"Would you make me whore?" Kitty asked.

The words jammed against my Protestant shelter. But my male ego tripped. Kitty would whore for me. She would do anything for me. All in the name of love.

"If it were profitable for both of us." I laughed and took her to bed. Our relationship was warm, uncomplicated. We never mentioned whoring again. But a month later, Kitty told me that she had a dinner date at the Waldorf Astoria (Count Basie had just opened). The following afternoon, Kitty gave me $50 to buy food. She was an excellent cook. Mentally, the dinner that night lacked flavor. Of course, I could have got stoned, beat up on Kitty, and put her down or rapped about the fabulous Waldorf, then changed gears and, ever so sincere, rapped about a poor, uptight writer who loved her. That's it: there's nothing else to know. Kitty was an occasional whore, and it brought her little joy, although I believe she enjoyed it in a subconscious sense: it was degrading.

Last year, a twenty-year-old addict asked me if I would take money from her. I needed money, and she wanted to help me. I was for real. Hadn't I from the very beginning respected her? I had never put her down, *made her feel like dirt.*

There are a variety of trees in the prostitution forest. My friend's wife doesn't enjoy oral sex, but tries to go along with the program. My friend, the father of two children, loves his wife. They have been married for eight years. A mistress would definitely complicate their relationship. The husband, father, lover, friend has whores orally.

THE EAST VILLAGE worms its way through a Ponce de León garden of drugs. But flowers dry, die. In the sun, in a musical cigarette box on a glass-top coffee table, in an oven, and, fenced in a newspaper blanket (limp as pizza dough), on a radiator. A *Reader's Digest* of scents, offering the fresh air of peace of mind or a hallucinating high.

Journeying into the interior of Welfare-Drugsville, where the last of the flowers were in the final stage of exile, I remember the sparse summer trees seemed unreal: models for Madame Tussaud's wax museum. In a ten-block area I encountered no police. The streets were monitored by junkies, thieves, pushers, a new breed of whores who sipped iced Cokes and coffee in the heat of afternoon. Domesticated hippies walked Doberman pinschers, German shepherds, or fashionable mongrels, while black and Puerto Rican teenagers, natives of "East Village" (the Lower East Side), motherfuck each other with words. The ancient tenements are monuments to the splendor of welfare. The poor, the uneducated are powerless against the government's yearly rape. Even whores get tired. Model tenements in Utopia! In lieu of flowers, garbage litters the pavement. Car arson is a big sport in the East Village (two cars in three days on East Eleventh Street between Avenues B and C). The fire department and police daily offer their services.

Social workers, VISTA (*vision*) workers, the Church offer ser-

[illegible] d [illegible] ing [illegible] T [illegible] a [illegible] o laugh [illegible] fi [illegible]
[illegible] still [illegible] Horn [illegible] la [illegible]
[illegible] the [illegible] w [illegible] ;bean [illegible]
[illegible] for two [illegible]
[illegible] st [illegible] gs [illegible] ll of the [illegible] p [illegible]
[illegible] na [illegible] u find [illegible]
[illegible] fr [illegible] th [illegible] et. The [illegible] C [illegible]
[illegible] a [illegible] blonde [illegible]
[illegible] sed, the [illegible]
[illegible] th [illegible] w [illegible] d to sell [illegible]
[illegible] T [illegible] y scenes [illegible]
[illegible] ves [illegible] n [illegible] y file [illegible]
[illegible] T [illegible] blue-e [illegible]
[illegible] S [illegible] t wait [illegible]
[illegible] was [illegible]
[illegible] to [illegible] e [illegible] somet [illegible] g [illegible]
[illegible] a [illegible] stim [illegible] uptown [illegible] u [illegible]
[illegible] the [illegible]
[illegible] e [illegible] th [illegible] d [illegible] ashed [illegible] sh [illegible]
[illegible] app [illegible] h [illegible] n subur [illegible] a [illegible]
[illegible] co [illegible] g men [illegible] e [illegible]
[illegible] c [illegible] l watch [illegible]
[illegible] g [illegible] ba [illegible] then [illegible] c [illegible]
[illegible] uter [illegible] c [illegible] ne mo [illegible] t [illegible]
[illegible] n [illegible] ns [illegible] ti [illegible]
[illegible] n [illegible] an [illegible] o [illegible] aid. "[illegible]
[illegible] T [illegible] p [illegible] s [illegible] tton wh [illegible] n [illegible]
[illegible] Ju [illegible] ef [illegible] urned [illegible] e [illegible]
[illegible] "[illegible] rea [illegible] o [illegible] get a pi [illegible].
[illegible] t [illegible] lw [illegible] sa [illegible]
[illegible] a [illegible] mo [illegible] A [illegible] B. "W [illegible] e [illegible]
[illegible] "You [illegible] ol [illegible] looking [illegible] r [illegible]
[illegible] n [illegible] of [illegible] s [illegible] alls to [illegible]
[illegible] b [illegible] my [illegible] l [illegible] ."
[illegible] care [illegible] s old wa [illegible]
[illegible] e [illegible] them [illegible] b [illegible] bout b [illegible] n [illegible]
[illegible] d [illegible] wa [illegible] g [illegible]
[illegible] hat [illegible] e [illegible]
[illegible] aug [illegible] l [illegible] ed [illegible] walking [illegible] k [illegible]

ambitious executive. At least the last of the flower children were interested in the pollen count. Anything goes! The New World's sexuality! Lord, sometimes I ask myself, Are they for real, are they free? Rimming, once a whispered desire of sexual swingers, is slowly surfacing from down under. And it seems somehow appropriate to mention human excrement and cannibalism as mankind prepares not to scale the summits but to take the downward path into the great valley of the void.

Thoughts pinballed through my mind; the questionnaire was almost blank, and I stopped off at Sam's; he lives in one of those medieval wrecks. The last of the communal flowers were limp in front of the building. They sat on the stoop, played guitars, sang on fire escapes, and got high on stairwells, seemingly placed there by a landscape architect, schooled in James Joyce's Nighttown.

Miss Ohio manned the second floor. Glowing with warmth, she had just returned from visiting her parents and giggled about her new silver-buckled shoes. Miss Ohio had been on the scene for almost a year. Nothing bad had happened to her—yet. Occasionally she gets high, talks about being "hung-up" on some "cat," spends most of her time with the neighborhood children. She seems so out of place in the East Village. She belongs to the world of babies, chintz-flowered bedrooms, country kitchens.

On the third floor, I had to step over a group of stoned children. Sam was talking with—let's call him Jerry. Sam works in Jerry's uncle's midtown office. We sat around listening to records, getting high. Then the white chick from upstairs arrived. She's got a Jones, a thing for black dudes. A hefty girl with a ban-the-bomb air. Her old man had split, and she wanted Sam to help her find him. "The bastard is probably in Washington Square because he knows I don't hang out there."

Meanwhile, long-haired Jerry had placed his booted feet on the lower shelf of the coffee table, his elbows rigid on his knees.

"I don't wanna cry," he whimpered. But he made no effort to check the tears. "I can't stand it. Last summer I was flipping out. Speed and every goddamn thing. Paranoid as a son of a bitch, and one night these punk kids tried to jump me. They were high, too. On pot and wine. I wasn't trying to cop a plea. I just didn't wanna fight. I started to run, and one of them comes after me. I gave him

against the babbling voices around me. I would play "Hey Jude" and "Revolution," knock down vodka, and make it. Sitting at my customary station at the bar, turned toward the street, I watched a chic *Harper's Bazaar* type of girl saunter in. She was Lady Brett Ashley, stoned on salvation.

"You weak bastards," she shouted. "Get back into the mainstream of life!"

The jukebox swung with "Can I Change My Mind and Start All Over Again?" The Bennington girl, masquerading as Lady Brett, wanted to dance. A real nigger type, carried away by the promise of the moment, asked me for a cigarette. "If you can't make it without a smoke, you're nowhere," I told him.

Meanwhile, the sotted sister threw her handbag on the bar and winked at me. A game, a happening, no matter, no matter. I knew her kind and gave her my Rover Boy smile. Lady Brett began dancing alone. A parody of a sensual grind. Surrounded by stoned but reserved men, she had for the moment forgotten her mission of soul saving. But the bartender, followed by his henchmen, threw Our Lady of the Bowery, kin of Hemingway and *Harper's Bazaar,* out the door. No one followed the lady's exit.

A dark, port-wine-drinking young man came up to the bar. Despite the warm night, he carried a leather jacket and had on black bell-bottoms, black T-shirt, and Swiss-hi shoes (in other words construction-worker high tops. Laces of tan leather, Dupont neoprene crepe soles. These shoes are extremely popular for comfort and durability, and offer the weight of a coffee cup's illusion of masculinity. In fact, knowledgeable people call them "fruit boots").

"Wanna smoke from a dead man?" Leather Jacket asked, offering a hand-rolled cigarette.

I accepted and discovered a man had died in the bar earlier. Men are always passing out, sleeping on the tables and floor, and the dead man was, well—on the floor. All Leather Jacket knew was that the cops went through the man's pockets, searching for identification. They laughed and joked with the regulars. A cop had given Leather Jacket the dead man's tobacco and cigarette papers.

Leather Jacket ordered two dark ports, before confession. Once again, I am working on my sainthood: I listen. A Catholic, [illegible] analy[illegible] [illegible] cross o[illegible] [illegible] that [illegible] the [illegible] fa[illegible] [illegible] the [illegible] question [illegible] him. [illegible] pur[illegible] [illegible] do[illegible] [illegible] learned [illegible] ask que[illegible] [illegible] he cou[illegible]

[illegible] look [illegible]

[illegible] she's [illegible] look [illegible] gled ou[illegible] [illegible] I sa[illegible] [illegible] his p[illegible] [illegible] king [illegible] bo[illegible] [illegible] think [illegible] three [illegible] sh[illegible] [illegible] M[illegible] [illegible] lack [illegible] [illegible] eve[illegible] [illegible] in[illegible] [illegible] fo[illegible] [illegible] ta[illegible] [illegible] class [illegible] fa[illegible] [illegible] [illegible]

"You're a smart son of a bitch. You got the whole fucking scene figured out."

"I'm not putting you down," I said. "But I've heard the story before."

Leather Jacket's brain was at the bottom of the wine barrel. "I'm all fucked up," he said, breathing hard. "I get so goddamned tired and lonely, and it's not all sex, you know. Hell. I could have almost any broad I want, and you know about the queens."

I understood, thinking: Jesus. I hope he doesn't start the waterworks. Leather Jacket was more honest than most twenty-five-year-olds from his prison. I remembered a Spanish queen who lived nearby. Her old man had left for P.R. The queen was alone and lonely. Perhaps Leather Jacket and the Spanish queen could, at least for the night, quench their loneliness. As we departed, I wondered where was my saintly halo, my recluse's cabin by the sea.

Coco gave Leather Jacket her Park Avenue welcome. We went into the living room. All the major pieces of furniture were covered in custom plastic, including the fluffy 9-by-12 white cotton rug. The art objects were holy: gilt madonnas with rosebud halos. Jesus Christ was everywhere. Plastic, coppertone, brass plate, plaster of Paris. The room was heady with orange blossom refresher. Large votive candles created a mood appropriate for a wake, séance, or Mass. Coco and Leather Jacket made small talk while I looked over the record collection. Already, I could sense they would work something out and that it would go well for them. I put on an LP, smoked a joint, very happy about the whole scene. Then Pepe, the ex-husband, lumbered in from the bedroom, yawning. He greeted me warmly and shook hands with Leather Jacket, and I knew that they would be enemies.

But Coco was in his glory. An amused queen enthroned in a red Easy Boy lounge chair. Pepe showed me the long knife he had bought on Forty-second Street. Leather Jacket was an excellent knife thrower. Coco cooed and teased. Pepe and Leather Jacket fought for his favors. Then Coco invited me into his neat little kitchen. He thanked me, and I inhaled Avon's Fandango perfume.

"Forget it, doll."

"He came back and I took him back, but I'll show him tonight."

The night danced on and on. We got higher. Pepe and Leather

FLASH! A CHICAGO POLL reports that segregation is flowering magnificently in America. Oh my God . . . interesting. Is John Wayne aware of the result of the Chicago poll? Once upon a time, John Wayne let Sammy Davis, Jr., wear that legendary hat in a Rat Pack western. John Wayne has given blacks two roles in films he has directed. One black was perfect for his role: he portrayed a slave. But American blacks are not responsible, according to Wayne. It was not surprising for him to announce in a May *Playboy* interview: "I believe in white supremacy."

Once upon a time, playing cowboy in an old wrecked house, imitating John Wayne, a nail zipped into my lower lip. I still have the memento today. But I want to tell you about Newport Beach, two years ago. Albert Pearl, my friend and tourist guide, pointed his finger in the direction of a palm-shrouded hill and said, "John Wayne lives over there." June Allyson also lives in Newport, I was told time and time again. I remembered her smile, husky intoxicating voice, the childhood MGM movies. But now I am a man; I know what kind of woman June Allyson is. Breathing the dry, clear air of Orange County, I always detected the scent of the far right. The only way I can describe the scent is to say: Inhale ether, or imagine facing a double-barreled shotgun ten feet from where you are presently standing or sitting.

Uncomfortable looking at the sterile, pretty pastel houses, the

matter, no matter! The Forest Hills protest is a Forest Lawn monument to American racism. Would the good people of Forest Hills protest if five hundred of their own kind, five hundred of their black counterparts moved in, early one summer morning?

We'll shift scenes here. On the Bowery, the ex-blue-collar workers rage in their drunken or dry leather voices about the mugging blacks, welfare, and what they have done for this country, rage about the lack of police protection. Clean-cut, always with a demitasse of coins, and chain-smoking—their eyes are a seismograph of hate. Is it because of my money, clothes, cigarettes, my deceptive youthful aura, or my blackness? One or all?

Last night I visited an old friend, James Anthony Peoples, who lives just below the frontier of Harlem on Central Park West. We had been out of touch for a long time. Now it was midnight, and the goodies had vanished. There was nothing to do but get a six-pack of beer. I crossed 110th Street and Central Park West and thought: Is it any wonder blacks and whites are walking out on the black Broadway musical *Ain't Supposed to Die a Natural Death?* Eighth Avenue beyond 110th Street is a living death. The rat-infested tenements remain. Neon-lit bars are gripped with fear. Was I the Man, a new pusher, a new junkie? One bar locked its door because none of the patrons recognized me. There were subway junkies on both sides of the street. Desperation in their eyes, they resembled black ghosts. Dachau survivors. Wearing colorless rags, they were not junkie cool. They were in the caboose of the junkie train. These men and women did not cop and hock stereos, color televisions. Watching their desperate street bits, my heart broke. Life had ended for them. *But not for the people who had created them.*

I finally copped a six-pack in a superette on 115th Street. It was now almost two in the morning. The superette jammed with bobbing, bad-mouthed teenagers. Vibrancy exploded from them like fireworks. But did they realize that life had already ended for many of them? You can destroy the future's futile dream, your own frustration, your helplessness with drugs, acts of violence.

Stunned, angry, returned to Peoples' apartment and casually asked, "Did Frankenstein's monster kill his master?" Peoples said yes, and I said, Yes, oh my God, yes! What a nice ending for a story.

became my epaulets. I considered America, the majority of people I encountered, dung mannequins wearing masks.

Harold and his wife, Lee, were unmasked. Harold and I had coffee and apple pie; then I went back to Madame Sophie's. At four that afternoon, ten men for "dish" (two Chinese students from Hong Kong), the race-track-addict chauffeur piled into a station wagon and drove to the celebrated Le Mansion in New Jersey. It's a mother of a place, a bad marriage between Greek Revival and New England colonial. Exquisite banquet rooms accommodate between twenty-five and three thousand people. And, ducks—total confusion. Parties breaking, parties beginning. Guests entering wrong reception rooms. They wore expensive clothes but lacked style. I suppose in their frantic race up the money-and-social ladder, they had forgotten good manners. Waiters, waitresses (the crudity of the waitresses is astonishing, especially a woman who looks like an apple-pie grandmother); the kitchen staff kissed, joked, and drank. "You ruddy-face old bastard. I'm gonna tell my husband!" Other crews arrived, then the young rabbi and *masgiach*.

The hired help ate in the gentile staff kitchen. I had chicken noodle soup and Dr. Brown's root beer, thinking, At least they feed you before the work shift begins—promising.

I don't remember the exact moment when things went bad. Our boss, Mary Louise, a plump vichyssoise black woman appeared, real, motherly. Her second, Uncle Tom's Shadow, was a dapper Dan, harmless. Our dish crew knocked out the previous party's dishes in no time. We were knighted with a cleanup detail in the Belmont Room, which was divided into two parts by a red satin curtain. Tables (set up for a wedding supper) were pushed against the wall of section I. The reception in section 2 was ending. But most of the guests did not want to leave. "Ladies and gentlemen," the band leader implored, "you are invited to attend the wedding ceremony." The well-dressed guests clamored for hors d'oeuvres, liquor. Waiters, waitresses appeared to be indifferent; they were partying too. A Puerto Rican of African ancestry said, "Everybody lapping up the booze but us. It's gonna be a long night, and I ain't got no grass. We'd better hit the whiskey sours. I know this place. It ain't no ball game."

The whiskey sours gave us courage to tote party paraphernalia

ends. Le Mansion had a reputation and even advertised in New York newspapers.) Then, a silence engulfed the kitchen. We continued working until 3 A.M. No overtime. The grumbling kitchen staff took over.

After dressing, we lined up for pay. They took out seventy-five cents for some nonexistent tax. A tip? Tips filter out before the dishwashers have washed the last dish. However, the host and hostess, who usually come into the kitchen after dinner, displaying benevolent smiles, are unaware of the theft.

We waited in the early-morning darkness for our chauffeur to arrive. The sun was up when we arrived in Manhattan.

...around the Valencia Hotel... overlooking St. Mark's Place... a
gathering of... chamber of-commerce... of... local... and... affluence) -
sally... roof... ... and glassware... paper too... are close in a
ugly... turbulent... thin... just... musicals... and *The Daily
Times*...

MEXICO SINCE MEXICO BY... BY...
FRAUD AND... FICIENCY

...her smell of my cigar, [la]... ed... at... she... ay eg. So i
... the... sitting in a comfort to... can ... a... the... club.?

...the investigations of the 9... 122 million... trag-gover y
...lan- ed claim chronic corrup... re... consists... that s...

...through... saint brandy,... in... 90.. I... ill... nav to... ne
...hat was many years go,'... n... ont... ued... d:

...'s... ac... na... u... ll ta e... ny... a... find... rw's ully... een go g
...i... e... in... .n. esource Ad... ta or, said a... u... em... as a s... t
...is... in at... mes...

...m... ea... wi... int ng... apor... o... an th... de. "T e Po... o
...ay... co d... wi... arts... d... ur... i... H.R.A. ... t... e -- ur... ti --
...he... ... r... n... s... omy!... Wc... l ... ojec s... l g... nc... rec... clean... to
...n... ig... il... ai... th strets, c...ng it... es... Pe on...

the poor. Three mini-vignettes of waste, money, time, inefficiency at a branch of H.R.A. are on the front lawn of my mind.

It's all there. Accounts in Swiss banks. A mysterious George José Mendoza Miller. An elderly man in a cubicle Wall Street office. The pulsating glamour of Las Vegas. Parked cars on a street in Los Angeles (straight out of a television detective series). A $52,000 check with Mary Tyler's private phone number on the back. Now, we'll switch to Amsterdam and it's not tulip time. H.R.A.'s money is so mobile—promiscuous dollars! Now, let's zoom in on the fabulous black "Durham Mob" from North Carolina. Out of sight! A rented car, the fuzz, and Forty-second Street.

Nina, a sensuous black divorcée, mother of three children, has appeared on the front lawn. She has an executive position at an antipoverty agency. Knowing of my financial hangup, she tried to secure a $ gig. I would write reports, Nina would school me. I had autographed copies of *The Messenger* and *The Wig* for her boss and went uptown on a fine, sunny morning.

"The switchboard service is lousy," I said, "and what are all those people doing in the lobby?"

Nina laughed. "Hustling, baby. Everybody wants a piece of Uncle Sam's money."

"But they're well dressed," I protested.

"I know. Only the poor suffer. Same old story."

"Enduring?"

"Yes," Nina agreed, then added: "Bad news, baby. Do you remember meeting a Mr. XX at a party on Riverside Drive?"

"Oh, him. I remember, and his pretentious old lady."

"He said you had a nasty mouth," Nina told me. "Bureaucrats don't like writers. The written word gets them uptight. All they know is numbers, percentages on charts."

"Now if only I was an out-of-work musician. A junkie or a jailbird," I fantasized. "Whitey and niggers dig them."

We laughed, saluted the gig good-bye. Nina sent out for coffee and doughnuts. While we waited, she talked about her program.

"Each time you come up with something that could help the poor, they veto it. I've been warned to cool it at meetings. Like the junkie program and the P.S. 201 thing."

The boy arrived with the coffee and doughnuts. Nina could

ographer and assistant director. Considering his experience, reputation, the lavish poverty giveaway, he was paid nothing—$100 a week. The teenagers were paid $45 a week to study voice and dance. Most of them were not interested in voice and dance. The boys and girls who were interested in voice and dance were in the Harlem tenements, the streets, sitting on stoops, standing on street corners. The boys and girls I saw at rehearsal had boogalooed under the wire with connections. I remember one girl, the color of hand-rubbed teakwood. Awkward, sullen, she knocked down $45 a week because one of the "big fish" was trying to make her.

Becham gave me the script to read. Only the author (the director and brother of the agency chief) could relate to the script. It was the type of musical MGM might have considered in 1886 and turned down.

"Can you believe we are opening next week?" Becham asked.

Another brandy, Nathanael West? Let's buy Eartha Kitt Calanthe harrissii orchids, jade, ropes of pearls. Let's listen to her rich, bitter laughter . . .

Before 'Mericans heard of Our Lady of Beautification, Lady Bird Johnson, and before all those black and white performers brought alms to poor blacks, Eartha Kitt, in the late '50s, had her own unpublicized antipoverty program at the Harlem Y.M.C.A. Miss Kitt's first love was dance, and she had been a member of the Katherine Dunham Dance Company. She sponsored the Eartha Kitt Dance foundation. Larl Becham taught the classes. Any black child could take free dance classes. You did not have to be a friend of a friend or have someone get sweaty hands, thinking about how you would be in bed with a couple of drinks, a little pot.

Revolting? I have an idea that one day black and white bureaucrats will succeed in eating Uncle Sam's beard, balls, navel, and the money itself.

Anyway, Birdie Greene, the maid, wants to clean my room, and I have to take the train to Philly, to the City of Brotherly Love.

Shot down in Manhattan, my mood was like F. Scott Fitzgerald's at Princeton. A lost writer in Philly, covering rock's elegant gypsies, Sly & The Family Stone. A taxi strike or what the hell? Popped a couple of pills, encountered the Doubtful Mushroom [illegible] Quaker [illegible] at last, [illegible] the S[illegible] [illegible] the [illegible] Now, [illegible] it was [illegible]

[illegible] managers [illegible] stopped [illegible] their bo[illegible] [illegible] these [illegible] don't [illegible] the [illegible] Clear[illegible] [illegible]

[illegible] their s[illegible] [illegible] the years [illegible] such [illegible] D[illegible] [illegible] seems [illegible] next to [illegible] the [illegible]

[illegible] swe[illegible] [illegible] stopped [illegible] competing [illegible] faces [illegible] Perhaps [illegible] blo[illegible] colla[illegible] [illegible] the [illegible] by the [illegible]

[illegible] a [illegible] [illegible] con[illegible] [illegible] probably [illegible] a pa[illegible] [illegible] flock [illegible] the pres[illegible] sincerity against her bosom like a contemporary Cleopatra with a humane asp.

Iron Butterfly gave a controlled performance. *Mucho* things working for them: a light show, fire, the drummer's hypnotic solo. Sly: a tough act to follow. One fact checked out: whatever followed had better offer more than peanut butter and jelly sandwiches and milk. The crowd's mood had changed. Let's-get-this-show-on-the-road! Little put-down remarks, peachy hands simulating megaphones. Twisting and turning in seats like the nursery-school set at a Saturday matinee. An orgy of fingernail biting. Two-fingered whistles. The gaiety of floating balloons cooled the action in my section.

Sly? I had watched the family arrive, single file. I caught a glimpse of Sly's father, little brother Sidney. Sly's aide-de-camp, loaded with cameras, directs the setup. Watching them drag out the electronic equipment, rock fans look bored. Young earthlings go on unorganized patrols. Then Sly & The Family Stone move through the semidarkness like secret agents boarding a ship at dawn. The spotlight doesn't hit Sly until he is at the edge of the revolving stage. Applause is polite. Guarded, as if the waiting, twenty little anticlimaxes had dried the applejack on the fans' hands.

Another delay. A cord, a connection, or some goddamn thing has been misplaced and the Family cannot perform without it. Two earthlings on my right look like the sons of prosperous farmers, but they have a good knowledge of rock. Resting their booted feet on the back of the chair in front of them, one says, "The fucking bastards are gonna take all night. Have you got the keys?"

The lost writer scans the lower arena. Primed with saliva, hoarded energy, they seem to rehearse sons-&-daughters-of-the-Lion's-Club retorts, handed down from generation to generation as the last heirloom in the American attic of—I am white and right and will not be kept waiting! Yes, a hard line separates this mood from that of a hard-drinking black crowd in an East St. Louis dive, or the silence of black balcony girls at the Apollo as blond Chris Connor comes onstage and scats, or the raunchy revolt of the Fillmore East audience. No, this unrest blew from the carved horns of legends, was removed from minds, lips by the second number. Sly & The Family Stone delivered. Through talent, a touch of sorcery,

hunts? A 21-gun salute to that fantastic broad, Miss Virginia Hill. Dorothy Parker, Ayn Rand, James Poe, and the smiling, talkative Elia Kazan. The cold, righteous years. General Eisenhower pirouetting into Korea that winter. We sawed open the wooden floors of our tents and hid the White Horse (white lightning) gin, were forced to march in the rain because our officers were afraid to let us relax in our tents, and our latrine slid down into a ravine when the ground thawed. Hysterical, stoned, bored, frightened, some of us shot holes in the roofs of our tents, tried to shoot bullets at the stars, shot heroin, sniffed cocaine, and went to the whorehouses with the zeal of aspiring politicians. Death had spared us; America was begetting a nation of zombies, or so we thought. "Back home," "back in the world," our countrymen had heads shaped exactly like golf balls. Years passed. I remember a brief moment of splendor and hope. Fail and enter the age of assassination. J.F.K., Malcolm X, R.F.K., Martin Luther King. Men and women protest, march.

They are still marching, according to *The Village Voice*. I'm losing my high and look at the *Voice* photographs: the pseudo-Nazi: upchuck pop art, and below it the chilling, precise portrait of the white-Right, advising: FIGHT THE JEWISH-RED ANARCHY! (Collegiate and apparently serious, the minted middle class are unaware of the Ronald Reagan South African waltz and as upright as backwoods Baptists.)

Next, a group photograph, notable for a girl resembling Susan Sontag. MP's frontlining. Ditto: Black MP's. An accident, or did the Pentagon believe uniformed blacks could cool the liberal white temper?

Norman Mailer with a part in his hair. Robert Lowell, Sidney Lens, Dwight MacDonald—a group photograph, intellectually heavy. The last photograph: another crowd scene with a banner reading: NEGOTIATE WITH THE NLF.

Smell the hot bacon grease; or are you waiting for it to congeal? Try a side order of cole slaw, dished out to the masses at a box supper. I had roast pork, rice, and beans with the neighbor's nine-year-old son. We clowned over wine and beer, then I chased the barefoot boy out into the street: we ended our cops-and-robbers game. On our block, real bullets ripped the air. The nine-year-old and I witnessed a Saturday-night double murder, a near riot.

[illegible] he, [illegible]
[illegible] ned [illegible]
[illegible] ew [illegible]
[illegible] day, Sunday. [illegible]
[illegible] in Brooklyn [illegible]
[illegible] the man wh [illegible]
[illegible] ing scen [illegible]
[illegible] What the [illegible]
[illegible] the Vie [illegible]
[illegible] ca [illegible]
[illegible] on [illegible]
[illegible] he [illegible]
[illegible] ngways [illegible]
[illegible] ard of [illegible]
[illegible] the [illegible]
[illegible] of wanderers [illegible]
[illegible] . Four [illegible]
[illegible] ang [illegible]
[illegible] t p [illegible]
[illegible] ous and [illegible]
[illegible] marvelo [illegible]
[illegible] plu [illegible]
[illegible] s, [illegible]
[illegible] p.

[illegible] orne [illegible]
[illegible] f us [illegible]
[illegible] as I [illegible]
[illegible] bbe [illegible]
[illegible] ining, I [illegible]
[illegible] utu [illegible]
[illegible] vad [illegible]
[illegible] cra [illegible]
[illegible] of [illegible]
[illegible] think is it [illegible]
[illegible] n sets." [illegible]
[illegible] no [illegible]
[illegible] te your [illegible]
[illegible] high [illegible]
[illegible] middle [illegible]

script that had to be shot at Universal or Allied Artists. Without realizing it, the GI protégés, we were rehearsing for the '60s.

Ah . . . the moment has arrived. Vietnam, our cancer, or life's booster. A television corn flake commercial, or shall we hum an abstract hymn to the liberal's menopause?

Another angry glance at the *Voice* photographs: Jiveass motherfuckers. Faces I have encountered in person and on the printed page.

A few years ago their kind were marching for the blacks. But nonviolent marching produced sore feet, fear, and the suspicion that one might truly, truly die for the "cause," and, too, perhaps the movement lost its kick, and like those beautiful rich women, who riding sidesaddle creamingly ejaculate, the liberals had quite simply, ladies and gentlemen, found a new cause, fresh with the scent of discovery. A challenge, a map of a situation on which they could embroider *Peace & Love*.

What should the peace-loving earthlings do? Marshal their forces and elect a President in the forthcoming election who will guide them toward a peace-loving future. That is our only salvation. If they are able to mainline moral reality into the American way of life. If. If. If—

At the moment, mothers, nothing's shaking. From the Pentagon whirligig, right on down to you and you. We are freaking in and out, in and out of the reality around us. But oh, what a marvelous show!

THE G[illegible] falls [illegible]
[illegible] the sky [illegible]
[illegible] gem. [illegible] days, ba[illegible]
[illegible] voices [illegible] *aise* grip[illegible]
[illegible] week not [illegible] but a stra[illegible]
[illegible] act [illegible] noti[illegible]
[illegible] war, [illegible]
[illegible] real [illegible] involve[illegible]
[illegible] seems [illegible] of [illegible]
[illegible] glass [illegible] an [illegible]
[illegible]

[illegible] (9 to 11 A.M.) [illegible]
[illegible] P.M.) [illegible] Thursdays [illegible]
[illegible] health ce[illegible] of a se[illegible]
[illegible] you abou[illegible] a Health [illegible]
[illegible] one time, [illegible] the center [illegible]
[illegible] the Ch[illegible] setting [illegible]
[illegible] *Man* [illegible] faintly [illegible]
[illegible] public school [illegible] housing [illegible]
[illegible] ends [illegible] an [illegible]
[illegible] two-story [illegible] seems so [illegible]
[illegible] men and [illegible] there to re[illegible]
[illegible] or a [illegible]

small building is the salvation of that dandruff-like disease, gonorrhea.

Mondays and Wednesdays are extremely busy, I was told, plus holiday aftermaths. S.R.O. But first you check in with the receptionist, avoid the children going to the dental clinic, the elderly waiting for X-rays. Male VDers go into a small, crowded waiting room with pale, pale green walls, almost the exact shade of gonorrhea semen. No smoking, please. Bright-colored plastic chairs. Bogart and Marx Brothers posters. Before interrogation and tests, you read, sleep, or watch your fellow travelers. Tense young men who usually acknowledge each other with a sly/shy you-got-it-too grin. The promiscuous earthlings are cool. Conversation between a teenager and his slightly older friend.

"What we gonna do after you get straight?"

"I don't know," the VDer said. "Go to the movies, I guess."

"Are you gonna take Marcia?"

There was no answer. The teenagers were seized with boisterous laughter.

Clapped by the same prostitute, two young mailmen also joked and laughed, crossing and recrossing their legs. An occasional elderly man (looking as if he's on a permanent down), homosexual couples—their faces a portrait of togetherness like expectant parents—are given the nonchalant treatment. But what intrigues me are the young men who arrive with luggage, knapsacks, sleeping and shopping bags. Some of them are from out of town and give false names, addresses, as do Manhattan males. I overheard one longhair give a Washington, D.C., address, complete with apartment number, then ask if a friend could pick up the result of his blood test.

"No," the smiling health aide said.

"Could my sister pick it up? She lives in the city."

"I'm afraid not," the kind, smiling health aide told him, "but check with your doctor."

From my observation, the majority of longhairs are not the supply clerk and other nine-to-five types. Heavy radicals and Marx you I Ching.

I've been down, much too black about the Chelsea Health Center. In the narrow corridor, in the cubicles, occasional funny vignettes.

not over. The social-worker interview. Everyone gets uptight. You are supposed to be very honest and name names and when and where. But there are the white lies, the loss of memory. Many VDers do not remember who they slept with and give the name of a foe/friend. You will never know the anonymous friend/foe who volunteered your name and address. Fake word-of-mouth also helps spread VD. And, too, it is much easier to detect VD in a man than in a woman. An ancient, misunderstood disease, often hereditary, VD is the thing this year. Our future. Aren't we promiscuous? Swingers in and out of bed? Aren't we top-of-the-morning Americans, seekers of fresh territories, and ever so mobile?

The drift? It continues. Frenzied days and nights. All I want to do is stay stoned; despair is the masochistic lover, chained to my feet as August spends itself slowly; time the miser with the eyedropper. Summer. Summer's end. Will the summer ever end? Will I escape this time?

Returning from another dish gig, I bought the Sunday *New York Times* and read the *Book Review*. You made the news today, boy. But that failed to ax despair. The frustration, the peasant's labor of the night before were still fresh in my mind. After showering, I feel less tense, prime myself with ice-cold beer. It's a mother of an afternoon. The sullen sky gives no promise of relief, rain. The murmurous St. Marks Place voices drift up as if begging for something which escapes them in this elusive city. But booze won't elude me. No. There's half a pint of vodka, and I made a pill connection on St. Marks Place, bought three pints of wine from a "doctor" on the Bowery.

And I sat in my room waiting, watching the sky turn dark, listening to radio rock, inhaling the Coney Island odors that wafted through the window from the nearby pizza parlors, hamburger luncheonettes. The night was a scorcher. Should I hit the streets? Visit air-conditioned friends/foes? Are you jiving, mothergrabber? What could they possibly do except accelerate the drift? So I showered again, opened the door, turned off the bed lamp. The Valencia is an anything-goes hotel.

Finger-popping, dance-marching around the room, wanting desperately to get higher; become incoherent, hallucinate, vomit, pass out. But that never happens. Once again, I was stoned in the

deflowered, hip, zipping middle-class Americans, off target, ricocheting—back home.)

"What's happening?" the girl asked.

"What the hell do you think is happening?"

"Wow, man. How you come on."

"Wow, how you come on," I said. "Must all of you say everything that I expect you to say?"

"Aren't the flowers lovely? Peace, flowers, and love, brother."

"Come on in." I smiled and let it pass, flicking on the light. "Let's share a stick of peace."

The girl executed a mock curtsy. In the light I could see her decadent infanta gaze. The infanta, concealing jeweled daggers under the crinolines, a girl-woman with small, hard, cold eyes, fixed on my penis.

"Good grass, man," the girl confided.

"Yeah."

"Your eyes look funny. Glazed."

"A black devil."

The girl giggled again. "No, you're cool, brother. We've got to put the flowers in water or else they'll die."

"Well," I said rising, "we can put some of them in the beer bottle."

"That's cool," the girl exclaimed.

We arranged the daisies in the beer bottle. The girl bounced on the edge of the bed, keeping time with rock on the radio.

"Do you think you can get me off?"

Silence.

"Come on, cookie. If you want some bread or a place to crash for the night, okay. But don't play. I'm a superb gameplayer. I don't like monkey games."

"Do you think you could love me?" the girl whimpered.

"No," I said, turning off the light. "But let's ball."

The girl, a knowledgeable child, sexually proficient, was kicked out at noon. "Do you love me?" she had asked.

Still high, seeking solitude, yawning, I had turned toward the girl: "What? Get out of here. You're out of your league. A lot of black dudes on St. Marks will buy that jazz. So you'd better get out and find one."

"I've got one," the girl replied bitterly, "and thanks for nothing."

AND ON THE FIFTH DAY, I left Manhattan, returned to the Catskills, my seasonal home away from home. I can always go to the Catskills and wash dishes. Real peasant wages, a peasant's caldron. Here—where it's green and serene—these flat, informal, manicured acres. The eye looks upward and sees dense treed mountains, a pearl-blue sky. Tall poplar trees ring the lakes and golf courses. Blacks and Jews may not share a passion for pork, but they do share a passion for Lincoln Continentals and Cadillacs. The Jews seem to prefer air-conditioned cars.

Early afternoon. The pool and cabanas are crowded. A bearded black tyro who will not speak to the black hotel employees plays light George Shearing jazz, which soars in the high wind. Far off, a woman sits alone and knits. Children play volleyball. A well-known Hollywood character actor frolics by the pool. This scene is visible from my window in the former children's dormitory. A pleasant vacation vista. The grind of Manhattan, Brooklyn, the Bronx is far away. Why move from the lounge chair? The entertainment director is trying to coax people to play games. The guests are indifferent. Perhaps they resent their vacation being regulated by a whistle. "And you're always complaining because there's nothing happening . . . Jesus," the director says into the floor mike.

The indifference flowers. A pleasant young man, a novice

stoned in the dormitory for two days. The salad man swaggers in with a fifth of Scotch and is escorted out of the kitchen. A middle-aged kitchen man, a professional, chases the smart-aleck second cook with a meat cleaver. The baker, a former marine, is stoned as usual. Between offering bear hugs, he throws wads of dough. A day behind the scenes in a Catskill hotel; you take it as long as you have to, or split. The working and living conditions are terrible. No unions or overtime, which is why hotels fail to secure stable employees. You work long enough to get wine money or "talking back" money and move on. But—Monticello, the mountain Las Vegas, beckons; the police wait; and it is ten and ten: a ten-dollar fine or ten days in jail, or both. Now you are no longer required to see a judge, go to jail. You give the policeman ten dollars, and he drives you to another hotel, regardless of whether or not you want to work. Labor Day is near; the hotels are desperate. This year, the Bowery men are not making their annual Catskill expedition. A man might as well panhandle, eat at the Municipal Lodging House on East Third Street, and sleep in a doorway. Why should they work twelve hours and get paid for seven? And may I wish the Bowery men a happy holiday.

At this particular hotel, the only happy people are the guests and the young black men from Alabama who will work the summer season and hope to return home with $500 or $300. Like the Puerto Ricans, they work hard, save their money, and stick together. A natural-born citizen of the world's most prosperous country, I tremble to think of what life back home is like. But that's another story. A chapter of the story is in the beautiful, legendary Catskill Mountains, in the great and small hotels, bungalow colonies, where once Jewish workers came to relax from Manhattan sweatshops, gangsters came to play and kill. Now, small towns and cities bear ancient Indian names, and progress and builders have raped the wilderness, and money, anxiety, anger, greed dance through the clean mountain air like a chariot filled with lovers.

Indifferent, unchanging world—that's it in the final analysis, I remember thinking one night. There was a full moon. With coffee and cigarettes for company, I went down to the lake. I thought of F. Scott Fitzgerald's Dr. Dick Diver. Yes. Tender is the night. I became frightened and left the following morning.

subtle electric-blue sky to the Chinese Garden. A solitary man slept on a cardboard mattress; half a loaf of Wonder Bread lay at his feet. The new lane of the Manhattan Bridge hadn't opened. Through the line of trees, I saw a squad car park on the lane. Two exhausted or goldbricking policemen sacked out. An old story. I had been coming here for a very long time.

I began knocking down drinks. When I looked up, a tall woman was coming toward me, moving with a slow, back-country woman's stride. Close-cropped gray hair, print cotton dress, and red-leather house shoes. She was like a curio, a ghost from Hell's Kitchen, a bit player from a Clifford Odets revival.

"Has a man passed through here?" the woman asked, her voice hoarse, hesitant, like a record played at the wrong speed.

"No. I've been here about an hour. I haven't seen anyone."

"I wonder where he went to. Some colored fellow has been following me all up and down the Bowery."

Jesus. One of *them*. Gritting my teeth, curling my toenails, I smilingly said, "Is that so?"

The tall woman nodded. She did not look at me. My vodka held her interest. "That's right. He just kept on following me and saying things. Every once in a while, he'd do something dirty."

"That's terrible. Why didn't you call the police?"

"What good are they?"

Chuckling, I offered the woman a drink.

She read the vodka label carefully. "This ain't wine."

"No," I sighed, "but it gets to you. One hundred proof."

When the woman finally released the bottle, she was panting. "Too strong. Wine's all right. Just like drinking soda pop, and you can get drunk, too."

"Cigarette?"

"You think I'll kiss it. But I won't."

"What?"

"You've got your goddamn hands between your legs."

"I've also got a cigarette in my hand. I have no intention of burning Junior."

"You can't make me do it," the tall woman said.

"Lady, have another drink and beat it. I'm getting a peaceful high, and I don't want you to zonk it."

Frowning, the woman reached for the vodka. "I won't do it.

The tall woman with the back-country stride did not move. I looked at her tired, middle-aged face, reddened from wine, the cold gray eyes, watery like tarnished silver. It would have been impossible to kiss the thin, pale lips, and her chest was almost as flat as mine. The idea of dogging this woman, who was descended from thin-skinned rednecks, didn't appeal to me. Unlike many American black men—I have never had a super-charged, hard-on for white women. All I saw was a masochistic woman who wanted to serve Head.

Laughing playfully, I forced the woman's head downward to get a reaction.

The tall woman kissed the head of my penis delicately once, the second time with feeling. She went down with the obedient movements of a child. She was a passable Head server. I wanted her door of life and pushed her down into the grass.

"You can't make me do it," the woman cried. "I don't know what you think I am."

"Shut up."

"Rotten bastard."

I stood up and couldn't control my laughter. "Get out of here."

"I wasn't bothering you, and I never said I wouldn't kiss it," the woman cried. "Could I have another drink?"

* * *

Skulled in the whitewashed cubicle, where the ceiling is high like in an old-fashioned mansion. Chicken-coop wire encloses the top of the cubicle. But there is no air. Only pine disinfectant, roach killer. Countless radios, two phonographs, and one television blast—this is the upper-class section of the hotel, and all the transient men are black.

The bed is lumpy with thin gray sheets, uncomfortable, like a bunk on a troop ship. No matter, no matter. There is a jug of mighty fine wine, a carton of cigarettes. I dismissed the voices, the music, the odors. I checked in to get my head together and write, but a few soldiers from the Army of Depression broke ranks. Now they brought up the rear. When would the bastards make it back to company headquarters?

Stoned, feeling surprisingly good, walking down Broadway, below Fourteenth Street. Less than a block away, I spot this dude on the opposite side of the street. There's something about his movements. Something isn't kosher, I'm thinking, as the dude crosses over to my side of the street and eases into a dark store entrance. It so happens this is where I turn the corner. Now, we're on the same side of the street. But he's in the store entrance of his corner, which faces Broadway, and I'm turning my corner, going west, picking up a little speed.

And who comes cruising along but "Carmencita in blue." Just tooling along like two men who are out for a good day's hunt in the country.

The squad car pulls over to the curb, and I go to meet them. The driver seems friendly. He's smiling. "Do you have any ID?"

"No. Some son of a bitch stole my passport, and I wish you'd find the schmuck."

"Where do you live?"

"Down the street. I'm sure I can find something that will verify who I am."

A brief silence. Calm as an opium head, I casually lean against the squad car.

"Are you the good guys or the bad guys? You see, I'm out to save the city from corruption like you guys. I'm working on my sainthood this year."

to cheap movies and bars where three drinks will cost the price of one. Not much has been written about the Homosexual Bowery, where masculine sex outnumbers "girlie" sex.

In moments of grand depression, I think of myself as the Cholly Knickerbocker of the Bowery, writing about young and old men in the last act of life. Men who sit in the foyer of hell as they wait to be escorted into the ballroom of death. But it is always cocktail hour for the "girls" who are sometimes called garbage and ash-can queens. Their past lives and wine have pushed them beyond *The Boys in the Band*. I'm thinking of one queen in particular. Now what kind of female would wear a ratty fur jacket on a summer morning? But once he/she sort of had it together: white-framed dark glasses, jet-black dimestore wig, white halter, lime-green shorts (before the hot-pants vogue), plus a wad of dirty rags. This queen not only wipes off car windows at Houston and Second Avenue, but tries to engage motorists in conversation and, like a visiting celebrity, hops up on the hood of a car, announces: "I've just arrived from Hollywood." You may laugh or choke with disgust but the queen is for real. Sometimes 5 P.M. traffic is stalled: the queen is dancing, waving to her fans.

The closet cases are another story. Masculine, they open under the toll of whiskey and wine. Masculine gestures give. A grand lady is talking, inviting, and to hell with the buddies, the bartender, the crowd of regulars. No matter, no matter, the closet is open. Until tomorrow. But we've been to that country before, too, haven't we? At least we have read the travel folders, and our friends have visited that country. Well, now we're heading down the trail, deep into Marlboro country (before the appearance of James Jones's *From Here to Eternity* Pall Mall cigarettes were considered effete. Now Pall Mall is the "hard-hat" cigarette, the jailhouse cigarette). The Marlboro men would be the first to admit it, sober or stoned. These men have been the backbone of our army, navy, and marine corps. Many of them were the heads of families. Most of them blame the opposite sex for their defeat. So they turned to whiskey, wine, and the company of men.

They do not hate women. They avidly watch and comment on the hippie girls and the blue-collar Puerto Rican and Italian women of the neighborhood. On payday and welfare day, most of them never get laid. But a surprising number of them have each

sitting near the streetlight. But did I really see the black man place his head between the other man's legs? No, my eyes are tired, my mind is tired.

Presently the two men got up and walked over and sat down under a tree, almost directly in front of me, the sidewalk separating us. But I could not hear what they were saying. All I could do was watch the black man stretch out on the grass, then turn to the young white man, who sat with his back against the tree. Finally, he stood up, and I heard him say, "I'll see you around."

The slightly older black man decided to pay me a visit.

"What's happening?"

"Nothing," I said. "I don't have a goddamn thing."

"Wish I could help you."

"But you can't," I told the man.

He thought about this briefly, then spotted a tall, long-haired blond man walking through the garden. He took leave of me and ran after the tall young man, who ignored him. Nevertheless, the black continued to run down his game. He puts his arms around the blond man. Suddenly the blond swung at him, and one, two, three, the fight was on. The blond had the slender man pinned against a tree and cursed him. The slender black man rubbed the blond's buttocks. The blond bolted up from the ground and walked away silently with the black following. They stopped and began talking. The slender black man tipped up on his toes and kissed the blond's lips. The blond young man protested but relented, and then they moved over into the tall grass and made love.

And why are they more comfortable talking about baseball than about their sex lives?

Mail arrives as if programmed by a doomsday computer: P.E.N. dues, Xeroxed McGovern letters, Museum of Modern Art announcements and bills, a request to subscribe to a new *little* magazine for twelve dollars per year; they would also like me to write for them, gratis. Another one of Maggie's HELP notes from Paris.

Dear Charles:

What the hell is going on? Are you all right? You haven't invited me to the States. In fact, you said nothing. Should I return to the States? Well, the goddamn French are out of town. A holiday and I am grateful. Received a

when—the United States Information Agency used certain passages from *The Messenger.* And one heard and read of writers who had received grants and hadn't published one book, or writers who had received grants and were reviewed on the back pages of the Sunday *New York Times Book Review.* One also heard of writers who received grants because they knew someone or had slept with someone.

Perhaps I should follow the advice that I've been given over the years: buy a tweed suit or whatever type of suit is fashionable at the moment and make the literary-cocktail *la ronde.* You know, even blacks do it.

And your father or my father might do it. I'll never do it: But I'll knock down more wine and go out on the fifth-floor fire escape of the Kenton Hotel.

From this distance the view is glorious. The pollution screen even filters the burning afternoon sun. There is no breeze. A sort of suspended quiet, although I can see traffic moving down Chrystie Street; children playing ball in the park; drunks in twos and threes, supporting buddies like wounded soldiers after the battle of defeat. Toward the east, a row of decayed buildings has the decadent beauty of Roman ruins. But only at a distance. Trained pigeons, chickens, and junkies inhabit those rooftops. Taking another drink, I think: I wish I could fly, fly, far away.

Here, there, again, and always, the Why of the last seven years. Skulled depression as I sit and watch the sun disappear. Aware of the muted, miscellaneous noises that drift up from the street, I am also aware of the loss of something. Thinking of all I've done and not done. Thinking and feeling a terrible loss.

"Man, they jumps," Sam exclaimed. "Didn't you know that?"

Sweet-potato brown, Sam has a Hitler, Jr., mustache. An ice-pick scar outlines his left cheek like a nervous question mark. His small bright black eyes seem to recede as if the sight of another pair of eyes was somehow indecent. We had worked together briefly in the Catskills, and I had helped him through several bad Manhattan scenes. His wife had taken the three children and gone to California with another woman. Sam's running buddy, "Two-Five," a thirty-three-year-old crippled Vietnam veteran, was beaten to death on the Bowery. But Sam was laid back now. He

was the hour of camaraderie, con games, great lies, illegal drinking, loneliness, anxiety.

Always skulled, I made my way through the crowd, exchanging brief, social greetings. Then, sat on the windowsill, trying to concentrate on the six o'clock news or staring out the window.

Against the deep blue of early evening, they turned on the spotlight at the Holy Name Mission and church at Mott and Bleecker Streets and you could see the white-and-gold-draped statue of Jesus Christ. It was not a life-size statue. From a distance, with the lights playing on it, Jesus Christ was larger than life. Sometimes He appeared to move. Extend His hand, turn slightly. Desperate, I needed a lift. Take me higher. Ground the motors of the stockcars racing in my brain. But "God never worked very well with me," Hemingway's Lady Brett Ashley said. Somehow I can't get in step with the masses and their current religious phenomenon, seeking belladonna for the soul. Tricky business, too. For what is religion but the act of levitation?

It would be much better if I read Malcolm Lowry's *Under the Volcano*. Through his despair, I might be able to understand my despair, to cut the loss, elevate hope.

Of course, I was unable to do this. I did not even reread *Under the Volcano*.

THIS CATSKILL SCENE is a Japanese watercolor: white poplar and pine trees command the fields; the mountains are shrouded in green. Serenity becomes a silent song. Then, suddenly, the sun is smothered by gray clouds. It's an Idaho sky, a pensive Hemingway sky, and you know you are in America. The eye travels out across the land: a buff-colored, shingled ranch house in a clearing of young trees. Fronting the house like emblems are two late-model cars, which spell money. Closer at hand, beer cans litter the wild grass like baubles from the moon. About a dozen butterball kittens are playing in the grass. Running, leaping, rigid before the moment of attack, their multicoloring becomes a shifting pattern in this unofficial season of death.

Originally this was hunting country. It still is, in a restricted sense, although No Hunting signs are everywhere. Vodka-mellow, I like to believe that Hemingway would have felt at home up here—Here where in summer young deer frolic like schizoid ballet dancers. But I wonder what Papa would think about the cats. "Any time you decide to shoot cats, it's the cat season," a man said yesterday. However, no one has said that it is the perfect season to hunt and harass men. Let me ease your mind: that, too, fuses in the clear air like the simultaneous orgasms of lovers.

The lower-echelon employees do not talk of love. It's always other hotels, booze, the Bowery, weapons. None of them own

We do not have to worry about domestic cat on the menu—or do we?

Certainly, I wasn't thinking about cats when I went to visit Joey. In the sunflower brightness of a Thursday afternoon, I walked four miles to Joey's hotel, stopping off at a roadside café for a cold six-pack.

Joey offered vodka at ten in the morning. Why not, as we used to say in Tangier. We began drinking and exchanging local news. Then, shortly before twelve, the sound of bullets interrupted our conversation.

"Whenever a hotel has too many cats," Joey, an old Catskill hand, explained, "they shoot them." At lunch Joey pointed out the two men who had killed the cats. The "second," a transient mental-hospital patient, was Mr. Clean. His head was shaped and glowed like a choice eggplant. The main man was lean and rather placid. I watched as he placed his elbows on the white trestle table and hand-rolled a perfect cigarette. The second scooped up the dead cats with a shovel and threw them down the hill. Joey remembered a record by the DC-5 titled "Bits and Pieces."

Postscript: Exactly one week later, at my home away from home, the local fascisti shot more unwanted cats at dusk. House cats and favorites survived.

On my dishwasher's day off, I walked four miles into the village of Monticello, shopped around, paid my respects to several bars, and returned to my kosher hotel. I hoped to spend a quiet day reading, finding out what was going on in the world. But it was payday. The transient workers were doing their thing, celebrating their past and future, the low cost of labor. I drank with them. Skulled in the middle region of my mind, returned to my room, and began reading *Time* magazine. The black print kept slipping off the slick white page. Sleep came down like a knockout drop.

Morning arrived gray and disfigured. The afternoon was a merciless drag. Skulled again, I watched reality enter the kitchen. The bearded Puerto Rican "captain" (the dining-room porter) sat down on the floor and removed his shoes. A melodrama would end if someone moved a stack of plates twelve inches. Tottering old drunks put iced-tea glasses in the wrong plastic rack. A young black takes exactly twenty minutes to put on his apron. Fat Boy

eyes, so despairing of the smell of booze and pot and used-up hope in bloodshot eyes of Negroes bombed at noon, so envious finally of that liberty to abdicate from the long year-end decade-drowning yokes of work and responsibility that he must have become in some secret part of his flesh a closet republican. . . ." Does personal despair, aging, the general mood of the times make a writer from the avant-garde uptight? Or was this "simple emotion" caused by the Reverend Abernathy's late appointment? Was Mailer looking for a fight? Years ago, he had written the famous *The White Negro*. He was the Father of Hip. He had almost single-handedly brought the world of Paul Bowles to the new frontier, exposing that world to thousands of middle-class youth and their elders. Certainly he had paid his slumming dues. Pot, pills, booze are old joys and nightmares to him—for he had touched the outer limits of despair in more than one instance. Even with his education, affluence, he went under in the dream, got flogged by the bats of hell. What could he possibly expect from American blacks in their situation? And now: "They had been a damned minority for too long, a huge indigestible boulder in the voluminous, ruminating government gut of every cowlike Democratic Administration. Perhaps the WASP had to come to power in order that he grow up, in order that he take the old primitive root of his life-giving philosophy—which required every man to go through battles, if the world would live, and every woman to bear a child—yes, take that root off the high attic shelf of some Prudie Parsely of a witch—ancestor, and plant it in the smashed glass and burned brick of the twentieth century's junkyard."

Prudie Parsely might have been incognito during the grass-green Eisenhower years. Indeed. But as I hunt and peck and go to press, Prudie has taken root and is trying to strangle anyone who opposes her. For years she has been the little sweet pea in the jolly green giant's pod; her small-town American heart (which is shaped exactly like a Norman Rockwell valentine) pulsed with security, a Dow Jones high of righteousness. Prudie was safe. Old Glory flew high, and God blessed the foreign descendants, and for a very long time they believed this was true. Heart of hearts! Vietnam, taxes, and black power made the beat irregular. Miss Parsely is aghast. She's a little afraid and is now working her army overtime. Anything goes. Why, the lady will take anything with two or four feet.

the image of her tits under the white nylon uniform stayed with me. Those tits seemed capable of guiding an ocean liner into harbor. I wasn't interested in Miss Mary's face, although it was attractive, unlined. She must have been at least forty-five.

Chuck won, and there were a lot of bravos. He left with Miss Mary, left in his yellow Thunderbird.

The Thunderbird's motor was souped up, and I heard it as Chuck zoomed up the hill. I ordered another double, feeling a little down, wanting a little loving. Then I ordered a six-pack and made it.

About an hour later, there was a knock on my door.

"Chuck," Chuck said. "Busy, man?"

"No." I yawned through the door. "Come on in. The door's open."

Chuck entered in his dazzling cook's whites. His dazzling boyish smile was wide. We were never buddy-buddy but got along well.

"Oh, man. I'm sorry. You're reading. You gotta let me read some of your books."

"Any time," I said, sitting up. "Wanna beer?"

"Sure could use one. Hot as hell this afternoon. Must have put away two six-packs in the kitchen this afternoon."

"Yeah." I grinned. "That kitchen is a bitch."

"You read a lot," Chuck was saying, "and I'm sorry to disturb you, but I came up to ask if you wanted a piece of ass."

This is just too goddamn much, I told myself. What's the angle? But already Junior was standing tall, waiting for me to put on my racing shoes.

"It's just down the hill," Chuck said. He wasn't looking at me then with that dazzling smile.

I stood up. "Anybody I know?"

"Yeah, man. Great piece of ass."

"Let's make it, baby."

"Man, you're ready," Chuck said as we made it down the hill. I kept on putting Junior in place, but the son of a bitch wanted to stand up and cheer.

The low-slung maids' quarters was a former chicken coop. Remodeling gave it the appearance of a jerry-built post-World War II ranch house. Hundreds of stamping feet had killed the grass [illegible] quarters. But [illegible] hard [illegible] h[illegible]; h[illegible] vital; her riotous colors were [illegible] the s[illegible] countryside and I was [illegible] ex[illegible] a[illegible] of B. B. King on a phonograph [illegible]

Chuck, grinning, unlocked [illegible] keys on his chain and [illegible] jingle [illegible] Christ[illegible]

"Well," he said, "[illegible]."

We walked directly into the living room [illegible] with a [illegible]ate design of garden flowers. [illegible] the scent of [illegible] thought I would pass out.

Chuck offered me a drink. "[illegible]" with the sweet [illegible] laughing, I nodded. [illegible] get [illegible] little uneasy. But I don't have to [illegible] den.

"Want another drink?"

"Nope."

"Okay," Chuck sighed. "[illegible] in the [illegible]"

[illegible] away on the wide [illegible] of muddy water [illegible] outlined her [illegible] face. She [illegible] strong supporting white [illegible] in magazines [illegible] s[illegible]ras.

Miss Mary had her eyes closed [illegible] idea that Miss [illegible] might [illegible] from her face [illegible]

"Hello, Chuck," Miss Mary [illegible] faintly.

"Hi," I [illegible]ed. There was no door between [illegible] and I could see Chuck sitting on the sofa. [illegible] window. He was looking straight ahead [illegible] walls. Junior was at [illegible] rest [illegible] Mary [illegible] But what the hell! [illegible] her thighs [illegible] chest. I thought that Junior [illegible] told myself, Baby [illegible]

Miss Mary opened her eyes briefly and touched my arm. "It's all right," she said.

I didn't answer her. My hot, greedy hands reached for the bra. Miss Mary's hand had engulfed Junior, who still seemed in the act of retreating.

Good God! There must have been twenty goddamn hooks on the bra. My short arms could not encircle Miss Mary. Besides, she was trying to rise and anoint Junior, who was beginning to march.

"Wait a minute," I said. Miss Mary appeared not to hear me. She had raised up, opened her mouth, was prepared to sing to Junior. He was at attention, and I had the bra off. Junior stood firmly at attention as Miss Mary lovingly caressed him, but depression touched my shoulder. I didn't particularly want to get blown. But I lay back on the bed and let Mary work out. There was nothing extraordinary about her tongue and lips. I raised up and grabbed her tits—mini-blimps; a man could fly high and safe between them or, buoyed by their softness, sleep the sleep of rapture. I pulled Miss Mary up toward me. Now she was crying softly. She held on to Junior as if she wanted to squeeze the breath out of him.

Miss Mary wanted to baptize Junior again in the name of desire; I wanted to get laid.

"Come on," I said.

Miss Mary was breathing very hard. She had a coughing spell, but I went ahead, while the woman who made crepe-paper flowers protested. Desire had reached its peak with me. All I wanted was to plow into those 180 pounds.

"Chuck—Chuckie, please. Oh, no—"

But it was pleasant with the pillow under her. Yes, lovely, for although she was a large woman, a baby cantaloupe couldn't fit into her vagina. It didn't take very long. Spent, happy, and grinning, I tried to pull away.

"No," Miss Mary cried. Her large sweating body shook, and the most terrible sounds I had ever heard, fast and painful, seemed to come from her stomach. Junior was getting uneasy, and Miss Mary's arms had me in a bind.

I took her again, took her slow and easy—this one was for her and the flowers. Those terrible sounds had stopped, and I could feel her pleasure as her body moved toward me.

Nathanael West
First Comfort Station
Purgatorial Heights

Dear West:

Por favor—forgive the delay. True, it has been almost six years. Hope
that it has been less than a day in your particular hell. It began in our New
York and followed me through the small transient rooms of all your depressing hotels. Now Absurdity and Truth pave the parquet of my mind. The pain
is akin to raw alcohol on the testicles. But I'm not complaining. Life's eyedropper is being sterilized with ant piss. Hallucinations? Joshing? West—I-
Am-Not-Spaced-Out, despite the East and West Village rumors. Slightly
skulled though. Celebrating the Day of the Dead.

I suppose the dead dog at the bottom of Malcolm Lowry's Mexican
ravine is almost home now. But the yellow-button white daisies have taken
root. I like that.

> Take care and watch the shit.
> Charles

P.S. Here's a little clipping from *The New York Times:* "Aosta,
Italy (AP)—Cold, avalanches, and lack of food killed about 20 percent of the wild Alpine goats and chamois in Grand Paradise."

CHARLES STEVENSON WRIGHT WAS BORN on June 4, 1932, in New Franklin, Missouri. In 1955, he moved to New York City, where he wrote and published three highly praised autobiographical novels about black life in Manhattan. He died at the age of seventy-six.

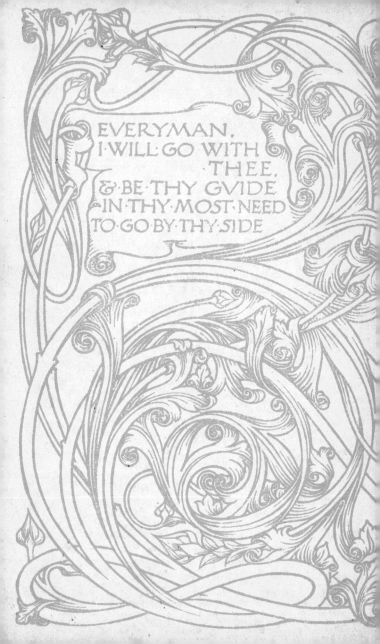

EVERYMAN,
I WILL GO WITH
THEE,
& BE THY GVIDE
IN THY MOST NEED
TO GO BY THY SIDE